Ronald E. Long, PhD

Men, Homosexuality, and the Gods
An Exploration into the Religious Significance of Male Homosexuality in World Perspective

Pre-publication
REVIEWS,
COMMENTARIES,
EVALUATIONS . . .

"Ronald E. Long takes readers on a provocative and wide-ranging tour of how religious traditions in a variety of cultures—from archaic to modern, and from East to West—have characterized homosexual relations and finds a common denominator: the presumption that sexual penetration connotes social superiority and sexual domination, which is the root of much homophobia and misogyny. But the modern gay man's assertion of a new kind of masculinity, in contrast to stereotypical views of homosexuals as feminized males, is part of a profound sea change, Long argues. The culture wars over same-sex marriage and gays in the military reflect a struggle against the old view of homosexuality as a signifier of perversity and weakness, and of sexuality in general as an act of conquest—views often implicit in religious prohibitions against homosexuality, Long explains.

Long is particularly impressive when he describes the challenge taken up by contemporary gay movements. The goal, he contends, isn't merely to 'deconstruct' a particular way of thinking about the interplay of sex and society. Instead, the promise embedded in gay equality and the diminishing of gay stigma is that we might 'free ourselves from thinking of sex as a matter of a man pushing himself into the body of a subordinate, and therefore subdued, person,' with profound and liberating implications for all of us, gay and straight."

Stephen H. Miller
Managing Editor,
Independent Gay Forum

More pre-publication
REVIEWS, COMMENTARIES, EVALUATIONS . . .

"Ron Long has gone where no gay scholar has gone before, and he has done so quite boldly. This is an important and significant work: important because it brings together such a broad cross-section of historical sources and examples, and significant because it provides a 'genealogy' of religious perspectives on male homosexuality. Long carries it off with a good deal of vigor and brilliance. He engages the reader by the sheer breadth of his academic research and expertise. This is what good scholarship should always be about: it is accessible, intriguing, and convincing. More significantly perhaps, this book is good *gay* scholarship, an all-too-rare commodity in these days of obtuse and often cumbersome queer theory.

The truly extraordinary thing about this book is its ability to see commonality in difference, and to perceive the one in the many. If only for its creative and audacious attempt at some comprehensive vision of homosexuality in diverse religious traditions, the text merits every serious consideration. Not many scholars would undertake such a risky task. Long does so very convincingly. Long's book helps us all understand ourselves and our world better. This outstanding book will add another very big notch to his already well-deserved reputation and growing influence."

Donald L. Boisvert, PhD
Lecturer, Department of Religion,
Concordia University, Montreal;
Co-Chair, Gay Men's Issues
in Religion Group,
American Academy of Religion;
Author, *Out on Holy Ground:
Meditations on Gay Men's Spirituality*

"This is one of the best surveys of homosexuality and world religions and will be a book to keep as a reference. Dr. Long takes the reader on a whirlwind trip through history and culture to discover the role of the religious significance of homosexuality. From Plato's Greece to the same-sex rituals of the Sambian tribes to the shamanistic role of homosexuals among the Native American Indian tribes, Long takes the reader inside the mythology and folklore and tells us what really happened.

This book goes much deeper than simply being a reference on the role homosexuality has played in world religions. Dr. Long finds the threads of commonality in each of these traditions and pulls them together, allowing us to see the underpinnings of the culture war concerning homosexuality in our world today. The book makes the powerful case that the fear of male homosexuality throughout history is tied to each culture's construct of what it means to be masculine and powerful. Dr. Long argues that the modern gay rights movement is more than simply a political or sexual movement, but at its core is a spiritual movement for good. If you are trying to make sense of the deeper understanding of the gay rights movement in our daily lives, Dr. Long's book is an argument you must read."

Rich Tafel
Author, *Party Crasher:
A Gay Republican Challenges
Politics As Usual*

More pre-publication
REVIEWS, COMMENTARIES, EVALUATIONS . . .

"**R**onald Long's book is an important and most timely survey of
the ways in which different religions
have endorsed and sustained norms of
masculinity of the dominant males in
any society. The greatest value of the
book is Long's proposition that contemporary homophile movements represent the first attempt to transform the
constructions of masculinity based on
war, domination, and penetration. They
do so by declaring that bottoms are real
men too, thus changing the way men—
gay, bi, or straight—understand themselves as sexual beings. Long's book is
an accessible and valuable resource not
only for gay and bisexual men but also
for everyone concerned with the inter-
locking questions of religion, gender,
and violence."

Michael Carden, PhD
School of History, Philosophy,
Religion, and Classics,
The University of Queensland,
Australia

HPP
Harrington Park Press®
An Imprint of The Haworth Press, Inc.
New York • London • Oxford

Men, Homosexuality, and the Gods

An Exploration into the Religious Significance of Male Homosexuality in World Perspective

HAWORTH Gay & Lesbian Studies
John P. De Cecco, PhD
Editor in Chief

Men, Homosexuality, and the Gods

An Exploration into the Religious Significance of Male Homosexuality in World Perspective

Ronald E. Long, PhD

HPP

Harrington Park Press®
An Imprint of The Haworth Press, Inc.
New York • London • Oxford

Published by

Harrington Park Press®, an imprint of The Haworth Press, Inc., 10 Alice Street, Binghamton, NY 13904-1580.

Unless otherwise indicated, all Scripture quotations are from The Holy Bible, English Standard Version, copyright 2001 by Crossway Bibles, a division of Good News Publishers.

Cover photograph, "Sandman," by David Vance.

Cover design by Lora Wiggins.

Library of Congress Cataloging-in-Publication Data

Long, Ronald E. (Ronald Edwin), 1946-
    Men, homosexuality, and the Gods : an exploration into the religious significance of male homosexuality in world perspective / Ronald E. Long.
        p. cm.
    Includes bibliographical references and index.
    ISBN 1-56023-151-3 (alk. paper)—ISBN 1-56023-152-1 (pbk. : alk. paper)
    1. Homosexuality, Male—Religious aspects. 2. Masculinity—Religious aspects. I. Title.

BL65.H64L66 2004
205'.66—dc22
                                                                                            2003022213

CONTENTS

Preface

The inspiration for this book lay in the research I undertook as I set about to develop a course in homosexuality in world religion for the Program in Religion of Hunter College of the City University of New York. The past thirty years have seen an explosion in scholarship in the general area of religion and homosexuality, but most published research has focused on specific areas or traditions, and collections of essays have been the exclusive vehicles of broader scope. This book is, as far as I know, a pioneering attempt at synopsis and, more important, synthesis. It is intended to be a brief, accessible analysis and interpretation of constructions of homosexual relations in a representative sampling of historical religious traditions and thinkers. Since different interpretive constructs can result in the religious tolerance—in some instances the requirement—of homosexual sex, as well as its prohibition, I am particularly concerned with the conditions that make any given construction of homosexuality seem not only plausible, but true.

I have chosen to limit myself to a discussion of male homosexuality, rather than homosexuality in general. One reason is that the literature is more extensive. Another is that historical religions have principally been concerned with male homosexuality. Why that has been the case is an interesting question and one that would extend beyond the scope of this study, but one which this study may help to answer.

Chapter 1 provides a general orientation to the topic, defining what will count as religion and what will count as homosexuality in the study. At the same time it introduces the cultural variability in conceptualizing what is normal and abnormal in male sexuality through a brief look at the vocabulary shifts apparent in the early-twentieth-century naval sting operation treated in a justly famous article by George Chauncey. Chapter 2, "Holy Homosexuality," discusses two ways in which homosexuality has been mandated or employed for religious ends. Chapter 3, "Holy Homoeroticism," explores two cases in which homosexual sex may have been frowned upon, but romantic attractions between men could be marshaled in the service of religious wisdom. Chapter 4 considers the case of the so-called Native American berdache, arguing that many treatments which emphasize the respectability of the berdache distort both the role and its sacred power. Specifically I side with those who see the role of the berdache as descended from a sexually humiliated enemy whose sexual penetrability makes him a living war charm. Chapter 5 centers upon the proscription of anal intercourse among males in ancient Israel. After surveying a number of approaches, I advance the argument that Levitical homophobia is the expression of a fear of male rape at the hand of enemy soldiers and, as a corollary, that a sexually penetrable man, by the logic of magical congruence, weakens the social body.

In Chapter 6, I turn to the Christian tradition, exploring first how the writings of Saint Paul embody a potentially salutary break from his Levitical heritage, and then turn to the writings of Saint Augustine. This section is, as far as I know, the first essay to consider how Augustinian theology provided the Latin West with the conceptuality by which homosexuality could be characterized as both the apogee of ungodliness and of unmanliness. The Buddhist tradition, which I treat in Chapter 7, shares much in its analysis of the problematics of human existence with Augustine but nevertheless, in a kind of reprise of earlier themes, could—at least in its Japanese forms—see how homosexual relations among monks might serve their enlightenment.

Each chapter can be read as an isolated study, but read together in the order of presentation, they mount an argument. Religious traditions have, in the interest of fostering and preserving the masculinity of socially significant men, historically presumed and/or exploited a fairly consistent gender paradigm by which full adult masculinity is sexually enacted in the penetration of social underlings—whether women, boys, slaves, or defeated enemies. Since implicit in this construction of gender is the presumption that penetration connotes social superiority or domination, I argue that it is in turn rooted in a metaphoric reading of sex as war and war as sex which has its setting in warrior culture.

Against the sweep and backdrop of the comparison of religions visited in the earlier chapters, the final chapter, "Struggles on the American Front," argues that modern homophile movements can be seen not only as advocates for the moral, legal, and religious equivalence of homosexual and heterosexual love but ultimately as bearers of a revolutionary poetics of masculinity that shatters the connections between love and war and makes way for the possibility that even the willingly penetrable man might be seen as fully masculine.

In all, this book represents my attempt to chart a reconstructive alternative to the deconstructive thrust of so much scholarship into historical forms of homosexuality inspired by "queer" and other critical perspectives.

*   *   *

In the course of writing, I tried a number of alternatives to the traditional footnote and bibliography format. In each case, the alternative proved more unwieldy than the more traditional approach. As it stands, for those who want to read further on any given topic, the notes provide a guide to the literature listed in the bibliography.

ABOUT THE AUTHOR

Ronald E. Long, PhD, is Assistant Professor in the Program in Religion at Hunter College of the City University of New York. He was formerly a Fulbright Scholar to Germany and has taught in the field of religion at Vassar College and in humanities at Columbia University. His essays and reviews have appeared in *The Harvard Gay and Lesbian Review, Theology & Sexuality, The Journal of Men's Studies,* and *The Journal of the American Academy of Religion.* He is currently a member of the Steering Committee of the Gay Men's Issues in Religion Group of the American Academy of Religion, for which he also served as Co-Chair.

Acknowledgments

We stand on the shoulders of giants. I and my arguments in this book are no exceptions, having benefited from the explosion in learning that has been seeded by gay and lesbian scholars since the Stonewall uprising. I know him only through his writings, but I—like many other gay scholars—owe a debt of gratitude to the late John Boswell, whose work on Christianity and tolerance almost singlehandedly established the field and occasioned the (sometimes all too acrimonious) discussions and debates that would shape the field of gay and lesbian studies. I owe a particular intellectual debt to L. William Countryman for his work in New Testament sexual ethics. Although I do not follow him in all particulars, my debt to him is apparent in the pages that follow. I also want to thank him for his personal encouragement when I was a rather abrasive scholarly neophyte. I owe a singular debt of gratitude to Professor Barbara Sproul of Hunter College, both for her personal encouragement and for the opportunity she gave me to develop the course on which this book is based when I was an adjunct, sine qua non. Rare in academia are adjuncts treated fully as colleagues in the way they are treated under her. I can only hope my own researches can live up by even a little to the work and stature of such giants.

Last, I want to thank my publisher, The Haworth Press, for its patience in repeatedly extending my deadline as though I were writing volumes instead of the more modestly sized book you now have in hand.

Chapter 1

Straight Thinking on Some Not-So-Straightforward Matters

GETTING OUR BEARINGS

Not so long ago, a graduate from an English university might typically have embarked upon a European tour. The theory was that exposure to foreign peoples and foreign lands would be edifying in a way that mere book learning had not been. To be sure, Europeans as a group were not all that different from one another, whatever their ethnic or national identification. Certainly they were not as different from one another as they would have been from the peoples of the Far East, for example. Even so, such venturing forth into new climes and places carried with it the shock of the new and different. What was ultimately and significantly to be learned, however, was something that could emerge only after the shock of the new and different had worn off and given way to something else. An exposure which was sufficiently long allowed one to perceive that below the level of the diversity of cultures was the commonality of the human. Such an insight required the kind of extended exposure that, until now, has not characterized the recently emergent study of the sexualities of the world. This is especially the case where the focus is on homosexuality. To be sure, the study of homosexuality in world history in general, and in religious history in particular, is still in its infancy. To date, explorers in the field have been overwhelmed, if not shell-shocked, by the new and alien—and have tended perhaps to overemphasize the variety in the ways humans have thought about and organized their sexual lives at the expense of what they have in common. However, the time has come to look below the surface of that variety to try to perceive the commonality that underlies all that apparent variation. Indeed, the argument which follows maintains that a surprising consistency of thinking informs the ways different peoples in different cultures have traditionally lived and thought about their sexual lives, and in particular the assumptions that are at work in any given take on male homosexuality. Simply put, religions have historically been concerned to empower socially significant men—that is, men who are significant by virtue of age or rank or simply by being men—to be men, and have traditionally been uncomfortable with them being anything else but "real" men. More precisely, in the variety of discourses in which their understanding of male homosexuality is couched, traditional religions are mediators of a fairly consistent understanding of masculinity—and have proven thereby to have been both direct and indirect supports for the masculinity of socially dominant men.

I do not want to underplay the often surprising cultural differences that do exist, demanding due recognition in their own right. Indeed, it may come as a surprise to discover that not all religious traditions have found male homosexuality ungodly or irreligious. In fact, some traditional religious cultures in Papua New Guinea mandate homosexual activity among their young males. If, in ancient Israel, the fear of God was the beginning of wisdom, the writer Plato affirmed that, among his Greek compatriots, it was homosexual romance which held the seeds of mature religiosity for men. Information on the variety of interpretations of male homosexuality in the religions of the world is part of what can be gleaned from this book. However, I am concerned with more than merely citing that eighth-century Confucians thought about homosexuality in one way, whereas fifteenth-century Christians in Europe thought about it in another. The real focus of the book is in the question of what lies behind and motivates any given religious assessment of male homosexuality, a task some scholars call "genealogy." It asks the question, what are the conditions that make a given way of thinking about male-male sexual relations seem right and fitting? Of course, one can legitimately ask such a question only when the historical variety that actually exists has substantially been brought to light. But the discovery and disclosure of this historical variety is a task that has only recently begun to happen, now that the Western habit of silence with regard to male homosexuality has been broken.

The degree to which the literatures of ancient Greece and Rome dealt with homosexual love—very often without a twinge of righteous indignation, and often with an approving eye—was not lost on

Victorian scholarship. The Greek celebration of love between males could be rationalized and thereby excused. Women, after all, were not brought up to be the intellectual companions of men. The prospect that their cherished Greeks would have countenanced, much less honored, a love between men that expressed itself carnally, however, was not so easily assimilated. However, by distinguishing the moral intent of a text from its literal meaning and then appreciating the latter in the light of the former, "[e]ven the work of poets of questionable moral propriety, such as Goethe and Heine, could and did in this fashion become moral guides" and "in the case of Plato they [the Victorians] hid from themselves the immense moral distance lying between Greece and their own day."[1] Thus, by a diversion of attention, the Victorian reader could appreciate the writings of Greeks who did not share their repugnance for homosexual sex—without being challenged by their very different sexual mores—and many Victorian thinkers would perpetuate a form of what had already become a well-esconced strategic avoidance of any sympathetic attempt at understanding sexual love between men on the part of Western scholarship. In the sixteenth century, Matteo Ricci wrote:

> In China there are those who reject normal sex and indulge in depravity, they abandon sex with women and instead they corrupt young males. This kind of filthiness is not even discussed by wise men in the West, for fear of defiling their mouths.[2]

It would have to wait until our own day for the silence to be effectively broken—and the veil of invisibility rent.

In America, even as late as the 1950s and early 1960s, a book such as this would hardly have seen the light of day. When even the suspicion of homosexuality was sufficient to ruin professional and social lives, and interest in the matter was sure grounds for suspicion, it is no wonder that scholars would be less than inclined to produce texts on homosexuality for public consumption. Nor would publishers find themselves inclined to print such texts had they been written. Potential buyers would not readily reach for such a title lest they be seen and their reputation compromised. Nor did any courses in "sexuality" exist to guarantee at least an academic market for such books.

This is not to say that nothing was known about the various cultural configurations of sexual codes and practices. Although explorers who were convinced of the moral superiority of the noble savage might very well have been inclined to overlook the degree to which such noble savages practiced what wise men in the West deemed un-mentionable, priests such as Matteo Ricci, in an effort to justify the need for conversion, were very alert to these practices. Yet they glossed over the particulars, rushing headlong instead to speak of all such non-Western values and practices as a generalized depravity. A rounded knowledge of the discreet sexual practices of a given cul-ture—much less the understanding thereof—would have to wait for another day. Indeed, it would have to await a generation of openly les-bian and gay scholars in the post-Stonewall era to shatter the tradition of silence, oversight, and ignorance.

The Stonewall Inn was a gay bar located in New York's Greenwich Village. In late June of 1969, a police bust for illegal sale of alcohol—an unfortunately common event at the time—resulted in the arrest of several patrons and the bar's staff. The released patrons, numbering around 200, were witness to the arrests and became incensed. The en-suing melee and subsequent rioting raised the Stonewall resistance to mythic status as the event that founded the modern movements for lesbian and gay liberation and civil rights. Men and women in large numbers came out of the closet and identified themselves publicly as lesbian or gay, refusing to acquiesce to a social practice that held their sexual orientation to be something they should be ashamed about. Simply by coming out, by refusing to recognize the legitimacy of the moral stigma that society generally attached to homosexual orienta-tion, out lesbian and gay scholars had freed themselves from the threat that the suspicion of being gay or lesbian might hold—and of-ten found themselves interested in exploring the questions of why and how other cultures might represent alternatives to the homophobic cultural practice and prejudice of the modern West. Since Stonewall, there has been an explosion in our knowledge and understanding of such cultural alternatives, and this book seeks to survey—and to un-derstand—what has been learned, if not generally about homosexual-ity in history, at least in religious history in particular.

The search for respected cultural heroes who could be understood to have been homosexual dominated the inquiries of the earliest pio-neering lesbian and gay scholars, but that project was to give way to the search for cultures in which homosexuality was not held in such disrepute as it is in much of modern American culture. However, what these brave pioneers began to confront was an almost bewildering variety in the ways people of various cultures have organized and thought about their sexuality. First, they came across some very alien sexual institutions. In the African cultures of the Azande and the Nzema, young men might form "marriages" with teenage boys until the former take wives and the latter take "boy wives" themselves. Among the Sambians in Papua New Guinea, prepubescent boys would be required to fellate pubescent elder boys. A boy would, traditionally, first ingest semen, then graduate to become an "inseminator" of young boys, before finally becoming an inseminator of women instead.

Nor have men from other cultures always been as loath as the contemporary American male to own up to homosexual sex. Among the Romans, for example, a man whose masculinity had been challenged could defend his virility by boasting of his homosexual conquests. It was what a man did in bed that could threaten his masculinity, not the sex of the person he chose to do it with. Besides, for the Romans, a real man was not a slave to his passions. Thus the exclusively heterosexual but obsessive womanizer would have been found less than manly, indeed effeminate, whereas the man who enjoyed sex with men could be counted as a man among men.

More surprising yet to Westerners for whom religion means the Judeo-Christian tradition was the discovery that the religious traditions of the world were not universal in their condemnation of homosexuality. Homosexual practices have been tolerated, honored, and even mandated by some of the other religions of the world. It is to the late John Boswell's credit to have pointed out that even the Christian tradition has gone through periods of time in which it seemed less antagonistic toward homosexuality than it now seems to be.

It is to this variety—the various ways the religious traditions of the world have taken up the question of homosexual relations among men—that this book is an introduction. The knowledge of cultural and religious variation is important not the least for the perspective it gives us on the present. We are all inclined to presume the world is as it is for us unless we are shown otherwise. As George Santayana (1863-1952) wrote, "Those who cannot remember the past are condemned to repeat it." Indeed, knowledge of historical variation frees us from the presumption that our folkways are indeed part of the wisdom of a universal humankind—thus freeing us from the cultural prejudice that would make male homosexuality always and everywhere an affront to "religion."

But ultimately, knowing that others may experience and organize their lives differently than we do does not go far enough. What we seek is not mere acquaintance with variation, but the whys and wherefores that account for a particular variation. Specifically, we want to ask what factors are involved in the religious embrace of homosexuality and what dynamics are at work when a religion is horrified by the idea of two men having sex. In other words, we want to inquire as to the factors that underlie, and seemingly influence, any given religious evaluation of male homosexuality. Nor are we interested in an exhaustive survey of all the variations out there, but only those that help us to understand ourselves. In other words, the focus of this study is less on the variations themselves than on the perspective on the classical religious traditions of the West gained by seeing them within a field of similarities and contrasts. Ultimately, of course, we want to see what bearing all this might have on understanding the "culture wars" of the present.

But first we need some disciplined reflection on the very terms of our inquiry for, in point of fact, knowing what we're dealing with is not as self-evident as it might seem. Take the idea of "religion," for example. On what basis do we recognize a religion as a religion, when such a religion is so very different from our own that it almost seems to be no religion at all? Whereas George Gallup may presume that the question "Are you religious?" and "Do you believe in God?" are one and the same, what do we make of those Confucian and Buddhist traditions that are technically "atheistic"? We need to reflect on such concerns before we set out on our journey of discovery.

HOW SHALL WE THINK OF RELIGION?

When it comes to religion, we suffer from what I like to call Parson Thwackumism. Parson Thwackum is a character in Henry Fielding's rollicking eighteenth-century novel, *The History of Tom Jones, A Foundling.* In one of his recurrent didactic moments, Thwackum said, "When I mention religion I mean the Christian religion; and not only the Christian religion, but the Protestant religion; and not only the Protestant religion, but the Church of England."[3]

The fact is, we end up positioning ourselves with respect to the religious traditions we have experienced, whether we accept or deny them, in whole or in part. And what religion amounts to for each of us is, by and large, that which we have come to accept, deny, or in some way affirm. But then we are left with the strange position that no other religion exists except ours, or at best, that other religions are religions only to the extent that they embody what religion is for us. In such a case, to seek what wisdom can be gained from exploring alternative religious perspectives is in vain, because, in point of fact, there are effectively no other religious perspectives to explore. If, on the other hand, we broaden our horizons to the point that we are looking at practices and beliefs that in no way seem related to the religion that we know, are we even exploring alternative "religious" perspectives?

An anecdote might help us to orient our discussion here. I have a gay friend who tells this story of coming out in his early twenties to his father. I was struck by the way he insisted that, if his actual words have blurred over the course of time, nevertheless the substance of his father's response remained seared in his memory: "But that's the kind of guy that other guys beat up!" his father had said. My friend was stunned by the matter-of-factness with which his father seemed to assume that beating up "faggots" was not only a fact of life but almost a right that normal males had in the natural scheme of things. To this day, my friend has been left pondering whether his father, known for being something of a bully in his youth, may not have been—once upon a time—what is today known as a gay basher. My friend tells me he was even more astonished when his father drew upon the language of religion to protest: "But it's a sin!" He does not remember his father as a very religious man. Although my friend's father could frequently be heard singing about the "little old church in the wildwood,"[4] he was not a church going man, although I understand he resumed a connection with the congregation of his youth when he retired to his hometown in Arkansas. The only time my friend even remembered his father using the word *God* in his presence was in response to a particularly striking Rocky Mountain landscape: "There must be a god who created all this beauty!" He was surprised and taken aback, then, when his father spoke of homosexuality as a sin, especially since he had never known him to use the term before. In this, my friend's father was but one of so many nonreligious Americans who resort to religious categories of condemnation when confronted by the realities of gay life. People who would otherwise care not a whit what the Bible says presume to know and promulgate as truth what the Bible teaches about homosexuality.

People use the language of religion, it seems to me, when they are hard-pressed to find an argument for a deeply held position. Sometimes, of course, they merely repeat themselves ever more loudly so as to drown out the spokespersons for alternative positions. On the other hand, the appeal to religious authority is likewise an "argument stopper"—it has the effect of positioning one's own opinions as somehow in sync with whatever realties count for more than anything else. What I am suggesting is that religion should be understood as the "language of conscience."[5] It covers the domain of those values that a person or group feels most deeply about and the rhetoric available within a culture by which people can be convinced of the truth of those values. Religions are an individual or group's basic way of valuing, and religious realities, in turn, are those things that constitute for a person or a culture a final "court of appeals."

In cultures that recognize a god or gods as religious authorities—powers thought to be the sources of life and life abundant—meaningful life is life lived in synchronicity with the gods. In the religions that have derived from the ancient Near East—Christianity, Judaism, and Islam—such "synchronicity" is often understood as a matter of obedience to the divine will. Sacred texts such as the Bible or the Quran are envisioned as repositories for expressions of, or at least clues to, the divine will. To others in the cultures which have descended from these religions who no longer believe that such a god exists, the idea of "life" may function as ultimate authority in the place of God. We are therefore confronted with what life teaches or demands of us.

However, where the gods are still alive to the faithful, there are yet other modes of god-relatedness. Just as Prometheus in the Greek tradition shared the knowledge of fire, so did traditions as diverse as the Aztec and the Hawaiian understand homosexual practice to be a thing introduced into humanity by the gods. Or the gods may be exemplars who are or can be imitated—so the story of Zeus and Ganymede reveals the "divine" pattern, and therefore meaningfulness of, the love of a man for a "boy." In other cultures, homosexual practice may be authorized by the teaching or example not of gods but of culture heroes or ancestors. This pattern of authorization is most typical in traditional China, where it is the homosexual practice of the emperors of legend that ground and authorize the practice. Although ancestors and culture heroes are usually inherited, one can "discover" one's ancestors or adopt the ancestors of a group one has joined. Thus the practice of *shudo*—the love of boys—among Buddhist monks in Japan was reputed to have been introduced into Japan by Kukai (774-835), the venerated founder of Japanese Shingon Buddhism and general cultural hero. Thus, we must attend to evidence of cultural sanctioning by the will, teaching, or example of cultural authorities.

Not all religious meaning is anchored by such authorities. Indeed, the power of the ancestors themselves often derives from their association with the mythic youth of the world. The ancestors are beings who lived when life was young and fresh and full—whatever fullness that we can have now will lie in recapturing the fullness characteristic of the past in the present. That is to say, the authoritativeness of the ancestors can derive from a myth of a golden or paradisical age, distant from the world of our time—the world as we know it.

But there are still other readings of history—other narratives—through which people recognize themselves and their vocations. American politicians continue to draw upon the biblical imagery used by the American Founding Fathers (the American ancestors) to cast the American experiment in democracy as a challenge to be a "city on a hill," the world's last, best hope, the vanguard of a future new world (order). Other peoples have a different sense of their national and/or personal vocations. Although modern Communists may aspire to be servants of the proletariat, ancient Israelites saw their nationhood—or so the story of the call of Abraham implies—as a call to be the medium of a blessing of all the nations. The meaning of homosexuality would then derive from the place homosexuality might have in the national vocation. The Founding Fathers of America envisioned that they were establishing a nation that, like Israel of old, could be a "light to the nations"—and its democracy could function as a beacon for the future, setting an example for other nations. When governmental agencies such as the FBI would later construct homosexuality as "un-American," the implicit moral censure derived its force from homosexuality's purported inconsistency with America's vocation. Historically, however, homosexuality has not always been seen as inconsistent with democracy. Indeed, in Plato's *Symposium,* the character Pausanias argues that the Athenian system of homosexual patronage helped to buttress Athenian democratic institutions and processes, while the all-too-compliant gratification of homosexual suitors in Elis and Boeotia and the proscription of homosexuality in Persia worked to inhibit the growth of democratic culture and practice respectively. Thus, both the FBI and Pausanias make implicit appeal to the national vocation to sanction—or morally discredit—the homosexual practices of their day.

The advantage of viewing religion this way—as a complex of basic values and practices, and the strategies by which they are justified— lies in the way it focuses the task ahead. Any given valuation does not take place in a vacuum but rather in the midst of myriad other inter- pretations and valuations. And any given evaluation gains plausibility through its interconnectedness, indeed its coherence, with the inter- pretive field in which it exists. In other words, what we want to do is inquire into those coimplicated factors that render any given religious evaluation its plausibility. What is it, so to speak, that makes the things of man seem like they are the things of God?

WHAT OF "HOMOSEXUALITY"?

Deciding what will count as religion for this investigation does not, however, deliver us from definitional difficulties. The notion of ho- mosexuality is every bit as slippery as the notion of religion. Take, first of all, the question of "sex" in homosexuality. What is the line that separates the sexual from the nonsexual and, by extension, the homosexual from other kinds of sex? It seems to me a coach's slap on the butt of one of his players can be construed as a social gesture, but I am not sure we would want to treat it as a specifically homosexual act. The problem gets compounded when we realize that no action typically taken as sexual necessarily is so. True, I might kiss my spouse, but then too I kiss my mother, my dog, my grandfather. Nor is a kiss between lovers necessarily a sexual act: a kiss good-bye as I go off to work is surely a different kind of kiss than one that is the pre- lude to lovemaking. Nor does genital contact guarantee that some- thing sexual is taking place. Among some traditional peoples in the Philippines, an older man may greet a boy by reaching into his pants, cupping his genitals, and commenting on how much the boy is grow- ing. In an interview with the author, the well-traveled photographer Kristen Bjorn, who has met and photographed men from around the world, tells the tale of a Filipino friend who was scolded by his father for rudeness when he pulled away from the friend of the family who was about to reach into his pants for such a greeting.[7] Something similar may have been characteristic of the mores of ancient Athens as well. The playwright Aristophanes, in his comedy *The Birds,* has an Athenian character say to a friend,

> Well, this is a fine state of affairs, you damned desperado. . . .
> You meet my son just as he comes out of the gymnasium, all
> fresh from the bath, and you don't kiss him, you don't say a
> word to him, you don't feel his balls! And you're supposed to be
> a friend of ours![8]

By the same token, although many people consider only vaginal or anal penetration "real" sex, surely we would want to consider fellatio, whether it leads to ejaculation or no, an act of sex.

And what about falling in love with a member of the same sex, even if the "love" is not consummated and leads to no "homosexual acts"? Surely, that should be construed as part of our subject matter, even if some cultural interdiction or personal hesitancy interposes itself and keeps such a romance from becoming, as we say, physical. Let me propose, then, that we consider the following as within the area of sex between men that is our chosen subject: sex, for us, will include those feelings and actions that, in any given culture, would—unless interrupted by interdiction—normally lead to physical engagement to the point of orgasm of at least one of the parties involved.

But even agreeing on what will count as sexual, we are still confronted with the fact that to search for interpretations of homosexuality among the religious traditions of the world in fact proves distorting. Over the past hundred years or so, first-world populations and thinkers (especially those of America and Northern Europe) have grown accustomed to dividing the human population according to sexual orientation, i.e., by the presence or absence of sexual interest in members of the same sex. Those in whom such interest dominates are homosexual, whereas those whose sexual interest is exclusively for members of the opposite sex are heterosexual—allowing, of course, for those who "swing both ways," the bisexuals among us. It is recognized that, in the absence of women (as happens in jail, for example) many men might turn to one another for sexual release. But the operative underlying assumption seems to be that when members of the opposite sex are present, sexual desire for members of the same sex is surprising, and perhaps horrifyingly so. However, this way of thinking has not characterized much of the world's thinking about sex among men, apparently not even in America—at least up until about a century ago.

In a celebrated article, George Chauncey diagnosed the various understandings of male "perversion" at work in a U.S. Navy sting operation that was conducted in and around Newport, Rhode Island, beginning in the spring of 1919.[9] In order to bring "perverts" who had presumably been "corrupting" the Navy's young men up on vice charges, volunteer sailors were dispatched into the neighboring community to have sex with men who made themselves available for such purposes. Apparently, the Navy—and the decoy sailors themselves—did not find what they were doing in any way problematic . . . as long as they enacted the role of penetrators in the act of sex. Only those who performed "invertedly"—that is, who were male but enacted something other than the typically male insertive role in sex—were stigmatized as perverted. In the culture of the time, men could be divided into a number of categories. There were those who were not interested in sex with other men. Then there were those who were available as insertive partners in sex with other men (with no attention given to the question of whether at other times these men might or might not want to have sex with women); such men would be called "trade" or "husbands" in the Newport underworld, depending on whether they were interested in one-night stands only or more enduring pairings. A third class of men comprised those who were available as the sexual "insertees" for such men. These men might be described as "fairies," "pogues," or "two-way artists," depending on whether they preferred oral sex, anal sex, or both. By contemporary standards, both of the two general classes of men—"trade" and "queers"—are deserving of the stigma of the "homosexual" label. By the standards of the Navy and the decoy sailors, only the third group—the queers—were the stigmatized group. In the ensuing trials of those who were arrested for "queer" activity, defense attorneys attempted to discredit the moral integrity of the decoy sailors who testified by trying to throw their motivation into disrepute. They argued that there must be something wrong with a sailor who would volunteer to have sex with other men. Clearly, then, in the arguments of the defense lawyers, we can see the new way of thinking about homosexuals making inroads into the culture of the time.

Most older cultures, and many contemporary cultures—especially those we call Latin—still operate with an understanding of male sex closer to that of the Navy and its decoys than that of the contemporary Euro-American societies. They seem more interested in the actions a man might be interested in undertaking than with whomever he might be interested in doing it. In such cultures, real men are sexual "tops"—that is to say, "inserters." To be a man who plays the role of insertee is, depending on culture, either deemed effeminate and/or boyish or servile. But whether it is the presence of desire for sex of whatever sort with a member of the same sex, or an interest in certain sexual acts irrespective of the sex of the "sexual object" (to use the term from the psychological literature), at stake is the masculinity of men. Desires and acts will be culturally frowned upon that are seen to compromise the masculinity of men—or at least the men who count socially. Religions traditionally will tolerate only those forms of sexual expression that do not compromise the masculinity of the relevant adult male population. Indeed, we might generalize by saying that religions (as we have defined them) are traditionally interested in shoring up the masculinity of socially superior males, whether that superiority is a matter of sex, age, or rank. Religions will endorse homosexual relations among men only where homosexual relations can be positively related to the religious and/or masculine development of men or where it at least does not detract from it.

Ultimately, the knowledge we seek as we explore the religious interpretations of male homosexuality is not a mere knowledge of historical variation and its conditions. We seek such knowledge for the perspective it offers on the issues and affairs of the present. We hope to put the present in perspective, to uncover what the real issues are that underlie, for example, the problems the contemporary Christian right in America has with homosexuals who insist on acting on the presumed moral indifference of homosexual desire, i.e., "flaunting their homosexuality for the whole world to see." Although evidence suggests that many cultures recognized what we would call "homosexual persons"—that is, people who find emotional intimacy and sexual satisfaction only with members of their own sex—that fact was not generally taken as particularly interesting and, more important, did not figure into discussions of sexual ethics. What the discourse of sexuality—as it is frequently referred to—does accomplish is to focus attention on the question of how people who share the homosexual "condition" can expect to be accorded the right to life, liberty, and the pursuit of happiness. But it is one question that ancient codes—framed with different concerns in view—were scarcely designed to address.

Although much has been made in the scholarly literature of the difference between older ways of thinking and the current language of sexuality, I would argue that at stake in the present is the interpretation and valuation of gay sexual love—the moral legitimacy of, to be specific, male-on-male sex. Prejudice against homosexuals as persons and against love between homosexuals is symptomatic of horror at the idea of male homosexual sex. Contemporary homophile movements are predicated, whether consciously or not, on the conviction of the moral equivalence of homosexual and heterosexual sex. The change that the discourse of sexuality has actually made is to have extended the stigma hitherto attached only to the insertee to the insertive partner as well. But what it has potentiated is the possibility of a movement to claim the masculinity hitherto reserved for the insertive partner alone for the receptive partner as well. Indeed, I will argue that the revolutionary importance of the contemporary gay rights movement lay in its—by no means clearly articulated as yet—revolutionary idea of gender, that male sexual receptivity is part of the repetoire of a normal, adult, fully masculine male. Simply put, the thesis of this book is that religious evaluations of homosexual love and sex depend upon the way male "bottoming" is construed—as does the resistance to male homosexuality in the contemporary period.

The idea of homosexuality groups together men and women who share a sexual interest in the same sex—specifically, gay men and lesbians. It cannot be doubted that they have common interests, political and otherwise. However, the contemporary gay male homophile movement is complex, for it also has a component that makes of it a men's movement—in that gay men have less in common with lesbians than with nongay men. It is in this complex character of the gay male homophile movements that the religious resistance and religious power of the social experiments now taking place are to be understood and appreciated.

The reader can, then, expect from this book three things. She or he can expect to be introduced to some of the major religious variations with respect to the question of homosexuality. I make no claim to exhaustiveness but have chosen examples for their representative nature and for their usefulness in leading to the second kind of knowledge we seek. The reader can expect to gain some understanding on how to understand such differences. Finally, she or he can expect to gain a new perspective on what seems to be the warfare of religion versus homosexuality that seems to occupy the religious establishments of America, and increasingly of the world, as American-style culture and American-style homosexuality come to typify the emerging contemporary world.

Chapter 2

Holy Homosexuality:
Of Men and Semen

THE SAMBIANS OF PAPUA NEW GUINEA:
IT WILL MAKE A MAN OF YOU

Eavesdrop on Americans in a public forum, a meeting among neighbors, students, or union members, or even a board of directors. When an individual comes to address the group, he or she will probably preface his or her remarks with expressions such as, "We've heard a number of interesting points, but it seems to me that . . ." or perhaps, "I've been listening to what the previous speakers have said, but I'm not convinced. I think . . ." The way we frame our ideas accentuates that our ideas are our individual and unique perspectives. In so doing, we present ourselves as creative, unique, and hopefully insightful individuals. It is a way of presenting ourselves that has a long and venerable history, and can trace its genealogy at least as far back as the "but I say unto you" of Jesus of Nazareth. We Americans pride ourselves on being unique individuals among our peers with unique insights, and our democracy works best when we volunteer ourselves and our ideas in the public forum.

But let us continue listening. Those who have roots in the South, in one of their folksier moments, might begin to invoke "what my dear old daddy used to say" or "as my sainted grandmother used to put it." Here we have a very different mode of self-presentation. Surely, it is the creative act of an individual person to figure out which of daddy's or grandma's words applies to the circumstances at hand. Yet the wisdom or insight espoused is not presented as that person's own, but rather as the wisdom of his or her elders, whether they are living or not. The individual is here deferring to the greater authoritative wisdom of his or her ancestors. Here our folksy American taps into one of the oldest styles of religious living in the history of humankind, characteristic of much of early tribal life as well as of traditional China, indeed, the entirety of traditional East Asian culture.

In many non-Western religious traditions, ancestors, not gods or spirits, are the focal spiritual realities. Ancestors are, of course, the "first" in a biologic line—into which females, typically, are grafted through marriage. However, ancestors are not merely the chronologically first among a group's members. They are also the originators of that group's traditions. Insofar as a group has a unique way of going about things—comprising when, what, and how they eat, how they house themselves, when and how they celebrate, etc.—those specific ways of going about life are traceable back to the foundational practices of the group's ancestors. To be a good and loyal member of the group or tribe one does things in the group's ways, and that is to do things in the ancestral ways. Ultimately, the ancestors are paradigmatic individuals whose lives are to be emulated. The lives of one's tribal ancestors delineate what counts for a fully human life, at least as far as the tribe is concerned. Life in the present attains to such fullness only to the extent that it imitates the ancestral pattern. Moreover, just as a person who acts childlike might be attempting to evoke the lost world of childhood, so too ancestral emulation might constitute an attempt to recapture the world of the ancestors—the time of the beginning when life was young and fresh. However, whether imitation of the ancestors is motivated by a desire to summon the freshness of the lost youth of the world or simply by the desire to lead a good life, the way of the ancestors is the authoritative pattern for the life of the group in the present.

The adult males among the Sambians, a tribal group living in the highland region of Papua New Guinea, are privy to a myth about their ancestors that runs along the following lines.[1] One of the two original age-mates who emerged from nature—from a local tree, to be specific—was troubled by the small size of his penis, but discovered through hands-on experience that pulling at it made it bigger and made it produce, in addition to urine, a snotlike substance. This age-mate, Numboolyu, wasn't sure what his penis was for, but noting that the snotlike substance also looked like the juice from a local food, he fed his penis and its produce to his age-mate, Chenchi, in an act of oral intercourse. The age-mate did not find the experience terribly pleasant until this age-mate slit Numboolyu's foreskin so that the glans could protrude even further . . . finding that this big penis was "tasteful" enough to suck on. Through continually donating semen to his partner, the first man lost all traces of childishness. His female-like childish puffy breasts grew flat like an adult male's pectorals—and his companion's breasts continued to grow more "enlarged" than they were in childhood, and indeed swelled with milk. Numboolyu's repeated inseminations "provoked" her femaleness, and in time also caused her belly to swell with child. She became pregnant through oral intercourse, but lacked any opening in her groin through which she could give birth. Finally, Chenchi's age-mate relieved her swelling by cutting a slit between her legs so that the first child could be born. The slit healed, but remained as the vaginal opening with which her mate could then have intercourse, an alternative to her mouth.

On one hand, this story about the maturation of the first man of the tribe (and his female companion) proves archetypal or paradigmatic for the way all men of the tribe come of age. At some point in life, they discover their penis, and then become semen providers first through oral intercourse and then ultimately vaginal. What is clear is that a man is—and is called to be—a semen producer and donator. But there is something unique about this first man's experience as well, because he lives in a world with only one companion. Other possibilities arise as the tribe becomes peopled with his progeny. Indeed, as the myth unfolds, there comes the time when his eldest son comes to him with his own erection and asks his father what he is to do with it. Numboolyu is troubled. He could send his son to Chenchi, but is reluctant to do so. He decides to send his son to his younger brother (that is, a younger member of the emerging tribe) so that his eldest son can be relieved of his erection through oral intercourse. This eldest son, then, will first experience himself as an (oral) inseminator of boys before he comes to experience himself as a donator of semen to a woman. In that sense, the experience of the two brothers is paradigmatic for all subsequent tribal men, because they will typically emerge from childhood as fellators of older boys, until they themselves begin to produce semen so that they in turn can "feed" younger men, and then eventually begin to donate semen to women. Although young married men may occasionally have oral intercourse with younger men, it is expected that a married man restrict his sexual activity to women after his first child is born.

This myth, then, describes the first instance of, and authorizes by example, a tribal sexual institution. Postpubescent young men have their younger male tribal members as their first sexual partners in oral intercourse. Obviously, this is one way to deal with the issues of raging adolescent hormones and erections. The social approval of using young men as sexual surrogates for females in situations in which sex with women is somehow proscribed or otherwise unavailable has parallels in other cultures.[2] However, among the Sambians—who are after all ferocious warriors—fellating older tribal boys is not just something one might do; it is in fact mandated and required of all boys, since ingestion of semen is, according to their culture, good for the boy. Without it, it is thought that even their bodies will not mature physiologically into the bodies of men.

We might say that among the Sambians men are recognizably made, not born, because their secondary sexual characteristics will not appear without the physical and moral influence from other men, much less their warrior virtue and prowess. In this society, men and women live in separate communal quarters. At a given point in the life of a male child, he will be removed from life with his mother and begin to associate and live with the men. Boys who remain with their mothers become "momma's boys." A boy needs to be surrounded by men, from whom the boy can learn how to be a man and among whom he can grow accustomed to behaving like a man. He will be made to bleed to rid him of any residual childishness and/or femaleness. At the same time, a boy has to ingest semen so that he will come to have a repository of semen of his own. Semen, it is believed, does not simply develop within a maturing male; it must first be "planted" in a boy so that the boy will begin to produce semen of his own—not to mention begin to display the secondary physical attributes of maleness.[3]

The importance of semen is an implicit, rather than explicit, theme of the myth of Numboolyu. In the myth, it is the ingestion of semen that makes the female capable of childbearing. It is semen that somehow causes the breasts to grow and become capable of secreting milk, the female equivalent of the male "nutritional" fluid. And it is semen that "causes" pregnancy. Although no one questions the fact that it takes a male and a female to make a child, we of Western European heritage tend to attribute fecundity to a woman. A man might provide "seed," but it is the female who "conceives." However, the Sambians are within a cultural circle of thought which believes the male is the fecund one. Among relevant cultures, the physiological processes involved in pregnancy are variously understood, but it is agreed that it is semen that is responsible for new life. It is semen that interferes with a woman's menstrual flow and constrains the menstrual blood to help form the child. Semen, on the other hand, forms the basis of the child. It may form itself into skin and bones, and the mother's blood coagulates into the soft tissues, or, as among the Sambians, semen develops into the child, while the mother contributes its blood.[4]

Semen, however, does not only make the female capable of childbearing, and cause pregnancy; it is productive of the masculinity of males in a male body. A boy needs semen to become a semen producer; he also needs semen to "harden" his childish body into the body of a man. Hence, oral intercourse between generational males does not merely relieve the sexual tension of the older boys but is, in fact, part of the process whereby the younger boys become masculine semen producers themselves. Sambian males ingest semen. Other New Guinea tribes implant the younger male with semen with ritual anal intercourse, whereas others may simply require that semen be rubbed onto a boy's body. However, without semen, the boy is destined to remain a child.

Semen, we may conclude, is a substance that feminizes women by making them ready for childbearing and ultimately turns them into mothers, and masculinizes males physiologically. To be sure, there is more to being a man than being a semen producer. Homosexual oral intercourse is accompanied by training in the arts of hunting and war, which are the provenance of Sambian men. But with the weight of ancestral authority, Sambian religious tradition involves the males of the tribe in a series of homosexual relations that have, as part of their aim,[5] the production of fully masculinized men. The masculinity of men, in turn, is a religious ideal. A fully developed man is a warrior, a hunter, and a semen provider. Fellating other males represents no compromise of a boy's masculinity but, by virtue of the Sambian understanding of semen, is the vehicle for actualizing that desirable goal. Although an adult male may find being fellated by other males something desirable even after marriage to a woman, adult males should have outgrown the practice and desire to fellate other males. Fellation of males is not necessarily a feminine thing, as other cultures might deem it, but is classed as either a female or a boyish thing to do. For an adult male to behave like a boy is unbecoming, not the least because it involves an abandonment of a fully adult gender in favor of the sexual amorphic character of childhood.

THE TAOISTS OF ANCIENT CHINA
AND THE PRESERVATION OF LIFE

Ancestors figure highly in the spiritual firmament of traditional China, as they do in traditional New Guinea. Yet it is the ancestors not of the "tribe" but of the individual "tzu," lineage, or family that are the focus of Chinese devotion. In China, however, devotion to one's ancestors results in deference to one's elders in the family and obedience to one's parents—rather than to the imitation of ancestral wisdom and practice. Parents are, after all, ancestors in the making and can be understood, by extension, to speak with the living voice of the dead ancestors. One's elders and parents are thus vested with the authority of the ancestors of the group, and devotion to the ancestors takes the form of filial obedience rather than ancestral imitation.

The followers of Confucius repeatedly tried to cast the emperor in the role of parent of the empire. However, such a view never really embedded itself deeply into the heart of the Chinese people. It was the family and its ancestral figures that repeatedly engaged the overwhelming devotion of the Chinese. This meant that in China imperial authority tended not to command the kind of obedience familial elders might. Nevertheless, the habits and deeds of wise old men were venerated and studied. The deeds, habits, and practice of emperors of old—factual or fictional—could set a precedent that was at least derivatively ancestral, thus establishing the social acceptability of a practice.

The Chinese circumlocution for homosexual love in fact refers back to the story of an emperor and his male "favorite." Once, when the emperor Ai was resting with his favorite, Dong Xian, he was called away to attend to some urgent matters. As a token of his love, he preferred to cut off the sleeve of his garment rather than awaken his companion whose head was resting on it. Thus, homosexual love came to be known as the "passion of the cut sleeve" as one translation has it.[6] Knowledge of, and lack of moral outrage about, such male favorites among the political elite of the Zhou, the legendary heroes of Chinese civilization, bespeaks a climate that has no particular moral objection to male-male love and sex merely because of the gender of the parties involved. Sexual attraction and sex between males was simply a natural part of life.

Taoism is one of the three great traditions of spiritual teaching in China, the other two being Confucianism and Buddhism. Taoism is best known in the West for its prime spiritual directive to live in accordance with Tao, the Chinese term for the "way" of things, to be accomplished principally through the cultivation of a kind of unforced action called *wu-wei*. However, for much of Taoist history, synchronicity with the Tao was valued above all as a vehicle for healthiness. Indeed, religious Taoism would come to center on the pursuit of a health so robust that death itself might somehow be overcome; whether immortality would prove possible, health remained the ultimate aim of Taoist practice.[7] In this view, what characterized something as "wrong" was its negative effect on the health of an individual and/or its impact on the social and environmental surroundings. Indeed, some early Taoist practices resemble a kind of health food movement. For example, these Taoists reasoned that, since we are breathing organisms, our wind power could be compromised by flatulence. Hence, in some forms of early Taoism, certain agricultural products, such as grains and legumes, were avoided because they led to loss of vital wind power and thus cut short one's span of life.

In the Taoist tradition, heterosexual sex is deemed spiritually problematic because it represents a kind of "unsafe sex" that threatens the full health of the male. Male ejaculation, like flatulence, is seen to involve the loss of an essential, vital element. Consider the belief— some might call it an "old wives' tale"—that lies behind the American high school coach's advice to players not to have a sex before a game. Such sex is seen to sap a young man's strength and manly vigor—and compromise his athletic performance. But why? It is not that sex takes that much energy. Rather, if semen is a vehicle of new life, perhaps it works by a donation of part of the male's "life force." It is a part of common wisdom that males grow tired after sex and tend to want to sleep. Perhaps, this is because ejaculation takes part of their life energy with it, and the vitality of men remains compromised until their reserves can be restored. A fear that ejaculation might signal a permanent compromise of the male's life force expresses itself in the folk tradition of China. Women can be potential vampires, sucking a man's life out of him through sex, whether oral or vaginal.

Evil spirits might assume the form of a woman, draining a man through intercourse.

One possible course of action would be to advocate that men could "preserve" their lives by avoiding sex entirely. Yet others found that sexual abstinence itself was unhealthy, placing the danger in having too much sex, rather than in the sex itself. That is to say, an occasional loss of vital fluid did not necessarily result in a compromised life force. Nevertheless, the loss of semen rendered any act of sex potentially dangerous. Still others opined that, if the "danger" in sex could be controlled, then sex might prove to be an actual path to spiritual health. The result, of course, was the practice of the "retention of the seed," whereby the male sought to have an orgasm without ejaculating.[8] To be sure, it took a great degree of discipline and training to gain that kind of control. (Scientists have suggested that the adept comes to have a kind of muscular control that so constrains the urethra that the semen backs up into the bladder.) Because there would be no ejaculate, such sex would be inherently a form of "safe sex."

At the same time, the Taoists were working with a psychosomatic understanding of human beings: what happens to the psyche has physiological consequences, just as physiological change has psychological and spiritual consequences. Taoists came to think, then, that the psychological sense of well-being which results from having sex especially with a young and attractive partner was the psychological corollary of the nourishment of a man's vital power, and perhaps even an aid in his longevity.

Chinese culture in general found the fact that some men might be sexually attracted to other men perfectly natural, a phenomenon that was attested even of the ancient wise and venerable rulers. If, in Chinese Taoism, heterosexual sex was inherently "unsafe" for the male unless appropriate protective steps were taken, one might think that homosexual sex would be considered "safe," since it presumably involved the mutual exchange of bodily fluid: what one lost through ejaculation would be supplanted by that gained from the ejaculation of the other. However, that is not how man-to-man sex is represented in the Taoist literature which is currently available to us.

To be sure, a great deal of the Taoist canon remains untranslated. Much of what we know about Taoist understandings of heterosexual sex is based on the translation of sex manuals for heterosexual couples. Collections of stories are, to date, our primary sources for Taoist views of homosexual sex. In stories such as those from the *Duanxiu pian* ("The cut sleeve"), young men seem to present exactly the same opportunities for enhancement of the vital power and the same sexual threat as do young women.[9] Indeed, demons that are intent on sucking a man's life away might assume the guise of a young man as well as a young woman. How can this be?

In thinking about homosexual sex, a modern American might think of it—if he or she bothers to think of it at all—as a matter of mutual oral or anal intercourse. But the modern American mind also might want to know, who is the "pitcher" and who is the "catcher," implying, of course, that sex between men involves a asymmetry of roles, with one being the insertive partner and the other the insertee.

I am told that, in Latin cultures, when one hears of homosexual relations between men, the knee-jerk question is regularly, "Who's the woman?" It is assumed that in homosexual sex and romances in Latin cultures, one man assumes the sexual role which is typical for women in a heterosexual relation. It is important to note here that sex by definition involves a man and a woman for Latinos. Therefore, if it is sex between men, one man must be "playing" the role of a woman, thus failing to conform sexually to common gender expectations of men. In such a line of thinking, the insertive partner who is penetrated is a gender "transgressor."

The Chinese, too, typically thought of sex as involving a penetrator and one who is penetrated. However, the penetrated partner was not seen necessarily as an effeminate man, since this role was not considered an exclusively feminine one. Sexual receptivity, rather, was the mark of a social underling of some sort. In sex, one man would be thought of as the "man." His partner might be a woman, a slave, an underling, or simply a "boy"—just as in Sambia where sexual receptivity on the part of a male was boyish, not necessarily gender transgressive. Indeed, the Chinese would typically want to know not who is the "woman" in a homosexual relationship but who is the "boy"? (Of course, it is important to remember that how people think about sex influences how they typically go about leading their sex lives. However, how people talk does not automatically mean that, in private, they always act in accordance with social expectation, nor does the available cultural discourse always prove a comfortable fit with personal experience.)

In such a construction of homosexual relations, "boys" will prove to be every bit as threatening and as life-enhancing as women. They are threatening because, presumably, they will be the respositories of their penetrator's semen.[10] At the same time, it is the very youthful beauty of the "boy" that is the source of the psychological thrill that betokens a physiological boost to their penetrator's life force.

What is salient in Taoist literature is the attention to how beneficial sex can be for the penetrator, whether in heterosexual or homosexual sex. Very little attention, if any, is given to what the penetrated partner might derive. Only modern spokespersons for the Taoist tradition have, in light of feminist concerns, argued that the "retention of the seed" works to prolong intercourse and thus make it more pleasurable for women as well as men.[11] Tradition focuses on the benefit accruing to the penetrating and usually older partner. Why a young man might want to penetrate an older one is a question merely registered with consternation in the literature. No attention seems to be given to the question of what benefit the younger man, the receptive partner, could expect in the sexual transaction. It seems that the adepts at Taoist spiritual cultivation could be counted on to be mature men who might lust after younger flesh, either male or female. The dangers and benefits are all on the side of the adept who would play the inserting role with either sex.

Before proceeding, we should consider nomenclature for a moment. Thus far, I have been speaking of penetrating or penetrated partners. The language is clinical. This represents an advance over the ideologically laden "active" and "passive" partners. Surely, the inserting partner is not necessarily "inactive." More important, it is not always clear who is "active." Who, for example, is the active partner in oral sex the fellator or the fellatee? (I suppose that would depend upon the relative degree of movement of the insertive partner compared with that of the insertee's mouth and head.) Although the terminology associated with the idea of sexual insertion is more accurate than that derived from notions of passivity and activity, the language remains unduly clinical and unwieldly, certainly more awkward that the vernacular. In common parlance, insertion is an act of "topping." Inserters are tops to their oral or anal bottoms, who "bottom for" for their tops. A man might top another in a specific sexual encounter, or a man might regularly be a top or a bottom in sexual encounters. In the rest of the text, for ease, I may use the vernacular "top" and "bottom" as both noun and verb as occasion requires. To summarize some of the territory we have so far covered together, we can say that Sambian boys are regularly oral bottoms for the older boys of the tribe, whereas an adult Sambian male is typically an exclusive sexual top for a woman. In traditional China, bottoming is a role appropriate to a social underling, whether that social status derives from one's gender, age, or social role (a servant, for example).

In neither Sambia nor traditional China is bottoming a role that is exclusively identified with women. Hence it is neither gender transgressive nor necessarily unmanly. Before proceeding, we might begin to speculate that the religious toleration of, if not the recommendation of, homosexual sex between males presumes that such sex is at least not unmasculine. In Sambia, an ideology about semen serves to relate bottoming to the process of masculinization, thus supporting the requirement of a homosexual phase for all boys. In traditional China, it is the absence of the stigmatization of the bottom in homosexual relations as effeminate that allows homosexual sex to be as spiritually significant as heterosexual coupling for those so inclined.

Perhaps, then, we are ready to begin to generate a thesis about religious tolerance of male homosexuality. The religions we have explored thus far are not loath to marshal and exploit homosexual sex for religious ends—in the case of Sambia, for the purpose of turning its boys into men and warriors, in the case of Taoism, for the purposes of a robust health that can prolong one's life. The presence or absence of tolerance depends upon how the ideas of masculinity and male-male sex are mapped. Such religious traditions either presume or draw upon a fairly consistent set of gender expectations as they relate to sex: age indicates the role a man is expected to take in both Sambia and in China. Sambian men are oral tops in homosexual relations; in China, social superiors are sexual tops of their social underlings, whether it is age or rank that determines who is the social top of whom. Such religious traditions either simply sustain by presumption or more strongly reinforce the notion that full adult masculinity is exercised in the sexual topping of others who are either women or not yet men—or perhaps even lesser men. Let us keep these ideas in mind as we consider "spiritual" cultivation according to Plato and Islam's Sufis in the next chapter.

Chapter 3

Holy Homoeroticism: Splendid Men and Splendor Divine

PLATO AND THE WORLD OF ANCIENT ATHENS

In his *Geography,* completed circa 23 C.E., the Greek writer Strabo reported not merely on the topography of the land of much of the world known to the Greeks and Romans of his day, but also on the history, manners, and customs of its inhabitants.[1] Purportedly, it had been the custom in Crete for a "lover" to "kidnap" a young man—having first announced his intentions publicly—and take the young man to a place where they would cohabit, feast, and hunt. There was apparently no question whether intercourse between the two would take place. Upon his return in two months' time, the youth had to own up publicly as to whether intercourse had been forced—apparently, any forced intercourse was subject to redress. Upon his return, the young man was also given a military uniform, a drinking cup, and an ox for sacrifice, then finally admitted into the "men's house" to which his abductor belonged.

In the wake of the discovery of Sambian homosexual initiation, scholars have debated the degree to which Greek experience paralleled Sambian practice. Some see in Cretan custom an echo of an ancient prototype that in turn helped to shape the sexual mores of Athenian and Spartan societies. William Armstrong Percy III argues that Cretan pederasty probably did not predate 630 B.C.E. when it was adopted as a conscious way of curbing overpopulation.[2] However, Robert Koehl discerns in Crete not utilitarian innovation, but an initiatory pattern of Minoan origin.[3] Whatever the results of the scholarly debate over the origins of Greek homosexuality, there is no question that homosexual affairs were pursued at least among the elite of Athenian society in classical times. Apparently, whether married or not, whether interested also in sex with women or not, Athenian men pursued romantic sexual affairs with younger men, that is, boys who were most likely in their late teens. The system in place resembled the system of "trophy boys" within contemporary homosexual society. The term, of course, is modeled upon the idea of the "trophy wife," a woman whose youth and beauty so far exceeds that of her husband that the casual observer concludes the bulk of her interest in her husband must lie in his worldly success and power. Whatever love may or may not exist between the spouses, the trophy wife is a public symbol of the man's social status. Among the ancient Greeks existed a system of patronage in which affluent men formed romantic, sexual liaisons with attractive younger men. A young man would grant his company and sexual favors in exchange for what he could anticipate as a social connection and a "start" in life. [4]

Presupposing this practice among Athenian men of Plato's time, Plato's *Symposium* is one of the prime sources for our knowledge of the practice—as well as evidence for the fault line that runs through Athenian thought and feeling about it. A symposium was the Greek equivalent to a dinner party, and Plato's *Symposium* purports to recount the events that transpired during one such dinner party hosted by Agathon in celebration of his victory in a playwriting contest in 416 B.C.E. The dialogue was not written until well after the death of Socrates in 399 B.C.E., probably later than 385 B.C.E., some thirty years after the events it supposedly describes.

The guests decide to celebrate not only with food and drink, but also by a contest of their own, each attempting to outdo the other by making a speech in praise of love. Phaedras, Pausanias, Eryximachus, Aristophanes, and Agathon each speak in turn. Socrates is the last to finish a speech about love, when the proceedings are interrupted by the appearance of a drunken Alcibiades whose speech about Socrates rounds out the dialogue and the contest. In his contribution, the comic poet Aristophanes concocts a myth about the origins of human sexual desire. It appears that, once upon a time, human beings were different than they are now. They were actually round figures with four arms and four legs who rolled instead of walking. (The very thought should alert the reader that Aristophanes is creating comedy and should be taken as speaking tongue-in-cheek.) In addition, each human had one head with two faces, and two sets of genitals. Some had female and male genitals, others had two sets of female genitals, and the rest had two sets of male genitals. Fearful of the pride and power of the humans, the gods decided to keep them preoccupied so that they would not storm the domain of the gods. Eventually, each human was split into two beings, with one set of genitals each, with the faces and genitals positioned on the front of their bodies. The result was that human beings were then so involved in the search for their "other half" that they ceased to be a threat to the gods. As one would expect, those beings who had had genitals of both sexes resulted in humans who sought out members of the opposite sex as their other half. Those who had two sets of female genitals became female beings who sought out the sexual company of other females, and those with male genitals became males who sought out other males for love and sex.

The relevant passage of Aristophanes' speech reads as follows:

> Any men who are offcuts from the combined gender—the androgynous one, to use its former name—are attracted to women, and therefore most adulterers come from this group; the equivalent women are attracted to men and tend to become adulteresses. Any women who are offcuts from the female gender aren't particularly interested in men; they incline more towards women, and therefore female homosexuals come from this group. And any men who are offcuts from the male gender go for males.[5]

Surprisngly perhaps for a modern reader, the very next sentence reads:

> While they're boys, because they were sliced from the male gender, they fall in love with men, they enjoy sex with men and they like to be embraced by men. . . .[6]

After glossing that such youths are the most manly of boys, the best of their generation, and members of the pool from which future public figures come, Aristophanes continues:

> [W]hen they become men, they're sexually attracted to boys and would have nothing to do with marriage and procreation if convention didn't override their natural inclinations. . . . In short, then, men who are sexually attracted to boys, and boys who love their lovers, belong to this group and always incline towards their own characteristics.[7]

Apparently, the male-male dyad is split into two beings, each of whom maintain a lifelong interest in other males, but Aristophanes' text is unable to imagine that this interest might manifest itself, as we contemporaries would, in anything other than an age-asymmetrical form. According to Aristophanes' account, in their youth, boys who are interested in other males will in fact be interested in men, while men who are interested in other males will be attracted to younger men. Although there is no inherit reason in the etiological myth that Aristophanes contrives to mandate that males who seek out other males must be of different ages, his text reflects the form relations between males would have taken in the Athens of his day.

Yet this insistence that male interest in other males will take an age-asymmetrical form makes it difficult to see how such partnerships might be lifelong, as he goes on to assert. Indeed, the text of Aristophanes' address adds that when the two men involved are in fact the halves of an original pair, there is a love match, and the two form a lifelong bond.[8] However, as he avers, when the relationship is between a mature man and a younger male, the younger male never, shall we say, grows into a boy-loving man himself, but will instead be frozen as a "youth" in a relationship despite his age. Aristophanes seems to combine two irreconcilably different understandings of male homosexuality into one. He wants to affirm the possibility of lifelong romantic attachments and at the same time insists on seeing such relationships on the model of an older man with a younger one, which implies one at least will outgrow the relationship in time.

The first speaker, Phaedras, avoids the seeming difficulty of speaking of lifelong love relations among men in his praise of the sexual love of comrades as the ground of manly virtue by concentrating on the dynamics of the relationship, not its longevity. He is clear in distinguishing the "lover" from his "boyfriend," arguing that virtue is inspired in each for fear of appearing shameful to the other. (The English word *virtue* disguises the force of the Greek, which otherwise conflates beauty *[kalos]*, moral virtue *[agathos]*, and manly, warrior prowess.)

The next speaker, Pausanias, begins his speech by distinguishing "common" from "noble" love. The love he calls common, it seems to me, is really a search for sexual release—a matter of, in the language of the street, "getting one's rocks off." For Pausanias, such love is "indiscriminant," in the sense that it can be satisfied by people of either gender, the dumber they are the better—whereas the more tasteful "celestial" love prefers the male, and a smart, admirable male at that. However, noble love, we discover, is that which a Greek nobleman would have for a promising youth, and not vice versa. Like Phaedras, Pausanias argues the civilizing effect of such noble love relations. Where they are forbidden, as in Persia, the populace is not free but is rather ruled by autocrats. Nor can the democracy that is the distinctive Athenian good coexist with a social practice in which young men are not taught to be discriminating in the choice as to which of their suitors they grant favors to—as in Elis and Boeotia. Athenians insist that potential boyfriends hold out for a good match, one that can be at least educationally beneficial, even as lovers will naturally seek out the most beautiful—and promising—of youths, and it is when both lovers and potential boyfriends exercise due choosiness that democratic institutions can flourish. However, one must note that Pausanias, like Aristophanes, maintains a distinction between the one who loves and the object of love: the elder is the "lover," whereas the younger is the "beloved" or the boyfriend. Love can apparently be predicated only of a man for a youth.

The Greeks could quite comfortably entertain the thought that males might form romantic liaisons with one another that would express themselves sexually. Yet, in general, many Greeks were apparently uncomfortable with the thought that a grown man might want—or allow himself—to be penetrated by another, but were apparently more comfortable with the idea of a willingly penetrable young man. Penetration by an older man did not compromise a boy's incipient masculinity—especially if it could be linked with the idea of his maturation and/or his education. Being penetrated was not thought to make the penetrated boy into a man, as among the Sambians, but it was acceptable for a young man to be penetrated—at least according to some—as long as it was part of an educational process.

The Greeks themselves, by the way, were aware of the inconsistency that existed in the way they modeled homosexual love in their minds. Popular culture understood Achilles and Patroclus to have been lovers. That Achilles was both the better warrior and the more beautiful, as Homer avers, caused havoc with the pederastic model of homosexual relations. Presumably, since Achilles was the better fighter, he was the top, but then he should not have been the more beautiful as well, since beauty is expected of the bottom. Hence the argument among the Greeks is about which of the two was the "lover," that is, the sexual top.

A "lover" would, in all probability, top his beloved anally. (Oral sex was primarily reserved, it would seem, for sex with prostitutes.) Anal sex, in turn, posed the danger of "feminizing" the young man. Anal sexual receptivity, in and of itself, held no shame, at least for a young man, nor did it compromise his masculinity, but some feared the boy might become "wide arsed," as it were. The danger was not physical, but metaphorical. A "wide-arsed" man was essentially a femininized man, a male without masculine restraint.

Contemporary American society operates with an inconsistent set of gender expectations. Although, stereotypically, men are held to be the more rational, and women the more emotional, when the two are in the back seat of a car, it is the woman who is supposed to have the power and presence of mind to say "no" when the man pushes his impetuous point—it is the man who cannot be trusted to be in control when sex is concerned. The Greeks were more consistent. Women typically were thought to be more emotional and less capable of sexual self-control. Men, on the other hand, were rational, and could be trusted to be in control of their sexual impulses as well. Failure to be able to say "no" to the self constituted the failure of appropriate masculine self-restraint. At least one scholar thinks that, out of fear of this kind of feminization, young men were encouraged to practice intercrural intercourse (the old "Princeton rub") rather than actual penetrative sex[9]—although I doubt the efficacy of such recommendations on the part of the morals squad, even if they were made. More important, this fearfulness for the moral integrity of young men resulted in the suppression of the thought that they might be motivated by such a thing as the compulsion of love. Boys might pair up with their admiring lovers, granting them favors, but the thought that boys might like being sexually receptive too much was, if not unthinkable, nevertheless a danger from which young men were to be protected. Although the speech of Aristophanes seems evidence to the contrary, scholars have hypothosized that the Greeks therefore maintained the social fiction that the younger man in a pederastic relation would endure, rather than enjoy, penetration by his lover—whatever might have been true in practice.[10] Since humans beings are the kind of social creatures who tend to accommodate to the expectations of the peers, such social fictions tended to dissuade young men from liking—or, perhaps, admitting that they liked—the sex they had with their elder lovers.

Aristophanes rounds out his speech with the thought that

> when someone . . . actually meets his other half, it's an over-whelming experience. . . . [I]t's hardly an exaggeration to say that they don't want to spend even a moment apart. These are the people who form unbroken lifelong relationships together, for all that they couldn't say what they wanted from each other. I mean, it's impossible to believe that it's their sex-life which does this—that sex is the reason they're each so eager and happy to be in the other's company. They obviously have some other objective, which their minds can't formulate; they only glimpse what it is and articulate it in vague terms.[11]

We have already considered the difficulties involved in thinking of lifelong love affairs given the contemporary practice and way of thinking about relations between men. It is the speech of Socrates that takes up the implicit challenge of Aristophanes in offering a substantive account of what lovers want—or, perhaps, more precisely, what the lover wants—when he is so strongly attracted to another sexually. Indeed, Socrates does not treat a case of mutual attraction, he presumes the asymmetry of love that informs all the other accounts. It is in this speech, traditionally taken as articulating the view of Plato himself, that the love of the homosexual "lover" for his boy-friend reveals itself to be the gateway to spiritual maturity, wisdom, and perhaps even immortality.

The bulk of the speech is represented, in fact, not as something that Socrates came by naturally, but something he had to learn at the foot of Diotima, a priestess of the male god Apollo. (It is indeed ironic that the man Socrates has to learn about the nature and import of masculine love through the inspired utterances of a female—or is it a man's idea of feminine inspiration?[12]) Humans are understood as inherently appetitive creatures, desiring beings who need what is outside themselves to complete themselves. All human motivation can be understood as a form of love, but it is sexual love that is paradigmatic for understanding what is going on in all human desiring. Love is understood axiomatically as a response to the beauty of that which is desired. This line of thinking is almost so obvious in Plato's *Symposium* as to be a truism. We are attracted by that which we find attractive. To find something attractive is to find it beautiful, the response to which is desire. But what is it we really seek when we are stimulated by the beauty of another human being and filled with desire for them? What we want, Diotima ultimately argues, is something beyond sexual satisfaction, in reality an unending happiness.

The argument that sexual desire is ultimately the want for something long-lasting begins with the observation that desire for the beautiful is identical with the desire to procreate in the beautiful. Since procreation in the beautiful (when it involves intercourse between a male and a female) might result in the creation of children, Diotima argues that children are an example of the kind of thing that we actually want when we think we want nothing but sex. The assertion is counterintuitive. More often than not, people are either surprised—and sometimes unpleasantly so—when sex results in pregnancy. Therefore it is not apparent that we have sex in order to have children. However, I think Diotima is invoking a notion of—to use a modern psychological term—subconscious motivation: what we appear to want is not always what we really desire. However, children are only one kind of procreative issue that might come from a love affair. In English, *intercourse* is a word that covers not only sexual congress but also social forms of interaction, such as conversation. Diotima's thinking moves along similar lines. Although sexual love between a man and a woman might result in sex, since by metaphoric extension, deep conversation is itself a form of sex, the issue of such sex can be thought of as progeny or offspring as well. Although sex between men and women may result in children, romance between men—whether it expresses itself in sexual congress or not—could be expected to impregnate lover or boyfriend alike with what we might call "brain children." Interaction with a beloved is the inspiration that may give rise to poetry or the making of statues. At an even greater remove, echoing the theme of Pausanias's speech, intercourse with the beloved may give rise to the inspiration that results in the creation of social institutions, such as democracy. For Diotima, each of these is more progressively long-lasting. Poems and statues can outlast the lives of their creators and their children, and institutions have the capacity to outlast even the death of civilizations and cultures. In an extrapolation, the logic of which is not completely clear, Diotima ultimately concludes that in wanting the beautiful we want the happiness and satisfaction such "having" provides—even as the possession of what we want gives rise to something that can apparently outlast our lifetimes. Putting the two lines of thought together, sexual desire ultimately reveals itself as the desire for an immortal, unending, happiness.

Love for the beautiful, however, not only reveals that which is desired in desiring anything—but actually opens upon the prospect of attaining that which we desire, if indeed such aspiration can be satisfied. Responding to a person's attractiveness with desire initiates a path to the wisdom and vision that could alone satisfy our craving, if our craving can indeed be satisfied. If, in the biblical traditions, fear of the Lord is the beginning of wisdom, according to Diotima, one man's love for another is the seedbed of maturity and ultimate satisfaction—if such a thing is possible. At first, the lover espies a beautiful young man and finds himself drawn to him. But a heart filled with romance finds itself in a new world to live in, a world filled with all sorts of beauties. Awakened to the beauty of his beloved, the lover first awakens to the physical beauty of others, then to the beauty of minds and hearts, and ultimately to the beauty of acts, what we might call "moral beauty." Our lover might also attain appreciation of the beauty of art and institutions. However, thus having awakened to the sea of beauties in which he is immersed, our lover may pass over into the recognition of a single beauty that is exemplified in each (thus accounting for their respective beauty), but exhausted by none (even the most beautiful thing is only more or less beautiful, and the most beautiful of those will eventually die or otherwise come to a disappointing end). This single beauty alone is a beauty that does not disappoint: It is a beauty that is not marred by imperfection, nor is it something that is changeable and can thus end. It is eternally perfect, that in virtue of which all other beauties are beautiful, since they more or less instantiate it—and it is the beauty in the light of which all beauties are recognized to be the beautiful things that they are. It is not merely an ideal, but the Ideal. Since this beauty is eternally beautiful, intercourse with it—the intercourse of vision—can satisfy our taste for the eternal. If the person who is enraptured by it could possess that vision eternally, it would answer to that which would satisfy us completely, granting us the eternal happiness that we seek. The later Platonic tradition would entertain the thought that we grow like that which we behold lovingly, that we can be immortalized by the vision of immortal perfection. The lover hungers and thirsts for the vision of his or her beloved, and drinks deeply of the beloved's beauty when in its presence. Food and drink become part of the one who is nourished by them. So too, immortal perfection communicates something of its own nature to the one who lives off the vision thereof. It shares its immortality with the person who beholds it lovingly. The *Symposium* does not go so far. It remains within the bounds of the conditional. If we could exist forever, it would be the vision of ideal perfection that would make our eternity a happy one.

At the same time, it is the vision of perfection that enables a person to judge correctly in matters moral. What is good but that which appears akin to the perfect? And the one who lives in accordance with sound judgment, holding fast and doing that which is good, is what we call a good person. The vision of the truly ideal is thus not only the source of whatever true happiness to which we can aspire, but also the vehicle of moral integrity and wisdom in life as well. The vision of perfection helps to make us good.

Enchantment with ideal Beauty cannot help but result in the relative disenchantment with all those lesser beauties that otherwise surround us. This is not to say that beautiful things cease to be appreciated for their beauty—their beauty is only a relative or lesser beauty—if still beautiful. Although lesser beauties continue to be appreciated as beauties, it is Beauty itself that now engages the fullness of our love, becoming the real object of our erotic interest. He or she who loves Beauty above all things will express that love in the hesitancy with which he or she judges and assesses all things in experience. He or she may be attracted by the glitter of something in the immediate environment, or the propects of following a certain course of action beckoning him or her at the moment—but the lover of the ideal will step back and ask just how beautiful these propects really are. The lover does not call anything beautiful until he or she has assured himself or herself that, yes, this is an instance, an example, of the truly beautiful. Since the Greek word for beautiful can also designate that which is good, the one who loves true Beauty above all things will correspondingly hold off from following a course of action until he can assure himself that such a course is right, because it exemplifies beauty. Because the ideal is the unchanging standard by which one judges relative beauty and goodness, he or she who loves the ideal above the real is delivered from fickleness, and one's judgment of quality shows a stability over time. In short, the lover of true

Beauty and Goodness becomes a man or woman of reliable judgment in matters moral and aesthetic—not to mention a person in control of his or her passions and emotions. The lover of ideal Beauty is alone capable of being a truly good person, possessed of "manly" self-control. But the lover of true Beauty and Goodness, the lover of the ideal, is none other than the lover of wisdom, literally, the "philosopher." For wisdom in itself turns out to be the love of the absolutely ideal— and the guidance of one's life by that allegiance.

However, if the philosopher has, through his realization of the compellingness of ideal Beauty, come to love it above all other beauties, how then does he relate to the beloved boy whose beauty was his springboard into the sea of beauties and from thence to the ideal? His love for the ideal has robbed his beloved of his overwhelming erotic appeal, since the philosopher's eros is now directed elsewhere. However, if his love for his beloved has lost much of its erotic force, his erstwhile beloved is still lovely and deserving of at least an attenuated love. Our lover will now see his beloved, however, not as the object of sexual desire. He will turn to him as a potential fellow philosopher and engage him in that more chaste form of intercourse, philosophy. He will become his young man's teacher. Through such intercourse, the lover hopes to "seed" the mind of his younger partner with a wisdom, virtue, and passion analogous to that of the mentor himself. Obviously, we have here a variation on the idea of the formative effect of intercourse that was foundational among the Sambians. In their case, however, what one man seeded another with was semen and the secondary characteristics of manhood. In the present case, what is seeded is wisdom, manly self-control, and virtue. (With the emergence of such manly virtue, we can imagine the sublimation of whatever desire a young man might have had to be sexually penetrated!)

At the conclusion of Socrates' speech, the dinner party is interrupted by the appearance of a drunken Alcibiades. The symposium was being held in honor of Agathon's victory in the playwriting contest concluded the previous day. Such contests were held in honor of Dionysus, the god of wine. So, too, we are meant to hear in the words of the drunken Alcibiades the judgment of Dionysus as to who wins the contest on who could speak most truly about love. After all, as the Romans would later say, in vino veritas—"in wine there is truth." Of course, Alcibiades has not been on hand to hear the speeches himself. Ultimately, he hails Socrates as the one who spoke most truly, since

Socrates is the most perfect embodiment of true love among the men at the dinner party, indeed among all men of his day. At the beginning of the dialogue, we see that Socrates has bathed for the occasion—an unusual action for him. He is wearing shoes, which is not his custom. At the beginning of his speech about love, Socrates characterizes the god Love as the offspring of Poverty and Plenty who shares something of the nature of each. The son of Poverty, Love is poor, lacking in what would complete him. The child of Plenty, he is filled with the knowledge of what he needs and the ingenuity required to attain to it. The reader is already prepared to see in the poor, bedraggled Socrates the incarnation of the god Love, and it is that which Alcibiades proclaims him to be.

Socrates, Alcibiades says, is like an ugly little doll possessed of the most beautiful interior beauty, a beauty with which Alcibiades is captivated—a beauty that lies not in his physical attractiveness. Alcibiades was reputedly one of the most beautiful and charming men of his generation. As such, he might have proven appealing to Socrates. However, it is Alcibiades the beautiful who is captivated with the beauty of Socrates, so much so that he wants to have sex with him. By the conventions of the day, Alcibiades would have been the younger, more beautiful man—and hence, the one who would probably have been penetrated in any sexual encounter with a man older than himself. However, Socrates proves oblivious to his obvious charms. It is Alcibiades who burns all too ardently to be loved sexually by Socrates. Obviously, he does not understand the kind of love that Socrates the philosopher can now offer him. At the same time, he manifests an interest in being penetrated sexually, all too inappropriate—by the canons of the day—for the younger man in a relationship. Such an interest is implicitly an effeminate, unmanly one—ultimately compromising his masculine virtue.

In fact, the historical Alcibiades was a follower of the historical Socrates, but the beautiful and charming Alcibiades proved to be a traitor to Athens during the Peloponnesian War with Sparta. It was after the war that the aged Socrates was brought up on charges of having corrupted the youth of Athens and condemned to death. To many, Alcibiades was living proof that the charge was true. In part, Plato's *Symposium* is an attempt to exonerate Socrates for what Alcibiades made of himself. The Alcibiades of the *Symposium* neither really understands Socrates, nor does he avail himself of the wisdom that Socrates offers him. Thus blame for Alcibiades' traitorous acts was laid inappropriately at the feet of Socrates.

Yet in the dialogue Alcibiades is a character sympathetic in ways that Socrates is not. Before the dinner party, Socrates meets a friend whom he invites to come along. In the meantime, Socrates becomes lost in thought and bids his friend go ahead and crash the party in advance of his arrival. There is something aloof about this Socrates, a man who seems almost bereft of even the most elementary of social graces. The modern reader, whose culture has trained him or her to be alert to psychological dynamics, cannot help but note the almost aggressive meanness Socrates shows in allowing himself to sleep with Alcibiades—while withholding sex. Plato has set the dialogue up as a third-hand report of what went on many years before at the symposium—told by someone who was not personally present. Plato invites us to be skeptical, not to accept everything we read. Are we to be critical of Socrates even as his compatriots would have been critical of Alcibiades? Are we to see, as Martha Nussbaum argues, the great cost, indeed perhaps the inhuman cost, of following in the footsteps of Socrates?[13] Are we to envision another path, equally as noble, but more humane and sensitive to the needs of those around us? Or is it, as Waterfield suggests, that we readers are to see ourselves in the figure of Alcibiades, as neophytes who have yet to start on the road to wisdom?[14] Plato himself may be seeking to undermine our doubts about the Socratic path since, by asking us to decide for ourselves with reference to the matters that have been related to us over the course of the dialogue, Plato the writer is assuming the role of mentor, the lover of the reader—who, in turn, is cast into the role of the beloved, a potential fellow philosopher.

Whatever one makes of the dramatic irony at work in Alcibiades in particular and the Platonic work as a whole, the import of Plato's *Symposium* for the inquiry of this book lies elsewhere. Plato, it strikes me, is not the great supporter of sexual love between men that he is frequently portrayed to be. In fact, in later books, the mature Plato will condemn homosexual sex as unnatural. I think his revulsion at the sexual practices of his contemporaries is already at work in the *Symposium*. However, even as he might condemn sex between men, Plato sees in homosexual romance the seeds of religious maturity. In the context of his society, where romances were more often to be expected among men than between men and women, it was in just such romance that the path to godliness lay. The Islamic tradition is even more explicit and severe in its condemnation of sex between men, but among the Muslim Sufis one can hear the echo of Plato: in a man's appreciation of the beauty of a younger man lies a path to God.

THE PLATONISM OF ISLAMIC SUFISM

If, in ancient Greece, sex between men was tolerated—albeit not always uncritically—the house of Islam has traditionally proscribed all overt sexual relations between men. Islamic life and culture seek to embody the values expressed in the revelation to Muhammad that is the Quran, the holy book of Islam. The Quran is explicit in its condemnation of homosexual sex. Although, as we shall see, the biblical story of Lot and the destruction of Sodom may have originally been more about the sin of inhospitality than any kind of aberrant sex, the Quran clearly understands the sinfulness of the men of Sodom, whom it calls "the people of Lot," to have included homosexual sex:

> What! Of all creatures do ye come unto the males,
> And leave the wives your Lord created for you? Nay but ye
> are forward folk. . . .
> And We rained on them a rain. And dreadful is the rain of
> those who have been warned.[15]

Another verse, which immediately follows a verse that mentions female homosexuality, seems to imply that whatever punishment the sin merits, it is light by comparison with that specified for other sexual transgressions:

> And as for the two of you who are guilty thereof, punish
> them both. And if they repent and improve, then let them
> be. Lo! Allah is Relenting, Merciful.[16]

An alternative rendering of the first part of the verse by the scholar Pinhas Ben Nahum sees it as applying to men, "If two men commit an unchastity with each other, then punish them both," and he concludes "it is obvious that the Prophet viewed the vice with philosophic indifference. Not only is the punishment not indicated—it was probably some public reproach or insult of a slight nature—but mere penitence sufficed to escape the punishment."[17] However, in point of fact, the punishment is not specified, leaving legal minds to search for guidance elsewhere.

Islamic jurists draw on the hadith literature—anecdotes and sayings of the prophet Muhammad independent of the revealed word of God which is the Quran—as well as the Quran itself in determining how to treat violations of the revealed path of life. Since this literature itself is inconsistent on the issue of the punishment merited by homosexual sex, and some of the hadiths are of doubtful authenticity, there is no universal legal position on the matter. Some Muslim jurists have deemed male anal intercourse a capital offense, whereas others treat it much more lightly.

However various the opinions about the severity of the punishment that homosexual sex might deserve, no traditional Muslim culture will avow in public any value that is at variance with those of the Quran. Homosexual sex remains taboo, unless and until contemporary Muslims—like their Jewish and Christian counterparts—begin to use the holy text against itself, arguing perhaps that the homophobia of the Quran is a culturally limited perspective that is out of sync with the deepest of Quranic values. However, that work remains in its infancy in Muslim circles. Despite the explicit proscription against man-to-man sex, Islamic culture has ironically proven to be surprisingly accommodating of the forbidden—as long as violations of the law remain private and unavowed. The standards of evidence required to substantiate guilt in homosexual relations in Islamic courts of law are high. Barring witnesses, the only effective evidence would be confession without physical or moral pressure, but the *sharia*—Islamic legal tradition—discourages such public self-recrimination.[18] Islamic culture was perhaps the first to practice what the U.S. military would later institutionalize as its "don't ask, don't tell" policy. Such homosexuality remains at best an open secret in Muslim societies.[19]

Among Jews and Christians, whose traditions likewise class homosexual sex as sinful, if not criminal, the proscription has, to a large degree, had a dampening effect on romance between men and male appreciation of masculine beauty. Not so in Arabic and other Muslim traditions, in which the male can be as beautiful as, if not more so than, the female. Whereas European and American poetry might typically speak of something being as soft as the cheek of a young maiden, Arabic poetry could just as well convey the same image in terms of the feel of the peach fuzz on a male pubescent's cheek. Muhammad himself is reputed to have been sensitive to the beauty of males. Indeed, one hadith has him warning that "beardless youths . . . have eyes more tempting than the *huris*," whereas another reports him as enjoining men to "keep not company with the sons of kings, for verily souls desire them in a way they do not desire freed slave-girls."[20]

In time, Christianity, and to some extent Judaism, assimilated the Greek suspiciousness of feeling and pleasure. They reflected the Stoic line of reasoning which asserted that, if procreation is the reason for sex in nature, then having children, not pleasure, is the only legitimate motivation for indulging in sex. Islam, however, never developed such a widespread aversion to pleasure. Although procreation might be the purpose of sex, the Quran explicitly permits sex for pleasure's sake.[21] Moreover, in Muslim perspective, there is sex in heaven, even if procreation ceases to be its point. The pleasure of love was generally thought a perfectly natural thing, neither undermined by, nor antagonistic to, devotion to Allah. With loved loosed from its bondage to procreation, the Arab theorist of love could explore the nature of attraction without preoccupation with the sex of the beloved, while the rigorist who feared male attraction to another male a dangerous temptation could still deem it unremarkable and natural. Indeed, in paradise, one could look forward to being attended by young men as well as by female *huris*. It is against this background that we can understand the Sufi "cult of the ephebe" (*ephebe* being the Greek word for "young man").

At the very least, a Muslim is one who lives and behaves as a Muslim behaves. One becomes a Muslim by saying the *shahadah*—"There is no God but God, and Muhammad is his messenger"—publicly before witnesses. Then, one is generally expected to conform one's life to the dictates of the *sharia,* the repository of legal opinions about the way of life enjoined by the revelation of the Quran. Such practice lays the foundation for thinking and understanding as a Muslim, as it were, "believing" as a Muslim. Sufism understands itself as the perfection of the Muslim path, completing the submission *(islam)* of body and mind with the transformation of the human heart. Because Sufism would prove innovative, particularly in the centrality it gave to the idea of love of, rather than simple obedience to, God, it would always bear the weight of the suspicions of the more orthodox, particularly in light of its cult of the ephebe.

This cult exploits the sensitivity of some adult men for the beauty of younger males in the ritual practice of *shahid bazi,* the gazing at a young man who is understood to be a "witness" to Allah. Muhammad is reported to have confessed, "I have seen my Lord in a form of the greatest beauty, clad in a garment of gold, on his hair a golden crown, on his feet sandals." One variant has this lordly youth wearing a cap awry rather than a crown, and another has him wearing green clothing rather than gold. In yet another related hadith, Muhammad simply claims that he saw his Lord in the form of a beardless youth.[22] To be sure, the authenticity of these sayings is open to challenge. Some could challenge them on the basis of the reliability of the transmitter. Others, rationally inclined thinkers, might doubt their reliability on theoretical grounds. For them, the sayings confuse the firm distinction between the creation and the Creator. However, those Sufis who took these sayings as reliable would conclude that if Muhammad could see his Lord in the form of a beardless young man, they could presume that the beauty of a young man could be transparent to the divine beauty, and that such a young man's beauty would be a testimonial or "witness" *(shahid)* to the beauty of Allah.

But who or what is God? Who or what is Allah? In Sufi tradition, God, we might say, is the Reality in virtue of which anything that is real is real. We might say He is the Existence in virtue of which anything that exists can have existence or "be in" existence. ("Know that He through whom existence subsists—greatly exalted is He!—is nondelimited Being.[23]) As such, God is not "a" reality alongside other realities, but the reality without which no real thing is real. As unmanifest or hidden, God is the inexhaustible depths of Existence. However, Reality shows or "manifests" itself as the existence of, and the Reality at the heart of, all real things. In this sense, whatever exists "manifests" the Reality without which it could not be. (Here, too, is another of those ideas that the orthodox thought smacked of heresy, for it seemed to them that the Sufis were confusing God with his creatures, compromising his transcendence!)

If all things "reveal" God, who is quintessential Reality presupposed as the background of all things, nevertheless not everything manifests Reality to the same degree. Reality, we might say, is a qualitative term as well as an ontological one. In this sense, things can be "more or less" real. When a thing is a good one of its kind, for example, we can say in English that that thing is "more real." Is not a good friend a "real" friend? Also, do we not speak at times of men or women as somehow being less than a "real" person, less than fully human? Can we not indeed speak of human beings who attain to the full stature of their humanity as being "real" men and women?[24] God is that Reality that manifests itself in the reality of things, in the reality that they have insofar as they simply exist—and in the reality that they have insofar as they "become what they are."

Human beings are unique creatures. A rock might be more solid and long-lasting than a human, yet a rock is merely material. A human being, by contrast, is not only physical—a human being is also a living being, indeed an animal. Beyond that, the human is possessed of a moral constitution. The human being is then, in contrast with the rock, "more real" because the human being manifests a greater degree of the different kinds or levels of reality. Further, human beings can cultivate themselves so that they can become "godlike" . . . in the imagery of Sufism, that is to say that the human being is the only creature that can embody all the divine names, the qualities of divinity itself. If God is merciful, so too humans are to be merciful. But to be godlike is to become fully what one is, a real, true, fully human human being.

Interestingly, God is not only "Reality" but also "Light." A stone merely exists, whereas a living being can have that glint in the eye that shows forth the "light of life." It is such a light that is eclipsed by death. In contrast to this light of life, the stone is but dark. For the Sufi, then, the human is a unique creature in whom the "Light of Life" manifests itself most brightly and clearly as the human embodies more and more of the attributes of God, the hundred divine names.

Some Sufis developed the spiritual practice of "gazing" at beautiful young men, not so much—as they argued—to appreciate the young man in and of himself, but as a "witness," a *shahid,* indeed a manifestation, of the beauty of divine Reality. In an intuitive jump reminiscent of the ascent to the ideal in Plato, the beauty of the young man supposedly facilitated an apprehension of the engaging beauty of all existence. The young man was to be the vehicle through which the splendor of all existence announced and manifested itself, and the boy functioned less as an object of erotic appeal in his own right than as an invitation to a passionate engagement with the whole of life.

The young man would be the cause not of love for his person but of a love for Reality, indeed of a love for God.

A young man, no matter how attractive, might not be the most morally developed of beings, but to the man sensitive to the beauty of younger men, the young man can at once manifest the beauty of Reality—*and* symbolize the beautiful luminosity to which we humans are called. The beauty of a young man, even a young man who is yet morally underdeveloped, can nevertheless symbolize and manifest the appealing attractiveness of manifesting all the qualities of the divine. It is not accidental, then, that the Islamic analog to the Western cult of chivalry would be the pursuit of *futuwwah,* literally the pursuit of "young manhood."[25] To be sure, we are not speaking here of the erotic pursuit of young men, but rather of the project of personally cultivating the virtues that were taken to be symbolized, perhaps even native to, young manhood. Those who were caught up in *futuwwah* were not necessarily Sufis—but Sufi theology permits us to see *shahid bazi* and the cult of chivalry as complementary spiritual practices.

As already noted, some Muslim theologians could be suspicious that Sufi interest in the "witness" went too far in allowing more god-likeness to the creature than was appropriate, thus compromising the transcendent otherness of God. More germane to our task, however, Sufis given to *shahid bazi* could be suspected of providing religious cover, and perhaps occasion for sexual license. In one tale from the *Arabian Nights,* a father takes his handsome son out in public for the first time. It turns out that the son is a real head-turner . . . and turns the heads of everyone in the marketplace, not the least being the head of a wandering Sufi who immediately insists upon an audience with the young man in his father's garden. The father, suspicious of the intentions of the Sufi, insists that the two be watched. As it turns out, the father is delightfully surprised to find that the Sufi did not, nor did he intend to, put the moves on the handsome son. The story ends with the watchful dad apologizing to the innocent Sufi for his apparently all too understandable suspicions.[26] Whatever the import of the tale, it at least trades upon the vulgar suspicion in some quarters that, among Sufis, religious intentions are masking sexual ones.

Given the pressure to conform at least publicly in Muslim society, it is not at all outside the bounds of possibility that the suspicions of our fictional Muslim dad might not have been groundless, and that actual Sufi practice may have been more sexually explicit than Sufis have been able to own up to in public. If so, inquiring minds would certainly want to know how a Sufi might have reconciled his overt homosexual activity with his identity as a Muslim, and what, if any, spiritual significance he might have attributed to it. However that might be, it is the practice of "gazing" to which Sufis have attributed spiritual significance. In the context of our exploration, the Sufi practice of *shahid bazi* is yet another variation of an already recurrent theme, that homosexual romance is a matter of the attraction of a mature man for a younger one.

Chapter 4

Holy Effeminacy: The Native American Berdache As Living War Charm

MEN AND MANHOOD

Barring a serious biological error, the possession of a penis is the decisive biological maker of maleness. However, as every boy learns in the course of growing up, having a penis is no guarantee that one is a man. Males are born, but men are made—with the help of nature in the form of timely infusions of hormones, of course. Becoming a man is as much a task and project as it is a matter of natural growth. Manhood—or, rather, masculinity—is part achievement. At the same time, it is not so much something that one "has" as much as it is something that is recognized by others. A male knows he is a man, or is masculine, if and as he recognizes his acceptablity as such among other men. He knows he has become a man when he can feel that he has become "one of the boys."

Psychiatrist Richard Friedman emphasized that men can be friends only with other men whom they respect at least as equals.[1] In civil society, a man may owe every other man, indeed all people, that minimal respectfulness we dub civility toward what we loosely call our fellow man, but he will find himself capable of friendship only with those with whom he can establish some rapport, and whom he can respect as a "fellow man." Equality among men is grounded in a masculinity common to each. Here, I believe, is the raison d'être for male initiations in tribal societies—every initiate can be counted as having qualified as a fully adult, masculine male, a "real" man of the tribe. The ordeals by which males establish and prove their masculine mettle may be less formal and more ad hoc in non-tribal cultures, but they exist nevertheless.

If masculinity is something that does not simply come with age, it follows that some men may fall short of the standard, that they will have proved themselves to be failed men. To be sure, the canons of manhood are at least to some extent culturally variable. However, masculinity will, in each case, be defined in terms of a masculine *style* and masculine *substance,* that is, one attains manhood as one masters typically masculine pursuits in a typically masculine style. To answer a Marine drill sergeant with the expected "Sir, yes, sir!" with a lisp would be to echo the right words but in an inadequate way. By the same token, "guy things" are what they are because they are the things typically done by guys. An interest in ballet, for example, was until quite recently in America something no red-blooded American male would be caught owning up to. Because one has to grow into one's manhood, some of those things that compromise adult masculinity amount to a residual childishness. "He's such a baby," we might say. Because such a thing may be said of a female as well as a male, childishness is that which compromises a man's maturity, not his manhood. That same boy might very well be called a "momma's boy" or a "sissy," in which case he is being chided for having failed to free himself from the embrace of women and thereby resembling them. The opposite of masculinity is femininity, not childishness. What seems to potentiate this latter is the psychological fact that, in the process of growing up male, a boy must distinguish himself from his mother with whom he is typically closely bonded in infancy and early childhood. A man is thus always psychologically vulnerable to the charge that he has not sufficiently broken with the ways of women.

Social theorists dub the set of expectations that any given society has of how males and females "ought" to behave as a "gender system." Modern homophile movements sometimes think of themselves at war not only with a given set of gender ideals but with the importance of gender distinction itself. Whether humans can or should aim for a completely gender-free way of living is an issue we will have to address. Here, it suffices to note that in the cultures we have explored thus far (with the exception perhaps of Islam proper, as distinct from Muslim civilization) sexual bottoming—whether oral or anal—has been construed as an act that can be legitimately performed by both males and females. When done by a male, it will connote the act of a boy—or of a number of other kinds of male social underlings. Fully adult, socially superior males are by definition both sexual and social tops. An adult male bottom would be perversely childish, or ridiculously servile. Other cultures—modern America, for example—construe bottoming as strictly feminine. Consequently, adult men are to be the tops of women, and bottoming is a token of effeminacy.

The cultures that stand in this latter tradition might, in turn, recognize two different ways in which a male bottom fails to be a man. His sexual deviation might signal a perverse distortion of masculinity. Others, society might allow, are actually transgendered persons, "women trapped in male bodies." Advances in medical science can now offer such men surgeries to bring their bodies in conformity with their gender identity. Barring the possibility of changing one's sex by penile excision or castration, if not genital reconstruction, a culture might simply assimilate the two conceptually. Alternatively, a culture might distinguish between men who are simply perverse in virtue of some salient masculine deficiency and others who are so effeminate that, although they are male by sex, they are so unmasculine as to have become not a woman but a nonmale. The photographer Kristen Bjorn, who lived and worked for some time in Brazil, was surprised to discover that Brazilian men recognized at least in practice just such a category of men.[2] Brazil, like most Latin countries, separates the men from the queers, the *homem* from the *viado,* the *macho* from the *maricón,* a penetrator from a willingly penetrable man. Despite the fact that a *viado/maricón* is a sexual bottom, he is still a man, and no *homem/macho* can be fucked by a *viado/maricón* without compromising his masculinity. However, Bjorn learned of *macho* men who could be fucked by men who were essentially preoperative transsexuals with no threat to their masculinity. Apparently, the penises of such men do not count as "real" and getting fucked by such a penis does not really count as being fucked because such men are, despite their penises, not really men at all.

BERDACHES: THIRD-GENDERED PERSONS OR UNMANNED MEN?

How the Native American holy men traditionally referred to as berdaches are to be mapped with respect to gender is the subject of some scholarly debate. Actually, the word *berdache* is something of a

misnomer. The word was orginally a term used by the French to denote "kept boys" or "male prostitutes" in the Middle East. When
French missionaries confronted the social type we are discussing,
they referred to these effeminate men as berdaches—and the term
stuck. More recently, Native Americans have argued that "two-spirits" is a more authentic and appropriate label. However, such a desig-
nation carries with it a questionable implicit interpretation of what a
berdache is. Accordingly, I will continue to use the more traditional
term *berdache* even at the risk of some imprecision because of the
lack of a better one. These people that the French confronted in Native American tribes were not prostitutes, but biological males who
dressed as women and did the sort of work the tribe thought of as
"women's work." In more recent times (in contrast with the sweep of
time during which Native Americans have inhabited the Americas),
berdaches might have been raised to be so from childhood. A young
boy might be put through an ordeal by which the tribe inquired into
whether the child was drawn to manly things, such as bows and arrows, or the things of women, such as baskets. The boy's preference
for the latter was an indicator that he was destined to be a berdache.
Or a dream or vision might indicate a boy's vocation to be berdache.
Sometimes, a man would become a berdache in adulthood. Berdaches were generally sexually active as bottoms. Thus, a homosexually inclined boy might very well have found himself gravitating to
life as a berdache. Homosexual sex would have been part of the "job
description" of the berdache, we might say. A homosexual orientation might have been a sufficient, but not necessary, condition for being a berdache. Some berdaches would take a "husband" for whom
they would be the "wife" both sexually and economically. (This "husband's" relation with a berdache, by the way, did not count against his
masculinity in any way.) Among many tribes of the Great Plains,
berdaches were discouraged from marrying so that they could "service" the young men of the tribe: the berdache offered a young warrior the prospect of a cheap date.[3] Berdaches, however, were not simply males who, for all intensive purposes, functioned as women. They
were "special," and tribes counted themselves lucky to have a berdache in their midst:

1. Berdaches were especially important for a tribal war effort.
   Typically, a berdache would accompany a war party but remain

apart from the fray, attending to sideline rituals. In some cases, they might fight, but were forbidden the use of bows and arrows, weapons reserved for unambiguously male warriors. Among the Miami, however, berdaches could take part in war with the proviso that, when they did so, they had to dress—and thereby, to function—as men.[4]

2. The berdache's potency in the war effort could be extended ritually. Among the Lakota, for example, a berdache might give a boy a medicine bag and a sacred name to "protect" him.

3. Because they were thus *wakan* or "holy," in some tribes they participated in tribal councils. Father Marquette, writing in 1673 about the Illinois, recorded that nothing was decided in the tribal council without first consulting the advice of the berdache.[5]

4. Berdaches were often ritual specialists in the more public ceremonies as well. Apparently the menstrual bleeding of women could contaminate a ceremony for warriors such as the Sun Dance. Among the Hidatsa, berdaches and postmenopausal women would make the preparations for the ceremony. Similarly, berdaches could do the "women's" work, such as cooking, in a ceremony that forbade female involvement.

5. Since the berdache was a power for the good of the tribe, he could take on any number of beneficial roles. In some tribal societies he might be seen to exercise a healing presence, much like a guardian spirit, especially at births. In a tribe where the berdache might be left behind when the men went to war, he might teach.

6. In some tribes, the tribal berdache would have a significant role to play in religious ceremonies.[6]

7. Although there is no scholarly unanimity, it is commonly held that berdaches could also be shamans. A shaman, of course, is one who in trances supposedly visits the spirit world and brings back messages.

Because the berdache was seen as embodying holy power and functioned in such significant ways, both religiously and otherwise, some scholars have concluded that it would be indeed appropriate to think of such beings as respected "two-spirits," one who is neither man nor woman but both.[7] Because berdaches are religious figures, so the logic runs, they must be thought of as respectable. Therefore, we must think of them in some way that avoids suggesting that their gender anomaly is in any way a freakish or ridiculous formation. Hence, when hailed as sacred two-spirits, such personages should be thought of as exemplifying a respected third gender all their own, whose sacred power would derive from the coincidence of what would otherwise be gender opposites. Indeed, in this line of thinking, the berdache's power and authority are derivative of the mix of gender and gender roles he embodies. By nature, the berdache is one who crosses boundaries and unites what is separate and distinct. He is sacred because he is a mediator and uniter of worlds. (Indeed, Roscoe thinks that the openness of the berdache to the white was an exercise of his priestly vocation of uniting worlds.[8])

The view has an initial plausibility. A shaman, for example, is one who can cross the boundaries that separate this world from the various spirit realms. However, in contemporary Korea, shamanism is strictly a female occupation. It could be that the berdache, like the "soft men" of Siberia who become shamans, qualifies for shaman status not in virtue of his androgyny, but because of his effeminacy. It is hard to see, moreover, how being a uniter of worlds could make the berdache a power for war. Nor is it easy to see how such figures who, by virtue of being sacred, would be subject to the degree of ridicule to which they were obviously exposed. The best those who insist that the berdache was a respected, not a ridiculous, figure can do in this regard is to argue that what the evidence reveals is a "joking relation" between equals, exemplified in a kind of frequently insulting banter characteristic of, for example, jocks in the locker room—guys who despite their mutual teasing really like one another way down deep.[9]

I suspect that at work here is an inappropriately anachronistic reading of sacrality and religion. First, the appreciation of mediation, of peacemakers, of the creation of harmony out of difference, is a distinctively modern preoccupation. In particular, the interest in minimizing gender differences is a particularly modern one. As discussed in the next chapter, many more traditional religions are concerned with the maintenance of difference, in letting men be men and women be women. We must be wary, then, of grounding the sacred status of the berdache in his embodiment of a distinctively modern virtue. More important, the theory seems to draw on a culturally determined confusion of religious regard and social and/or moral approbation, of social tolerance and social acceptance—as well as a misunderstanding of what counted for religious power among the Native Americans. To be *wakan* was not necessarily to be good, but to be, in some significant way, powerful.

Modern Euro-American religiosity is a product of its history. The late existentialist philosopher Karl Jaspers argued most mainstream contemporary religious traditions have their origins in what he called the Axial Age. This was a period of time in which the religions of the world underwent revolutionary change. Plato was an axial revolutionary in charging Homer with blasphemy for speaking of the gods engaging in immoral activities. Within the same age, the prophets of Israel were declaring, "[W]hat does the Lord require of you, but to do justice, and to love kindness, and to walk humbly with your God"[10]— even as Confucius in ancient China was insisting nobility was not inherited, but a moral character that humans were called to cultivate. In short, in the Axial Age, religions were coming to identify goodness with the divine, and religion with moral virtue. Much later, the European deists of the eighteenth century, wearied of the violence occasioned by confessional differences, began to view religion as important not for its metaphysical and doctrinal claims, but for the virtue it sought to instill. These deistic thinkers influenced the founding fathers of America—and the modern use of the word *religion* is heavily colored by the direction of their thought.[11] The point of this little historical diversion is to show that, by contrast, Native American spirituality is pre-Axial in character. It has not been refined by the fires of morality. Although we post-Axial thinkers may expect religious power to proceed from moral goodness, pre-Axial spirituality responded to power, period—power that might be marshaled for good, but something that is amoral in and of itself. Nor would the mere fact that a person would be a principal in a religious ritual necessarily imply that he or she was expected to be a socially admirable or respectable person. Consider the jester in a medieval court: he was not necessarily the kind of man a mother might want her son to grow up to be, but he had an important function. People can be tolerated, and society can provide a significant place for them without admiring them. For example, the transvestite RuPaul for a time had a TV talk show, even though he remains, in the eyes of most, a ridiculous figure. Something of the sort was going on with the berdache, I believe. Indeed, the berdache was a ridiculous figure. He was subject to more than a little teasing and not a little ridicule. The humor was not, I suspect, a sign of affectionate equality, but purchased at the berdache's expense. An adequate account of the berdache will have to account for his or her ridiculousness as well as the berdache's sacred power.

First and foremost, the berdache is especially valued for what he can contribute to a war effort. Obviously, his value in this regard cannot lie in his warrior prowess. Since, in most tribes, the berdache was not allowed to fight, and in others his participation was restricted, his value in this regard could not lie in his warrior prowess. Walter Williams has pointed out that, among the Plains Indians, women warriors could also take part in war, as long as it was understood that they had ceased menstruating.[12] That is to say, women could be thought warriors, as long as they had ceased to be bleeders. In general, women in their prime menstruate regularly. It would not be presumption to think that males, who after all only bleed when wounded, might have thought women were periodically "wounded." Thus, to go into battle with a bleeding woman would be to go into battle, as one of my students so pointedly put it, "already wounded."[13] Perhaps, by contrast, to engage the enemy with a berdache at one's side was to enter the war, as it were, already victorious. In other words, the berdache was *wakan*—or sacred—because he was a living war charm.

Ramón Gutiérrez seems to have gotten the matter right—a position which gains in plausibility in the light of Richard C. Trexler's study of gendered violence throughout the Americas at the time of the European conquest.[14] The origins of the social institution of the berdache are rooted in the tendency of warriors to rape and pillage—or simply to rape. The soldier's job simply is to penetrate enemy bodies. When he has exhausted the urge or need to penetrate with a weapon, he may go on to penetrate enemy bodies with his phallus. He may rape the enemy's women, or he may humiliate the enemy even more by raping the enemy himself. It is instructive to note that the Nahuatl word for "powerful warrior" can be literally translated as "I make someone into a passive."[15] Such humiliated men would thus be both a badge and symbol of warrior prowess and of victory. They could be kept to be routinely penetrated and taken into battle much as a football player might decorate his helmet with symbols of past wins. These defeated enemies might very well be kept around for just such occasions, dressed as women and forced to work as women as befits their humiliated, penetrable, status. It might have become so important to have such a living war charm, that if the tribe did not procure one in battle, then one could force a member of one's own tribe to become one. Alternatively, dreams and ritualized trials could reveal which of the tribal members were most called to be such a "pathetic excuse for a man."

The additional roles the berdache came to perform can be seen as the extension of the "power" that they derived from testifying to the warrior prowess of the tribe as a whole. A good luck charm in battle might very well have become a good luck charm in illness and childbirth, where other kinds of enemies needed scaring away. In further development, because he was holy and powerful, his words might be trusted, and the berdache would find his way into tribal meetings as a reliable counselor. By his feminization, the berdache would have been classed with postmenopausal women for ritual purposes—and likewise become a candidate for being a shaman. Finally, the berdache outlives the stigma of shame, as ridicule replaces humiliation—even as he continues to serve the men of the tribe sexually. (Why might We'wha have wanted to talk to the whites? Perhaps because no one took him in his tribe took him seriously, and here was the white man ready to see in him a kind of priest!)

The consequence of treating the berdache as the successor to a humiliated prisoner is that the berdache can no longer be hailed as an honored third-gendered person. At best, he becomes a socially valuable gender misfit in a two-gender system, his gender blending making him more ridiculous than admired, even as he was honored for his power. Indeed, society found a place for such a gender freak, a role that is important—but social usefulness does not an admirable person make.

All this has political consequences. I suspect, like Gutiérrez, that treating the berdache as an admired two-spirit is rooted as much in political interest as it is in the desire to do justice to the facts. The revelation that there were societies in history in which gender variance was honored might go a long way in undermining the sense that disrepect for gay men is natural and inevitable. However, the theory would have political weight only to the extent that gay men are conceived as gender-variant men, as "queens" rather than real men. No doubt some gay men think of themselves and handle themselves as "queens." They might assume that gay sex involves someone playing the part of a woman, and so they might signal their availability by dressing in drag and/or expressing effeminate gestures. More generally, they might simply interpret the love of one man for another as a feminine thing, thereby interpreting a homosexually inclined man as a "gender transgressive" person. However, many contemporary gay men refuse to think that their homosexual desire is at all feminine or compromising of their masculinity. Although such men might refer to one another from time to time as "she," they do so with tongue in cheek. For them, bottoming is not so much a matter of being feminized as of being "man enough to take it." Consequently, the discovery of the veneration of male nonmen in other cultures does not really advance the political cause of these latter gay men.

In light of this historical investigation, however, it seems the berdache is an instance of a man who is humiliated through sexual penetration. In such a construction, sex is less an act of love than an act of domination. But once again, this is a variant on a common theme, that fullness of masculinity enacts itself sexually in the penetration of social underlings. In this case, it is the act of sex that not only symbolizes the status of the social underling, but it also turns him into one. The really interesting question that arises is, can sex be used to humiliate an enemy because it is already understood as a matter of social domination? Or is penetration seen as an act connoting social superiority because it has been refracted through and interpreted in the light of warrior culture and sensibility? I would argue that sex can be seen to involve the assertion of social superiority only because penetration is understood as an act of domination. To see sex in such a light is to presume that an act of sex is analogous to an act of war. In other words, the construction of masculinity as a matter of sexual topmanship depends upon a metaphorics of sexual warfare derivative of warrior sensibility.

Whether such an association of homosexual sex and social domination characterized the ambient culture of the Bible is a question we shall have to keep in mind as we seek to understand the proscription of homosexual sex in the book of Leviticus in the Hebrew Scriptures.

Chapter 5

Holy Homophobia
in the Hebrew Scriptures

HOMOPHOBIA AND THE FEAR OF EXILE

The word *homophobia* is actually of relatively recent coinage. It was invented by George Weinberg on an analogy with words such as "agoraphobia" (irrational fear of being in public) or "arachnophobia" (an irrational fear of spiders) to designate the almost irrational disgust and horror that so many typically manifested, and which many still do, when confronted with even the idea of homosexuality.[1] At the time of Weinberg's coinage in 1972, homosexuality was still officially classified as a psychological disorder by the American Psychiatric Association, although that assessment was soon lifted in part by the pressure from studies such as those conducted by Weinberg. Weinberg himself was arguing that there was indeed such a thing as a "healthy" homosexual, and it was the homophobic—not the homosexual—person who should be classified as pathological. History attests to the way the word caught on and is today deployed to designate all kinds of resistances to homosexuality. The word *homophobic,* however, can be applied literally to the Hebrew Scriptures, those biblical texts which the Christian tradition has dubbed the "Old Testament." In the Hebrew Scriptures, the fact that the issue of homosexuality is only minimally mentioned might be taken as an indication of its relative unimportance in the vast sweep of Hebraic concerns, were it not for the fact that at least some acts of homosexual sex are proscribed because they are arguably so horrific as to be downright dangerous and deserving of capital punishment. Indeed, such proscribed acts are, in the words of Scripture, "abominations" (*to'eba* in Hebrew) which threaten the whole people of Israel with exile from their land.

The only explicit references to homosexual sex are the proscriptions against homosexual anal intercourse in Leviticus 18 and 20:

> And with a male you shall not lie the lying down of a woman; it is a *to'eba*.[2]
> And as for the man who lies with a male the lying down of a woman, they—the two of them—have committed a *to'eba;* they shall certainly be put to death; their blood is upon them.[3]

Although a technical cultic term at base, an abomination is something that is sickeningly disgusting. Apparently, the author of the proscription, as well those followers who included it with the Pentateuch, considered male anal intercourse so disgusting that it would sicken the very land itself and cause it to vomit forth the people who harbored the perpetrators. That is to say, homosexual anal intercourse was an act that threatened the people of Israel with exile, or more specifically, *another* exile.

According to the outline of history offered by the biblical texts themselves, Israel had become a nation among the nations—that is to say, a kingdom ruled by a king—with David's assumption of the throne. Technically, Saul may have been the first king, but David was the first real king to leave a dynasty to succeed him. David bequeathed to his successors not only the kingship but presumably also a degree of public unrest. Some would have been unhappy with permanent dynastic rule itself, some with David's decision to relocate the cultic center of the nation to Jerusalem from its traditional home in the north. In any event, when rule passed through his son Solomon to his progeny, the nation split into two kingdoms, Israel to the north, and Judah to the south. Recent archaeology has cast doubt on the accuracy of the account of the early history of the nation. It is not at all clear that there ever was a united kingdom under David which later split into two:

> There is good reason to suggest that there were *always* two distinct highland entities, of which the southern was always the poorer, weaker, more rural, and less influential—until it rose to sudden, spectacular prominence *after* the fall of the northern kingdom of Israel.[4]

The actual history here is beside the point, since whatever political entities existed did so as independent kingdoms only because they grew to be such during a period in which there was a relative power vacuum in the area. In time, however, the Assyrian empire would begin to cast its imperial net westward, ultimately swallowing up both the northern and southern kingdoms. The ascendancy of the city-state Assyria would eventually give way to that of Babylon, but the political practice remained the same. Conquered states lost not only their independence but also their effective local leadership. The intelligentsia and the religious and political leadership were transported to the empire's capital, where they were settled into a ghetto so that they could be watched, even as their absence from their native land minimized the threat of revolt back home. This is what is known to tradition as the period of the Babylonian Exile.

In the ancient Near East, it was generally assumed that, when one people was victorious over another, the gods of the defeated people had been likewise conquered or even killed. However, there appeared among the Israelites individuals, or perhaps even schools of thinkers, who were known as "prophets." The thinking of some of these prophets—or at least the ones whose thinking proved sufficiently prescient for their sayings and writings to be preserved—resisted the common assumption. Neither soothsayers nor fortune-tellers, prophets were— like Martin Luther King Jr., in a latter day—essentially visionaries and "advisers" to the nation. However, unlike Martin Luther King Jr., they protested that their visions and insights were not their own, but that of their god. They offered diagnoses of the social, political, and religious dynamics of their respective day, as well as prognoses for what would happen should countermeasures not be taken. This, they would say of their deliverances, is how the God of Israel sees things.

As the power of Assyria grew by assimilating other city-states and peoples into the empire, the prophetic witness was thus to strike an innovative chord. If Israel (or Judah) were to lose its national independence at Assyrian or Babylonian hands, the prophets argued, it would not be because of the superior strength of the gods of their enemies, but the work of their own god. Indeed, the decisive step toward monotheism was taken when the prophets asserted that exile, should it occur, would be something their own god had brought about by means of the Assyrians and their gods. Thus, they were implying that the Assyrian gods were nothing but puppets in the hands of their own god.

Loss of national independence and exile would be the work of the God of Israel, punishing his people for the failure to live up to their potential and their calling to be his people. But many of the prophets would not rest content with the mere thought of punishment, stepping away from any thought that the god who had brought Israel into being as a people through Abraham and later as a nation under their kings would disown them. Perhaps exile would be as much opportunity as punishment. Through exile, Yahweh, the God of Israel, was offering his people a chance at repentance and reform so that, when restored as a nation among the nations, they would finally be the light to the other peoples of the world that they had been created and charged to be.

The literature of the Bible is heir to the prophetic point of view. It not only includes representative writings stemming from the schools of thought that together interpreted the exile along such lines, but much of it is the product of the self-reflection and soul-searching of those in exile, reflecting upon what had gone wrong, and attempting to divine the contours of a new constitution for a restored Israel—one whose virtue would preempt future exile. The book of Leviticus is the product of such critical self-reflection. Scholars such as Jacob Milgrom argue that its laws and precepts reflect ancient preexilic practices and sensibilities.[5] Others argue that it is the product of a priestly imagination, conjuring up the constitution of an ideal state that has never been.[6] In either case, it is a digest of what priestly writers thought the revelation of God required of them.

The proscription against homosexuality occurs in the part of Leviticus (Chapters 18-20) that scholars have dubbed the "Holiness Code," or "H" for short. It is arguably a single document that has been interpolated by an editor or editorial committee into the surrounding body of laws, authorship of which is attributed to "P," the priestly writer or school. The impurities that are the concern of the "H" author are those which are so contaminating that they mark the perpetrator with an indelible stain, not unlike the "damned spot" of Lady Macbeth. These impurities are so sickeningly disgusting that the very presence of the offenders among the people constitutes a threat to the landedness of the people as a whole. (Other categories of impurities include those that are unavoidable, such as being sullied by the act of defecation. Such unavoidable impurities—and many avoidable ones—are less serious, since there are steps to be taken by which they can be "washed" away or otherwise drained of their contaminating power.) Hence, the severity of the offense that is homosexual intercourse was deserving of the death penalty. The susceptibility to being disgusted seems to come with the territory of being human, but the range of things that typically cause disgust is culturally variable. One culture, for example, might be sickened by the idea of eating cooked dog or cat, whereas another might relish the same prospect. Since we have already seen that homosexual intercourse is not universally condemned, we will have to inquire into the grounds on which biblical disgust in these matters is apparently based.

The Holiness Code is a strange collection of laws. For one thing, the sequence of laws is itself odd. Laws regarding various forms of incest and other sexual matters, for example, are interrupted by a proscription against worshiping the god Moloch. Moreover, the lawgiver moves quite abruptly from the seemingly momentous to the trivial: the injunction to love one's neighbor as oneself in Leviticus 19 is followed immediately by the prohibition of intermixing different kinds of cattle, different kinds of seeds in the same field, and different kinds of clothing. At the same time, other prohibitions are striking by virtue of their absence. Sexual relations with the wife of a father's brother are expressly prohibited—but a law against relations with the wife of a mother's brother goes unmentioned. The omission is particularly glaring because the immediately preceding rules concern the sister of *both* father and mother. Last, some laws concern rather outlandishly envisioned hypothetical situations: a man, for example, is forbidden to have sex with women in three generations of the same family. Who would've thought?

All of these surprising irregularities can be accounted for if we follow the ingenious suggestion of Calum Carmichael,[7] that H is not a collection or handbook of laws based upon the systematic envisionment of hypothetical situations but is rather the reflection of a legal mind examining the shortcomings of the ancestors of Israel as evidenced in whatever form of the story of Genesis he would have had in hand. Indeed, the laws of H seem to correlate rather well with episodes in the lives of the ancestors as recounted in the Genesis narrative. The H author enjoys the presumption that he now knows better than the founding fathers of Israel since he is the beneficiary of the revelation to Moses, which did not occur until after the events related in the book of Genesis. Our author is probably an exilic or even postexilic thinker striving to discern the path for the future occasioned by a critique of past Israelite actions.

Many traditional cultures—the Sambia of Papua New Guinea, for example—presume that the present should emulate the past. Ancestors are exemplary figures whose lives embody practical and ethical paradigms for the present. The people of the Bible have a different experience of time. Biblical religiosity—whether of the Old or the New Testament sort—is free to break with the past. Indeed, biblical writers inhabit a world that needs not simply recycle the past but that is free to move into the truly novel. Those who followed the prophets were free to critique the present and the past on the basis of an Israel that could and should be, but has never been. In the New Testament, Christians will be enjoined to think of themselves and to act as citizens of a new world order that they will hail as the "Kingdom of God," an order that is at best prefigured—but not yet embodied—in history.

The H author presumes a progressive understanding of revelation. It was Moses who mediated the full sense of the values according to which Israel should live, and the ancestors of Israel who predated Moses could not have had the kind of fullness of understanding that was available to those who would come after. Pre-Mosaic ancestors led lives that were compromised by non-Israelite ways. Only to post-Mosaic eyes, however, would the anomaly have been apparent. Thus, it would fall to exilic and postexilic thinkers such as the H author to sift through the past to discern what is an authentic expression of Israelite values and what is not. The ways of Israel are not the ways of its neighbors, and the author of H is attempting to discern how Israel should live in the midst of exile and/or in some future reestablished Israelite kingdom. What is at issue is not how all the peoples of the world are to live, but how Israelites are to be true to themselves, their traditions, and their god—above all, how they are to avoid future exile.

THE FEAR OF DEATH: ANAL INTERCOURSE AS "UNSAFE SEX"

In Carmichael's understanding, the proscription of male anal intercourse in Leviticus 18 represents the conclusions of a legal mind meditating on the story of Sodom in Genesis 19. Two angelic visitors come to town, and Lot, a hospitable man, insists that they stay the night under his roof. In the course of the evening, the other men of the town gather at Lot's door, insisting that he turn over the strangers to them so that they might "know" them. Lot is so horrified by the demand and the prospect that he offers to give his daughter to them rather than to hand over the men who have accepted his offer of hospitality. The angelic beings eventually escape mistreatment by striking the men blind.

Scholars debate whether the "sin" of the men of Sodom lies in their violation of "hospitality," the protection of strangers not infrequently being a principal concern of the deities of nomadic peoples and their successors, or whether it lies in their violation of sexual propriety in homosexual intercourse—or perhaps even both, violating hospitality by homosexual rape. What is the reason for Lot's horror, a horror so great that he would prefer to let his daughter be repeatedly raped? Is it that the men of Sodom would violate the laws of hospitality? Or that they would do it in such a way? Apparently, nowhere in the Hebrew Scriptures or in the Apocrypha nor in the Talmud is the sin of Sodom identified as homosexual intercourse.[8] Nor do the New Testament authors use the story of Sodom in their discussions of homosexuality. It is, however, so identified in the writings of Philo and Josephus, who are roughly contemporaneous with the New Testament, and in the Pseudepigrapha. If our legally minded Levite was to think that the sin of Sodom was homosexual sex, he would represent the only author in the Hebrew Scriptures who would be thinking along the lines characteristic of a much later period. The fact is that the story, in and of itself, is ambiguous. There is no reason why our author could not have seen homosexual intercourse as part of the sin of the men of Sodom: homosexual intercourse was the way in which they would be violating the laws of hospitality.

However, nothing about the story helps us to understand why our Levitical lawyer would find homosexual intercourse so objectionable. His choice of the word *abomination* to characterize it does provide us with a lead. The force of the word can be understood only in the light of the theological presumptions of the book of Leviticus as a whole.[9] Although the God of Israel is a cosmic power, he has also a local habitation among the Israelites. He is thought to be enthroned on the ark in their midst. The ark—and later the Temple itself as the "house" of God—was a source of power. The enthroned God is a kind of power source whose presence radiates and vitalizes the land and energizes the society from the center outward. This power dissipates in efficacy as it reaches the far extremes of Israelite territory. Equally important, however, this enthroned God is vulnerable to being driven away by, and must therefore be protected against, "impurity." Only "pure" things can come near him, and "impure" things must be kept at a distance from his localized dwelling. The proximity of impurity threatens to drive him away—unless the 'impurity" can somehow be eradicated. In some cases, impurity dissipates with time or can be washed away. Other impurities so severely compromise people that they have to be exiled or put to death. An abomination is a serious impurity, one that cannot be tolerated in the whole territory energized and animated by the presence of the god.

Just as the approach of death can seem to drive life away, so some scholars think that the ritual system that protected the god from impurity is a way of protecting the divine power of life from contamination by death in any of its forms. An "impurity" in this line of thinking is something that is contaminated by death. We are not speaking of hygiene here. For example, a man is rendered impure by the physiological process of ejaculation. It isn't sex that is impure, rather it is ejaculation that renders a man somehow compromised by "death." In our discussion of Chinese Taoism in Chapter 2, I noted how semen can be construed as the bearer of a man's life force, which he "donates" in intercourse for the sake of a new being. His ejaculation, then, involves a little dying, since it means suffering the loss of a little bit of his life. In the present context, a similar line of thinking might lead one to see his "compromised" vital power as a matter of being temporarily "contaminated by death." Thus a priest who had ejaculated could not do his priestly service near the Holy One until his impurity had been waited out or otherwise washed away—that is, until his fullness of life had been restored to him.

To think along these lines, the abomination that is male anal intercourse—for that is what the proscription in Leviticus is finally about—must constitute a "deadliness" of a particularly severe sort. It has been proposed that the deadliness of homosexual intercourse must be a phenomenon similar to the impurity acquired as a result of intercourse with a menstruating woman. Blood is another one of those bodily fluids that, in ancient modes of thinking, is the bearer of life. Too much bleeding and a body dies. A menstruating woman, then, could very well then be understood as, during her menstruation, contaminated by death. Sex with a menstruating woman would thus mean that a man was depositing vital fluid in a vessel in which death had manifested itself—and it is this blatant mix of life and death that makes such intercourse an abomination. Such a mix—because of its blatancy—would represent a particularly powerful, and thereby even dangerously explosive, mix. Such mixing of life and death would then be too dangerous to tolerate. Homosexual intercourse could be construed as dangerous on similar grounds. Ejaculation in the act of anal intercourse involves an explosive mix of life and death—if the rectum is somehow understood as a "vessel of death," that is, if excrement is associated with death. For then, the act of male-male intercourse would involve the depositing of the fluid of life in a place of death.[10]

Interestingly, it is again in the Far East that we find just such an equation of shit and death. Shinto is most easily understood as the indigenous tradition of Japan that became aware of itself as a unique spiritual path when Buddhism was introduced. It is a religion whose practices are particularly concerned with keeping the things of life and death fully separated from each other. In early Shinto practice, for example, the death of a ruler so contaminated the place from which he ruled that his successor would have to establish a new capital city. Interestingly, it is not certain that early Shintoism found in male homosexual relations the same kind of violation that the Israelites found. The *Nihon Shoki,* one of the oldest Japanese books, contains the story of two male lovers, Shinu no Hafuri and Ama no Hafuri. When one dies from an illness, the other commits suicide so as to be "with" his beloved in death. His friends, taking this desire literally, bury the bodies in the same grave. The story notes that thereafter the sun—the life-giving sun, we must gloss—did not again shine on that spot. Not until, so the story goes, the grave was opened and the bodies buried separately. The story involves some kind of offense against the sun, but it is not clear whether the impropriety lay in the homosexual relation or in the mere fact of a common resting place.[11] Nevertheless, it is in the Shinto creation story that we find evidence of an equation of excrement and death.[12] Susa-no-o, the spirit of the dry—and thus potentially deadly—west wind, defecates under the throne of Amaterasu, the sun-spirit, the shining-she-in-the-sky. In the morning, when Amaterasu rises and assumes her throne, her realization that she is sitting where someone has shat drives her fleeing into "eclipse." That excrement can drive away the power of life that operates through the sun establishes an association of excrement with the power of death.

That the depositing of semen in the anal canal was explosively dangerous apparently underlay the Zoroastrian proscription against male homosexual intercourse. The Zoroastrian tradition descends from the reforms of the Iranian prophet Zarathushtra (Zoroaster, in Greek). For him, the world was the theater of action in a war between Ahura Mazda, the Spirit of Bounty, and Ahriman (Angra Mainyu), the Spirit of Aridity and Death, in which Ahura Mazda could be trusted to be ultimately victorious. At stake, of course, was the bounteousness of the earth, for when Ahura Mazda comes into his own as the unchallenged ruler of all, the world becomes the bounteous Kingdom of (the good) God. Since service to Ahriman could ultimately be understood as leading to aridity and death, those who served the "evil" one as if he were the power that vivifies the living are deceived—and Ahriman is thus also the Spirit of the Lie. By contrast, service to Ahura Mazda is service to the trustworthy one, the Spirit of Truth. (Of course, behind this idea, lies a "competition" among cults.) Effectively, Zarathushtra began to think of some of the divine pantheon of the people among whom he was born as "aspects" of Ahura Mazda. Others, the *daevas*, were understood as evil spirits in service to the Evil, Deceiving One. Apparently, it is the creation of the world that awakens Ahriman into ruinous action. But before he attacks Ahura Mazda's creation with disease, death, and decay—to mention only a few of the evils he brings upon it—he creates a legion of evil cohorts through self-sodomy.[13] Indeed, it is his intercourse with himself that results in an explosion of evil power hell-bent on anticreation.

Cyrus of Persia, who ended the Babylonian Exile, was a Zoroastrian. Conceivably, the writer of the Holiness Code knew of the Zoroastrian hatred of male anal intercourse and was influenced thereby. In the event that the author of the Holiness Code was writing during the exile, we would have an instance of the convergence of minds in the same part of the world. However, if the concern of the writer is with the mixing of the fluids of life with a vessel of death, one would presume that he would go on to rule out all anal intercourse—whether heterosexual or homosexual. However, the author does not. So per-

haps we need to look further in search of a justification of this proscription in another line of thought that might be taken to ground a hatred of explicitly homosexual anal intercourse.

THE FEAR OF DISORDER:
HOMOSEXUAL SEX AS DEFORMITY

It might be thought that homosexual intercourse is associated with
death because it is reproductively sterile.[14] However, to stop there
would be to overlook the real logic that is at work. It is because homosexual sex is something other than vaginal sex that it fails to be even
potentially procreative. However, this is to see homosexual sex as a
kind of deformed, freakish formation. Deformities, according to the
theories of scholars know as structuralists, result from the confusion
of categorical distinctions.[15] That is to say, what if the problem is not
the deadliness of homosexual intercourse resulting from the confusion of life and death, but simply the fact of confusion itself? In the
previous line of thinking, what is feared is the deadliness of the conti-
guity of death contamination with the power of life. What is feared is
the power of death itself. But perhaps it is disorder and chaos that is to
be feared instead. After all, according to scholars, the priestly school
of thought that is responsible for the book of Leviticus is also responsible for the story of creation in Genesis 1. There God is seen as creating by separating things and putting them in their appropriate places:
first, light is separated from dark, then the waters above from the waters below, then land from water. He goes on, of course, to create sky
creatures, water creatures, and land animals, each having their own
domain before he eventually creates humans and then takes his rest.
Humans are created in the "image and likeness" of the creating one—
a biblical way of saying that humans are local sheriffs whose job is to
see to it that, in this creation of God's, God's will continues to be
done. That means, humans—or at least those humans who are Israelites—are to follow in the divine footsteps. First, they, like Him, are to
work for six days, and then take the (one-day) weekend off. More
generally, the human vocation is to maintain the divine order and to
extend the ordering process. Things are to be categorized and kept in
their places. Although the importance of keeping a kosher kitchen
would be a later development within the Jewish tradition, already in

this story, the created order is a kitchen in which things that are separate are not to be mixed. The world is to be kept kosher. Indeed, later in the story of Genesis, it will be the desire of heavenly beings to mix it up with the daughters of men and, second, the desire of earthlings (humans) to storm heaven by building the tower of Babel that occasions the divine wrath which almost returns the entire creation to the chaotic void that was at its beginning.[16]

"Impurity" or "dirt" can be thought of as "matter out of place." When that out of which one's garden grows finds its way onto one's pretty white skirt or shirt, soil has become "dirt," something that is to be washed away. Here, cleanliness is not only next to, but is, the practice of godliness. The project is to avoid getting dirty to the extent possible. Unavoidable dirt is to be dealt with by any number of forms of washing. Avoidable dirt is to be simply avoided. When the dirt that is avoidable is so deeply staining that it cannot be washed away, those who have been rendered impure must be run out of town or otherwise disposed of. Homosexual anal intercourse would apparently be one such dirtying act. But wherein is the dirt? It is not clear how the slogan—dirt is matter out of place—helps us to understand the matter of homosexual impurity.

It was the venerable eighteenth-century philosopher Bishop Butler who penned the philosophically seminal truism "Everything is what it is, and not another thing."[17] Indeed, we frequently understand a thing by distinguishing it from what it is not, what is other than itself. Sometimes, we define things in relation to an opposite. A man is not a woman, for example, nor is a woman a man. "Purity" requires that things be what they are. Effeminacy in a man is dirtying since he is now characterized by that which characteristically belongs to something else—namely, a woman. Most things do not have clear opposites, but can nevertheless be understood as "not this, and not that." For example, a cow is a land animal and is thus other than a fish and other than a bird. A cow that had fins would have that which properly "belongs" to something else, namely a fish. Such a cow would be literally a kind of "mixed breed" and thus impure by virtue of the mixture makes of it a deformed monstrosity. But a thing need not be a mixture of "two kinds" to be impure; a thing may be deformed simply by having that which does not properly "belong" to it. Humans typically have five fingers on each hand, and one head. A six-fingered hand or a two-headed human are considered deformities. Finally, it is deformity that makes something impure. The slogan "matter out of place" is a circuitous way of getting at what makes something a deformity.

It is important to note, however, that the notion of deformity requires a norm of "good form" from which the deformity is a deviation. The atypical is only atypical in reference to a concept of the typical—or we might want to say, the stereotypical. The notion of a deformity requires a kind of paradigm case that functions as the standard of good form. Leprosy is a disease that causes the skin to whiten. The whitening of the skin does not happen all at once, so that for a while the leprous person is blotched, having patches of normal and of leprous skin. In the purity system of Leviticus, the leper may have been clean prior to the onset of leprosy, and is "pure" again once his body is totally whitened. However, the blotched condition renders him or her impure—since it violates the sense that, stereotypically, the human is to be of one hue. The color of the skin is of no consequence. What is of consequence is that the skin be of a consistent color. Severely blemished or mottled skin is a deformity. So too, the cow may come to typify the condition of being a land animal. To be a land animal is to be cowlike. Those animals that are not sufficiently cowlike—such as the pig—are atypical, and thus deformed, land animals. They have about them things that do not properly "belong" to the idea of land animal. In purity religions, some deformities have consequences. Happily or unhappily, impure lepers are shunned. The not-so-noble pig is spared the knife on the sacrifical altar—as well as the "altar" in the kitchen.

Arguably, homosexual anal sex can be seen to involve one of two "deformities." Physically, a man is a penis-bearing person. But a man is a man not only by what he is, but how he handles himself. By definition, or shall we say typically, or stereotypically, a man is a penetrator in the act of sex. Anal intercourse between men involves one man assuming the (typical) role of a woman—an abominable mixture of roles! Alternatively, male-male anal intercourse may represent deformed sex. If real sex involves a penis in a vagina (vaginal intercourse), then a penis in the anus is a deformity. By the same token, oral sex would be deformed sex as well—or, as some men think, not "real" sex at all! The Levitical text does not seem to be interested in a rod being in the wrong hole. Otherwise, we would expect the condemnation of homosexual anal intercourse to be followed by reflection on oral intercourse. Instead, the proscription of male anal intercourse finds itself imbedded in a list that also contains a proscription against bestiality, suggesting that the real issue is not the *hole* that the rod is in, but *whose* hole it is. In short, the real issue has to do with the transgression of gender norms in which one man is unacceptably behaving as a woman with another man.

Interestingly, however, Leviticus finds both partners in male-male intercourse culpable. If male anal intercourse is a dangerous and deadly practice, a line of thinking we explored earlier, then both partners might be thought equally guilty of transgression. In the line of thought we have been pursuing here, guilt seems to accrue to the willingly penetrated one, the man who in his own self confuses male and female sexual roles. Whence the guilt of his top? Perhaps he is guilty by virtue of complicity with another man's self-betrayal of his masculine identity. Perhaps he is guilty of a betrayal of his own masculine identity. That could be so only if sexual manhood is defined in terms of being the top of women only. We have already explored a variety of cultures in which men could be tops of younger males and social underlings as well as women. In context, the author of the Holiness Code would seem to be the exception. What kind of social conditions might lead a culture to identify men as tops of women only—excluding from them a whole range of sexual partners that other cultures allowed them? This question is, it seems to me, related to the question of why the author of the Holiness Code seems interested in male homosexual intercourse exclusively, showing no corresponding interest in homosexual relations among women.

There is no question that homosexual anal intercourse fits the Levitical framework because it can be construed as a kind of impurity. However, I have already noted that, if Carmichael is indeed correct and the H lawgiver is reacting to the story of the men of Sodom whose sin so many other contemporary authors saw as a violation of hospitality, we are left with the question as to why H would single out the impurity of homosexual anal intercourse as the one he felt bound to prohibit. Many different things can be construed as improper mixings of life and death, or simply as improper mixings of any number of sorts. Why would this particular mixing be a concern while other possible mixtures go unmentioned, especially if the story about the ancestor with which the H author is dealing at any given time is suggestive of such a plurality of impurities. Additional considerations must be in play to cause the author to focus on the particular impurity of homosexual sex.

ALIEN WORSHIP, ENEMY WAYS IN WAR

Just as Carmichael correlates the proscription against male homosexuality of Leviticus 18 with the story of Sodom, so too he correlates that of Leviticus 20 with the story of Tamar contained in Genesis 38. The story involves an episode in the life of Judah, brother of Joseph, which takes place after Joseph has been sold into slavery. It seems that Judah had a daughter-in-law, Tamar, who was married to his first son, Er. In the course of time, Er died without leaving an heir. According to the custom that would in time come to be known as "levirate marriage," the brother of a man who dies childless is expected to take his brother's widow as a wife and to father a child on his brother's behalf. Thus Onan, Er's brother, married Tamar. However, whenever they had sex, Onan withdrew before ejaculation, apparently uninterested in fathering a child that would be his dead brother's more than his own. For this, the God of Israel killed him. (By some strange logic, the sin of Onan later comes to be identified with masturbation rather than "coitus interruptus" in violation of a brotherly duty.) Apparently, Shelah, Judah's third son, was too young to marry Tamar after Onan's untimely demise. That is, he was not yet of an age to begin to ejaculate. Tamar was sent back to her natal family to live until such time as Shelah became "marriageable." Time passed, Shelah came of age, but no marriage happened. By this time, Judah's wife had died, and Tamar—still eager to do her duty of bringing forth progeny for Judah's family—disguised herself as a "cultic sex worker." Judah, apparently ignorant of her real identity, then sired a child by her. When Judah realized Tamar had become pregnant, he accused her of prostitution—apparently of the cultic kind. When he realized, however, that her child was his, he admitted his culpability in not giving her to his son Shelah. All was forgiven, and all was well. Judah refrained from having any more sex with Tamar.

Our H lawgiver, reflecting on this story, extrapolates two laws: a man is forbidden to have sex with his daughter-in-law, and men are forbidden to have sex with other men in a way that involves one man playing the "woman's" role. He apparently takes no note of the fact that Tamar played the role of a "temple prostitute" before passing directly to the impropriety of a man having sex with his daughter-in-law. Although the idea of temple prostitution is not mentioned, it remains the missing link that leads him to the thought of male-male intercourse: we Israelite men, he seems to be saying, do not even have the kind of sex that is typical of a male temple prostitute, much less include it in the cult of our god. That kind of sex is simply not done . . . at least not among us!

Other strands of biblical tradition are explicit in condemning such cultic practices as alien to the religion of the God of Israel. Deuteronmy 23:17-18 expressly forbids the daughters of Israel from becoming *kedeshah* (a temple functionary distinguishable from a *zonah*, or "ordinary" prostitute) and the sons of Israel from becoming *kadesh*, a word that is coupled in verse 18 with the Hebrew word for "dog." Whereas in those traditions that stem from the Bible, interaction with the divine is accomplished in sacrifice and/or verbal intercourse—"prayer." The author of Deuteronomy seemingly testifies to a religious practice in which devotees seek to influence the gods—the mother goddess specifically (the divine figure who arguably survives as our "Mother Nature")—through physical intercourse with one of her representatives. One could rouse the Holy Mother to one's cause by having sex with one of her priestesses—or one of the men who gave themselves to the service of this mother. Sex with devotees was apparently part of the job description of the ancient Near Eastern equivalent to the nuns and monks of later years. In the Christian tradition, it became customary to think of a nun as having (symbolically at least) "married" Jesus Christ, and thus her vow of chastity could be understood as her pledge of fidelity to her spiritual husband. But the ancient Near East seems to have known of a service to the Mother Goddess that required the sexual servicing of the devotees. Presumably, in order to protect bloodlines within the family, women in general—both married and marriageable—could be expected to restrict their sex lives to intercourse with their husbands or the husbands they might be married off to. Males, therefore, were the ones that were likely to seek out the services of such godly functionaries. That males might be available to male devotees would certainly help solve the potential problem of unwanted pregnancies within a temple.

If the idea of cultic prostitution is indeed the conceptual link by which the story of Tamar leads the H lawgiver to the proscription of homosexual male intercourse in Leviticus 20, the idea remains unmentioned. Apparently, H is less interested in the purity of the cult of Yahweh, the God of Israel, than he is in Israel's independence from such alien practices. In short, homosexual intercourse among men is "constructed"—to use the scholarly jargon of the moment—as a "foreign" practice, typical perhaps of non-Israelite culture, but certainly not a practice native to the men of the House of Israel: "That sort of thing is not done among us! It isn't done, and it isn't to be done!" The construction of male homosexuality as a foreign vice is a recurrent move in the history of the world. Indeed, it baffles the mind how the ideological machinery of Communist China could turn a blind eye to the evidence of homosexual practice in China's literary past to pronounce homosexuality a Western vice. It is to the lasting credit of gay pioneer historian John Boswell to show how homosexual practice was tolerated among many Christians until well into the medieval period.[18] Mark Jordan has shown how the medieval Christian mind could nonetheless construct male homosexuality as an Islamic failing (and Islam, a Christian one!).[19]

Clearly, the construction of homosexuality as foreign presumes an ignorance—either real or willful—of evidence of actual homosexuality in one's community or in one's tradition. On the basis of his research among American males in the 1940s, Albert Kinsey estimated that one in ten males would likely to be predominately homosexually inclined.[20] Let us say one lives in a small rural community (and scholars now think that the original Hebrews were rural folk, indeed pastoralists who settled in small communities in the hill country outside the Canaanite cities). If there are only ten menfolk, and Kinsley's predictions hold true, then presumably there would be only one homosexually inclined man in the group. Chances are, if he didn't sense anyone else in the community to be like-minded, no one would know of his "proclivities." His homosexuality, and homosexuality itself, would remain hidden unless a more significant public presence existed. Since under rural conditions, the presumption of heterosexuality would hold sway, one could very well find all homosexuality as characteristic of groups other than one's own. Perhaps it was as an alien practice characteristic of city folk that the Israelites came into contact with homosexuality. That confrontation might have been sufficient to set the pattern of thinking of homosexuality as something that is not of "us," but something characteristic of "them." Perhaps the

H lawgiver simply stands in a tradition stamped by that experience, or perhaps the public face of homosexuality was overwhelmingly the face that homosexuality wore among the aliens that he knew, and his understanding of homosexuality was informed by the character he read in that face.

What kind of public face might homosexuality have worn in our lawgiver's experience? First, he lived in a world that knew and had known a great deal of warfare. He lived and worked, after all, among people who had been uprooted and exiled because they had suffered defeat at the hands of the imperial powers of Mesopotamia. For much of the history of the world, warfare has tended to make rapists of victorious soldiers. Raping the enemies' women is a way of humiliating them, showing that they lack the power to defend their women and children. But even more demonstrably yet, raping the enemies themselves is a way of showing they lack the power to defend even their own persons, whether that assault is with the spear or arrow or . . . the erect phallus of the victor. Homosexual intercourse in this case is not an act of love but a demonstration of complete power over and humiliation of another. Indeed, the rape of the unwilling male may so impress itself on the mind that it overshadows knowledge of homosexuality among one's own people and eclipses the sense that homosexual intercourse might be an act of love.

Second, some Egyptian wall paintings depict men who are apparently among a ruler's slaves down on all fours, in "doggie" position, looking back over their shoulders at the ruler with their posteriors raised.[21] Having examined the figure of the berdache, it does not take a stretch of the imagination to see in these Egyptian figures slaves—perhaps even former enemies, now slaves—who are expected to offer their anuses to the whim of their lords and masters. Again, homosexual sex is the service of a slave, not a freeman. Perhaps it is even an ongoing demonstration of the victor's power over his former enemy, now enslaved. The penetrator now is master, and the penetrated one a humiliated man forced to serve the will of another, irrespective of his own likes or dislikes, his enjoyment or his pain.

Finally, something must be said of the temple prostitute. Of late, in the absence of any archaeological support, scholars have begun to doubt whether the male temple prostitutes of Deuteronomy were anything more than imaginative, literary constructions. However, we do know of men, the *galli* of Roman times, who did enter the service of the Mother Goddess by castrating themselves and assuming, in part, feminine attire. Latin literature pictures them resembling the drag queens of today, with an exaggerated feminine style. If our lawgiver had confronted such men, it would be impossible for him to experience their sexual receptivity—as I think we can assume—other than as part of an offensive feminization. It is not that being womanly is bad—for a woman. What is horrifying is the emasculation, the unmanning, of men. This effeminacy among "religious" men could only reinforce the lawgiver's sense that homosexual sex—as evidenced by wartime rape, peacetime slavery, and now religious effeminacy—could reinforce his sense that homosexual sex constituted a humiliation. The top humiliated his bottom by unmanning him, and the bottom, if willing, could be nothing other than complicitous in his own humiliation at the hands of his dominant top. Interestingly, we can now see what would be so horrifying to the lawgiver about the request of the residents of Sodom to "know" Lot's houseguests. For they wanted not merely to have sex with the visitors. They wanted to humiliate them by topping them—forcibly if they proved to be unwilling. This truly would be a violation of their persons, not to mention Lot's hospitality.

As an aside, one might note a not-dissimilar line of thought at work in Islam. Jim Wafer has pointed out the widely recognized fact that, within Arab culture in general, a man's masculinity is seen to be compromised by taking the so-called passive role in sex, and that a challenge to a man's masculinity is, among Arabs, a particularly egregious affront. In context, one might think of the "submission" required by Islam as a kind of masculine intitation—with the sword as a stand-in for the penis—which enables the initiate to identify with active masculinity. As such, he would seek to subdue and dominate what is non-Muslim. The Muslim, therefore, would resist all temptations to be sodomized, a rebellious, non-Muslim desire of the self. So, too, one can understand the tolerance—even in the face of the Quranic condemnation of the people of Lot—of a poet such as Abú Nuwás, who sought to sexually penetrate and subdue non-Muslim young men, the important aspect being that these were non-Muslims being subdued to a Muslim. Wafer opines that it is ultimately this linkage of ideas that lies behind the proscription of homosexuality in the thought and practice of Islam.[22]

The idea that the Hebrews considered homosexual sex less an act of love than a power play by which one man humiliates his willing or unwilling partner, and that such a view lends force to the more explicitly religious considerations of impurity and cult, gains in plausibility when seen in the light of ancient conceptions of body ownership. For indeed, the presence of pathetic passives within a group is particularly dangerous to the degree the social body is more important than the individual.

WHOSE BODY IS IT ANYWAY?

In his work on biblical sexual ethics, New Testament scholar L. William Countryman traces the lineaments of a second ethic at work in the Levitical literature. He begins with a helpful distinction between "morality" and "ethics."[23] Morality—or a moral praxis—involves the actual do's and don't's expected of individuals within a given group or by an individual of himself or herself. An ethic, on the other hand, refers to the principle, the rationale, for distinguishing just these dos from these don'ts—and/or a systematic listing of obligations and taboos explicitly developed from attention to such a principle. Let us invoke Countryman's own example. A person or group that avoids meat may do so for any number of reasons. One might expect that a vegetarian might want to avoid complicity in the violence involved in butchery. However, in point of fact, the vegetarian may be more concerned about eating the most healthy diet possible, and finds meat far too fatty to be healthy; or he or she may simply be thrifty, convinced that the price of meat is far too expensive to justify the pleasure—if not in pennies, perhaps in the amount of grain it takes to feed the cattle before they can be butchered for food. Thus, nonviolence, health, thrift, and ecological responsibility may all be invoked as rationalizations for vegetarianism, and are thus equally ethical principles justifying the morality of the avoidance of meat. If one were to take one of these principles, nonviolence, for example, and show how the principle can be followed in any number of situations beyond that of the table, one would have an ethic in the second sense.

For Countryman, many of the moral practices outlined in the book of Leviticus can be justified on the basis of a "purity ethic," but many can be seen equally well as following from what he calls a "property ethic." The prime directive of a purity ethic is "Be as clean as possible," or, negatively put, "Avoid dirt to the extent possible." The prime directive of a property ethic, however, would mandate the avoidance of using the property of others as if it were one's own to use as one pleased. Some of the laws of Leviticus lend themselves to justification within both systems. On the basis of a purity ethic, incest—the paradigmatic case of which in ancient Israel would involve a son having sex with any one of his father's "wives" (the Hebrew term is simply that for "women," as it is in many East European languages)— would be seen as wrong because it involves the inappropriate "mixing" of social roles, that of son to his father, and at the same time "husband" to one of his father's women. However, this same action could be seen as a violation of a property ethic in that a son would be "using" one of his father's women as if the woman were his, and not his father's property.

We might find it uncomfortable to speak of a "wife" as the property of her husband. Yet ancient Israel is not modern America. In modern America, we would consider the rape of a man's wife as first and foremost a violation of her person. But in the book of Job, Job complains that the rape of his wife would be an abuse of him, while what we might think of as the putative abuse of his wife in her own person goes unremarked. Yet it is not so much that a woman is the property of her husband as she is the property of his family. That this is the case is borne out by the practice of levirate marriage. If a married man were to die childless, it would have been the responsibility of one of his brothers to take the widow as one of his own "women" and to sire a child on his brother's behalf. To put the matter crudely, a man's wife is first and foremost a family womb (and, since the children of her womb should be of the same bloodline as her husband's, she should be virginal when she marries into the family so as to keep the lines of heredity clear).

This not to say that the "husband" is an independent agent, a patriarchal power who might dictate to others according to his whim, at the very least an authority unto himself. As Countryman makes clear, a man who is head of a family is essentially "owned" by that very family.[24] He is not free simply to do as he might wish. He is charged with the responsibility of managing and hopefully improving the family's wealth—however that be measured, whether in sheep or shekels—and with protecting the family's honor. Interestingly, he, too, is—in a sense—reduced to his genitals, since they are in a very literal way the "family's jewels." A married man might be enjoined from visiting a prostitute—I would argue—not because he is arrogating his body for his own pleasure but because he is risking siring a child outside the family context.

Modern Americans may find such a line of thinking as strange as they might find thinking of a wife as the property of her husband. Among us, our bodies are our own, and we can do with our bodies what we want, as long as—so the saying goes—"we don't hurt anybody." That is because, as a result of a long process of historical development, we have come to value the individuality of the individual as the most important social fact about him or her. We are individuals, who may or may not join social groups and social bodies. Corporations, literally "group bodies," are initially formed by the voluntary banding together of individuals. We even tend to think of the bodies that we are born into as having this voluntary character. Is not the regnant ideology the social fiction that societies are formed by the consent of the governed to a social contract? Individualism even infects our natal families, for we tend to see them as realities whose ongoing life we can opt out of. How else can one account for the amount of popular cultural material preaching to us about, indeed arguing us into, the importance of family?

How different this is from life in traditional China where an unfilial child could be complained of to the government and punished by the civil authorities. Anthropologists and historians alike have shown time and again that ancient men and women, like men and women in more "traditional" societies, experienced themselves more along the example of the Chinese than the modern American. A person was first and foremost a member of a social group, whose identity was—if not totally, then practically—derived from his or her role within that social group. A person was in essence a cell of a larger social body and expected to behave as such. In ancient Athens, women, children, and slaves would have been "owned" by the patriarch of the family, but free men, that is to say, citizens, were both functionally "owned" by their respective families—and by the polis. Although prostitution, both male and female, was an accepted fact of Athenian life, citizens could lose their rights of citizenship by prostituting themselves[25]— showing that they could be bought or otherwise used to do another's bidding, and thus not sufficiently trustworthy to represent themselves in the public forum. Ancient Israel was a "nation" made up of tribes, which were in turn made up of households, for both of which we would use the term *families.* Individuals derived their principal identifies from, and owed their allegiances to, Hebrew family life.

The point is that Countryman claims that, although some of the laws of Leviticus can be justified as part of either a purity ethic or a property ethic, not all can. The proscription against homosexuality, he argues, for example, can only be justified within the operative purity system. We might doubt his claim if homosexuality was thought of as something that might occur only outside the household, such as the use of a prostitute. That is to say, having sex with a prostitute could be thought of as a matter of indulging in sex in the interest of satisfying the urge for pleasure in a kind of willful blindness to the claims of the family. Of course, the parallel would not work were we to speak of homosexual relations *within* a household. However, were we to think of homosexual sex as generally taking place with a person not of one's household, cross-cultural comparisons would still argue the weakness of such a line of thinking. In ancient China as well as in ancient Rome, a man was free to use his genitals as he wished—with slaves, concubines, prostitutes, or others—as long as he did his family duty. That is why I stated earlier that consorting with prostitutes on the part of a married man was proscribed because it posed the threat of children born out of wedlock. Exclusive claims on one's genitals could be based only on the supposition that semen was a scarce natural resource which had to be conserved. Likewise, the non-procreative nature of homosexual sex could be found as an abuse of family property if—and perhaps only if—semen was thought of as a resource not to be wasted.

To be sure, among the Sambians, men feared that their semen reserves might become depleted. I can personally attest to the high school gym teacher who confided to the boys that we had only "ten thousand shots, and we should use them wisely." Although the sense that semen is a limited resource might crop up cross-culturally from time to time, no evidence exists that the ancient Israelites thought of semen in such terms. The story of Onan in Genesis 38 might be thought of as involving such a construction of semen, but, in point of fact, the story revolves around a case of coitus interruptus, whose offense lies in Onan's refusal to perform his responsibilities within the tradition of levirate marriage, rather than in the traditional imputed wastage of seed as such.

However that may be, whether or not the proscription of homosexual intercourse is understandable within the Israelite assumptions operative in its putative property ethic, it is the manner in which Countryman defines "property" that proves so fruitful in this context. Indeed, property, he argues, is an extension of the owner's body.[26] If the individual is but a cell within a wider social body, then it is also a microcosm of the whole, and an isomorphism exists between what happens to it and what happens to the larger body of which it is a part. Let us recall how we argued with respect to the Native American berdache and women warriors. The berdache could accompany a war party—as a kind of war charm, but not as a combatant—because his humiliated status guaranteed the war party would be going into battle already victorious. More relevant to the present context is the observation that a woman could go into battle as a combatant if she could be understood as having ceased to menstruate. Otherwise, the war party would be going into battle already wounded because one of their party was already a vulnerable "bleeder." Indeed, I submit that ancient Israel was a culture that existed within the wider warrior culture of the ancient Near East. The sexually penetrable man was seen as a martially weak man. His sexual penetrability threatened to transfer over to, indeed possibly infect, the wider social body with vulnerability to all sorts of alien, especially enemy alien, penetrations.

At first glance, we might dismiss such a line of thought as primitive superstition, but perhaps our dismissal would be premature. Perhaps it is a similar line of thought that underlies discussions about the contemporary issue of gays in the American military. Gay philosopher Richard Mohr is worth quoting at length on this point:

> Straight soldiers' skittishness, which the military uses to try to justify the suppression of gays, is a mere surface phenomenon masking a much deeper and wider cultural anxiety about gay men—anxiety over understanding the male body as a penetrable object. For the military, the real person, the full citizen, is defined as one who must penetrate while never being penetrated. Conversely, it defines the enemy as a potentially penetrating but actually penetrated body. The citizen warrior first "penetrates" the enemy's lines and then penetrates the enemy himself for the kill.[27]

Thus, the Levitical proscription against male homosexual intercourse could be rooted in the very same fear for the integrity of the social body that underlies the concern over gay bottoms in the modern American military.

As a general theory, such a "magical" isomorphism between microcosm and macrocosm that is here evident goes a long way in filling the gap in the structuralist theory of impurity. Structuralists such as Mary Douglas have argued, as with one, so with the other. But they have failed to show the compellingness of the connections that a theory of magical congruence does. More important, this arguable isomorphism between the part and the whole allows the student of the history of homosexuality to understand Boswell's claim that the Christian West became ever more intransigent in its horror of homosexuality as it worried more and more about Islamic penetration of its borders and culture. The theory seems particularly relevant in trying to understand what lay behind modes of thinking within ancient Israel, a tiny society vulnerable to the potential threat of the imperial designs of Egypt from the West, and ultimately the actual threat of Assyrian and Babylonian penetration from the East.

Let us sum up this already overlong chapter. It is my contention that the Israelite take on homosexuality is strongly influenced by the martial practices of soldiers in the ancient Near East. Israelite men were so horrified by the sexual humiliation that victorious foreign soldiers might inflict on their hapless victims, that they insisted that no Israelite man would treat another Israelite man in such a manner. Effectively then, the horror of sexual humiliation eclipsed any sense that men might have sex with one another for pleasure or out of love. Male intercourse was exclusively a matter of one man humiliating another. Moreover, by the logic that what happens to the part happens to the whole, the Israelite feared that male-male intercourse created penetrable men in the populace, the presence of whom consequently weakened the body politic. If Israelite men were not to have intercourse with one another, would they not be free, like the soldiers of other cultures, to humiliate their enemy? However, it is not hard to think that they were so horrified of this abuse of the enemy on the part of alien victors that the practice itself became in their eyes too horrible to countenance in general. In addition, if their God was their champion on the world scene, as we know they thought of him, then their horror of the practice would have been transposed to God himself. Thus, male-male intercourse would have become something unthinkable on the part of Israelite men, not to mention, in violation of the will of their God. We cannot overlook the characterization of homosexual sex as an impurity, and thus fit to take its place in lists of other impurities. Nor can we overlook the fact that homosexual sex was associated with the worship of foreign gods. All these more specifically religious considerations, however, would lose in force if it were not for the fact that in the ancient Near East, as in the Americas, a powerful warrior is "one who makes another into a pathetic passive."[28]

Of course, if the circumstances of war were to change so that war becomes something other than a matter of hand-to-hand fighting in which one penetrated another's body with one's weapon, the analogy between sex and war on which the idea that sex can be used to humiliate an enemy would be undermined. So too would the presence of women in the military serve to undermine the idea that sexually penetrable soldiers weakened the whole. Raise the possibility that sex between men might be a matter of pleasure or love rather than humiliation, and the whole edifice is threatened with collapse. Each of these developments would have to wait until the present day for their full flowering. At the moment, it is meet, right, and fitting that we should inquire as to what early Christianity would make of its Hebrew, in particular its Levitical, heritage.

Chapter 6

Early Christianity:
A Revolution Aborted?

PAUL: FOOD, SEX, SIN, AND TASTE

In the fall of 1999, Jerry Falwell, the self-proclaimed leader and spokesman for the so-called Moral Majority, and Mel White, a one-time staffer for the same who subsequently came out as a gay man, held a "summit" in Falwell's backyard of Lynchburg, Virginia. What each sought from such a summit is not clear, although it does seem that Falwell was trying to overcome the image problem he had by emphasizing that his opposition to homosexuality was a matter of hating the sin, not the sinner—whereas White seemingly wanted to impress upon the Religious Right through one of their most well-known leaders the danger of ill-considered diatribes and antigay rhetoric in stirring up violence against those very sinners they purported now to "love." As gay journalist Steve Bolerjack reported in the *New York Blade News,* White and his colleagues apparently "gushed" about Falwell's hospitality, while the fact remained that the

> hospitality consisted of serving only bottled water to White and his group. Falwell had decided against serving food to his guests because he interprets an uncited Biblical passage as a prohibition against breaking bread with the "sexually immoral."[1]

I have not been able to track down Falwell's explicit biblical reference. But more germane to the point is the way the whole affair reprised one of the basic conflicts within the early Church. Indeed, Falwell appeared to be following the path of the so-called Jewish or Torah Christians whose way of being Christian long has been left in the dust by mainstream Christianity.

Jesus of Nazareth had, of course, been a Jew, but he was a Jew who was executed by the Roman authorities by crucifixion. To be sure, by any accounts, crucifixion is a particularly horrible way to die. But for a Jew, crucifixion was a way of adding insult to injury. Indeed, the Torah proclaimed that by such a death the victim had been rendered a "cursed" (that is, impure) thing. According to Deuteronomy 21:23, "a hanged man [i.e., one who is hanged on a tree] is cursed by God." And yet within not so many years, Christians writing the New Testament Gospels would attribute to Jesus, however anachronistically, the saying, "If anyone would come after me, let him deny himself and take up his cross and follow me."[2] Discipleship had evidently become the way of the cross, a way that the Judaism of the day would have found a path of impurity, thus not religious at all. This relative indifference to the dictates of Torah would not be easily won by the early Church. It would have to be worked out through a series of controversies and crises.

The Gospel of Matthew—and gospels are less biographies in the modern sense of the word than sermons or interpretations of the life of Jesus—seeks to represent Jesus as a second Moses through whom Israel supposedly received her Law. He groups the sayings of Jesus into five blocks in an echo of the Five Books of Moses, and ultimately has Jesus say, "Do not think that I have come to abolish the Law or the Prophets."[3] Yet the early Church remembered that Jesus—perhaps even more characteristically—was not a slave to the letter of the Law. Apparently, he felt quite free to eat with "prostitutes and tax collectors," those disreputable outcasts whose presence sufficed to render one's table impure. He reportedly felt free to heal on the Sabbath, the day of rest, even as he justified his disciples when, on a Sabbath, they "began to pluck heads of grain" by saying ultimately that "the Sabbath was made for man, not man for the Sabbath."[4] Jesus was a Jew, and during his life he spearheaded a movement principally among the Jews of his day. As the movement spread after his death, particularly among the gentile population, the question whether one had to be a Jew in order to be a follower of Jesus as the Christ, where "being a Jew" was tantamount to being "Torah observant," could not be avoided.

Saint Paul, who had never known Jesus prior to his crucifixion and death and who early in his own life persecuted the Jewish remnants of the Jesus movement, nevertheless came to feel that he had been personally commissioned by the risen Jesus, whom he beheld in a vision, to be an apostle to the gentiles. Jesus had, of course, been Jewish, and the question could not be suppressed: since Jesus had been Jewish, did one have to become Jewish to be a follower of Jesus as the Christ? Since Jewish males were required to be circumcised, the potential gentile male convert who would not have been circumcised—circumcision has not been the general practice among the peoples of Europe even until the present day—would have had to face the prospect of being circumcised as an adult if being Jewish was to be required of Christian converts. Such a painful prospect, one can only imagine, could not have but hampered Paul's potential success. Whatever the ambiguities that haunt Paul's full understanding of the Jewish law, it was not lost on him that Jesus' death had been occasioned by and/or condemned by the law, and that fact served to undermine the absolute claims of the law. By being resurrected, God had effectively reversed the condemnation of Jesus by the law. Hence, Jesus' resurrection had effectively freed humans from any slavish obedience of the Jewish law. Hence, in an early "council" of the Church recorded in the Book of Acts, there would be a meeting of the minds between Paul and Peter in concluding that circumcision would not be required of male converts to Christianity.

However, the issue would raise its ugly head once again with regards to table fellowship. Table fellowship had already emerged as central to Christian worship. Among those whom scholars have dubbed Jewish—or Torah—Christians, the presence of a person whose actions had rendered him or her impure would have been sufficient to render the "table" impure as well, and hence was to be avoided. Apparently, the congregations of Corinth and of Rome, with whom Paul would correspond, were made up both of such Torah Christians as well as those who felt no real compulsion to obey the dictates of Jewish law, chiefly in the matter of the emergent kosher culture of contemporary Judaism. These latter Christians might have felt perfectly comfortable eating such forbidden foods as pork. Alternatively, since parties in the Roman world were generally thought to be hosted by a god or goddess, they might have partaken of food or drink that would have been construed as having been "offered" to idols. Hence, in an effort to preserve the peace and unity among the respective communities, Paul addresses the conflict in sensibility that has arisen in both in the letters he writes to each. Combining what he has to say in both 1 Corinthians and in Romans—even at the risk of sacrificing nuance on the altar of caricature—we can say that he develops his own version of a "don't ask, don't tell" policy. He hails the latter type of Christian as the "strong"—a term that can, in context, just as well be read as "strong-stomached." By contrast, the Torah Christians he dubs the "weak" or "weak-stomached." Since, he argues, idols are not so much false gods as nonexistent, there is really no impurity in eating food dedicated to the nonexistent. Further, the Christian is really freed from the religious obligation of following the Torah's regulations regarding food entirely. Nevertheless, the strong-stomached, although technically in the right, are not to antagonize the "weak" among them in the interest of unity, even if it means they have to refrain from food that is otherwise allowable to them. However, at the same time, the weak-stomached Torah Christians are to refrain from asking the strong about their diet, and—again in the interest of peace and unity of the group—are themselves to refrain from any condemnation of the strong.[5] Essentially—and this is the important point—impurity has ceased in Paul to be a matter of religious obligation, but is instead relegated to the realm of personal taste. In matters of keeping kosher, a Christian can decide for himself or herself according to his or her taste, but it is nevertheless a matter of taste that is at issue, not religious obligation, much less a matter of sin.

We might expect a very similar approach from Paul with respect to another matter that would presumably have been a point of friction between Torah-observant Christians and their "stronger" compatriots in the Christian movement—let us follow the scholars and call them "Gentile Christians." Roman sexual practices were very alien to the Jewish tradition. Just so long as a man did his family duty, he would have been free to use his genitals for his pleasure, free to use them especially in sexual congress with prostitutes and slaves of both sexes. Actually, the Roman was free to enjoy the charms of young men, although—unlike among the Greeks—the sons of Roman citizenry who were themselves destined to become citizens of the empire were forbidden to him as sexual partners. In fact, the sons of Roman citizens frequently wore a *bulla* (a locket containing an amulet shaped like an erect phallus) around their neck to announce to the world their incipient masculinity, which was not to be compromised by undergoing a "woman's experience."[6] Sexual receptivity compromised the masculine dignity of both the adult citizen and the youth destined to be one.

As historian Craig Williams observes, "First and foremost, a self-respecting Roman man must always give the appearance of playing the insertive role in penetrative acts, and not the receptive role."[7] What might have gone on in private was another matter. Although Williams contests that the Latin *exoleti* denotes male prostitutes who were sexual "tops" for their male clientele, as it has been understood by other scholars, he nevertheless admits that such men existed[8]—in which case, Roman men might very well have found themselves willing to pay to be penetrated. However, penetration was as much an assertion of power as it was an act of sex. Hence, to be known as one who has been or could be topped—especially by a social underling—was, for a Roman man, a compromise of his masculine dignity. Indeed, it may have been the reputation that Caesar was "every man's wife and every woman's husband"[9] that contributed to his political demise, especially when it was thought that Caeser could be topped even by his lieutenants! The matter is relevant to our discussion of Paul because there might very well have been—indeed, probably were—men among his converts who were homosexually active, since homosexuality carried no stigma by itself and was deemed to be perfectly well within the acceptable repertoire of adult males of the wider Roman empire.

Paul identifies homosexual activity as a specifically pagan or gentile, and thereby alien, practice, but it is not clear what such categorical distancing entails. Would he have proven amenable to considering homosexual sex on an analogy with the way he approached the question of nonkosher food and food sacrificed to idols, were he to have been challenged? In the course of his Letter to the Romans, for example, he argues that the existence of God is something which should have been apparent to all peoples of the world from their beginnings. However, pagans had not recognized God, but had followed an idolatrous path instead. Then follows the only passage in which he unambiguously refers to homosexual sex. As a consequence of such idolatry,

> God gave them up in the lusts of their hearts to impurity, to the dishonoring of their bodies among themselves, because they exchanged the truth about God for a lie and worshipped and served

the creature rather than the Creator, who is blessed forever!
Amen

For this reason, God gave them up to dishonorable passions.
For their women exchanged natural relations for those that are
contrary to nature, and the men likewise gave up natural relations with women and were consumed with passion for one another, men committing shameless acts with men.[10]

The characterization of homosexual sex as "contrary to nature"
owes its roots to Plato.[11] However, it is Stoic rationale for such a characterization that would have been the ambient and decisive one for
Paul and his audience. In Stoicism, the well-being of a person (his or
her "true" happiness) lay in virtue, where virtue was life in accordance with nature. "Nature," however, was a word that denoted a
number of things equivocally. In the first instance, "nature" could refer to the universe as a whole which, for the Stoic, was generally conceived of as an organism. A human, by such a reckoning, was part of a
larger body with its own necessities. If, for the health of the whole, a
part must suffer or be sacrificed, then the Stoic was bidden to accept
the dictates of necessity without protest, vocally or merely emotion-
ally, in that mood of general *apatheia* for which the Stoics have been
historically famous. One was to be satisfied with doing one's duty
and playing the part that fate required of one in the ongoing life of the
whole. But nature and duty were also conceived along a second line
as well. One's duty, in this second line of thinking, lay in the living of
one's life in conformity with the "reasons" for things in the way the
world worked. Since sex existed in nature for the sake of reproduction, so one should indulge in sex only for the sake of having children.
Ultimately, any other reason for having sex was "unnatural"—as
would be any form of sex that would not be open to procreation. What
is salient here is the setting up of vaginal sex, that is, penis in vagina,
as the only form of sex that is real. Other forms of sex could only be
deformities when compared with the norm of "natural" sex. Note that
this is the same logic by which something was, in the Levitical
scheme of things, deemed impure. Calling something "unnatural"
thus reveals itself as no real argument at all but the college-educated
vocabulary for calling something sick or disgusting. So in Paul, the
charge that God gave gentiles up to homosexual relations among
themselves is simply synonymous with saying that he gave them up
to all sorts of impurities. But we have already seen that, barring any

additional considerations, impurity for the Christian was *not* something that needed to be assiduously avoided on religious grounds.

Consequently, scholars debate how Paul should be read here. Is he to be seen as a consistent thinker, such that the passage from Romans quoted earlier can be glossed, "Because of their idolatry, God gave the gentiles up to such tasteless behavior as homosexual sex," as L. William Countryman argues?[12] Alternatively, Paul is to be understood as an inconsistent thinker with regard to the moral status of impurity, too much a product of his Levitical background to allow homosexual sex to be anything less than sin. Such is the view of Bernadette Brooten.[13]

For guidance as to the most appropriate way to understand Paul, we might turn to other related passages. However, those other passages in which Paul is arguably speaking of homosexual sex do not help us to adjudicate the matter. For example, the list of those in 1 Corinthians 6:9-10 whose vices will disqualify them from participation in the future kingdom of the deathless whose firstfruits the resurrected Jesus is and which can thus be counted as "sins" rather than merely tasteless behavior runs as follows: "neither the sexually immoral, nor idolaters, nor adulterers, nor men who practice homosexuality, nor thieves, nor the greedy, nor drunkards, nor revilers, nor swindlers will inherit the kingdom of God." The English Standard Version (ESV) phrase "those who practice homosexuality" is, however, a highly questionable rendering of the Greek *arsenokoitai* and *malakoi*. Literally, Paul writes that *arsenokoitai* and *malakoi* are among those who will be excluded from the kingdom of God. *Arsenokoitai* is used by itself in the list of sins cited in 1 Timothy 1:10, and is also again questionably translated in the ESV as "men who practice homosexuality." *Malakoi* are literally "soft men." Although the term may refer to sexually penetrable men, it actually denotes "men who are effeminate"—and effeminacy is not cognate with sexual penetrability. I would suggest the word covers much the same ground as the English term *sissy*—together with its ambiguities. Not all men who are effeminate in manner are in fact willingly penetrable sexually—nor are all men who are willingly penetrable effeminate. However, sexual penetrability is yet taken as symbolic of "sissiness." Beyond that, *malakoi* fails to map fully with sissies, because in the ancient world uncontrollable desires were more decisive in determining effeminacy than was sexual penetrability. In fact, as noted earlier, a "ladies' man"—in the thought of the day—might very well be the very model of an effeminate, hence soft, man.

Arsenokoitai is even more difficult to translate. New Testament scholar Dale Martin argues that the term seems to be associated (in the Pauline lists) not with the sexual sins, but with the economic ones. The term connotes sexual relations, but the thrust in meaning may have less to do, he argues, with sex itself than with economic exploitation which might involve sex. Martin admits that he finally does not know what the term means. He suggests, however, that it is just as likely—if not more so—that the term most directly denotes the exploitation of others through sex rather than homosexual sex.[14] Perhaps we would not be wrong then in seeing that *arsenokoitai* might be more profitably translated, in the language of the street, as "johns," patrons or clients of prostitutes—with the proviso that the *arsenokoitai* would be those who use money to top others sexually. In this case, penetration would connote economic domination. Or perhaps we are to number among the *arsenokoitai* also those who use their position to exploit others sexually, as a master might exploit his male or female slaves. Summarizing, then, Paul would be excluding effeminate men and exploitative penetrators, not specifically homosexuals, from the kingdom.

Paul would probably have been forced to be more explicit if his sayings on the matters at hand were met with protest. Perhaps he would have had to think through the issue more carefully and consistently, particularly if, as Brooten argues, he was in fact a less-than-thorough thinker in his reduction of impurity to a matter of taste. In the case of the debate about pure and impure food, Paul confronted congregations with people who represented both sides of the issue. Perhaps, in regards to sex, Paul's sayings are being met with nodding, uncontesting approval. In short, he may be—as it were—"preaching to the converted." We need to take into consideration what kind of people might have comprised Paul's audience. Robert Jewett, recognizing that "sexual freedom was granted to freeborn males in relation to all slaves, clients, and persons of lower standing, so that sexual relations were clearly an expression of domination," goes on to say,

> I wonder if Paul's rhetoric may not provide entrée into the . . . unhappy experience of slaves and former slaves who had experienced and bitterly resented sexual exploitation, both for themselves and for their children, in a culture marked by aggressive

bisexuality. Their countercultural stance as members of the new community of faith entailed a repudiation of such relationships and, from all the evidence available to us, a welcome restriction of sexual relations to married, heterosexual partners. For those members of the Roman congregation still subject to sexual exploitation by slave owners or former slave owners who were now functioning as patrons, the moral condemnation of same-sex and extramarital relations of all kinds would confirm the damnation of their exploiters and thus raise the status of the exploited above that of mere victims.[15]

The central issue in Paul, then, would not be homosexuality per se, but homosexual sex that was not chosen but forced upon people by those in position to exploit them.

Actually, I wish I could say that I thought Paul was an inconsistent thinker with regard to food and homosexuality out of a concern for the social inequity of ambient Roman sexual practices. However, I rather doubt that Paul's repudiation of homosexuality is actually based on sensitivity to the politics of sex and an abhorrence of the humiliating subordination implied when one man penetrates another. To be sure, I have argued that the proscription against Leviticus had its origins in a fear of male rape and the fear that sexual "passives" in the community would threaten the whole. However, by Paul's time, the social context had changed, and Paul is simply perpetuating in a rather unthinking way what had become a habitual prejudice that classified male homosexual sex as impure and, what amounts to the same thing, unnatural. Paul is not forced to explore the full ramifications of his position on impurity as it relates to sex because his repudiation of such unnatural sexual relations was falling on receptive ears. Among his audience would have been those who were sensitive to the sexual abuse of males that Roman sexual mores tended to sanction. Neither Paul nor his audience found homosexual relations acceptable, but their respective rationales were different. The failure of nerve that kept Paul from inquiring into the status of sexual impurity for Christians had the consequence of simply allowing the presumption that homosexual relations are all too often, perhaps even of necessity, a matter of abusive power relations to stand uncontested in his audience. Moreover, at the same time that the practice of the penetration of males is contested, the presupposition that penetration connotes subordination is not. Thus Paul simply passes on what we can recognize by this point in our study as a traditional construction of the political nature of masculine sexuality.

If Paul proved a veritable reactionary when it came to the construction of masculinity and the act of sex, he was nevertheless at the forefront of another dimension of the Christian revolution. In the passage cited earlier, Jewett remarks in passing about the countercultural shift in thinking about sex and marriage that the Christian community championed. However, that revolution was wider in scope than his comments would suggest. Even as the Christian movement was to curb the rampant bisexuality that expressed itself outside of marriage, it was nevertheless the bearer of the power that would dethrone the absolutist imperial claims of the ancient family as it existed in Rome, Greece, and Israel. Simply put, marriage was virtually universally expected of adults in the ancient world. Christianity came onto the scene insisting that one did not have to be married to be part of the Christian movement. One's identity was first and foremost derivative of one's status as a member of the Body of Christ—and only secondarily derivative of one's place within a family. One might choose to marry, but marriage was not incumbent upon one as a person or as a Christian. Jesus had, in all probability, not been married. For whatever reasons, probably because he thought that Jesus was going to return any day to transform the world into a totally new world order, Paul thought it would be best if one did not involve oneself in the entanglements of family that marriage represented. Indeed, early Christianity may owe part of its success to the freedom it gave its members from the obligation to be part of a family, and because—to use the words of Countryman—"owned" by it, bound by its needs. Of course, in a famous phrase, Paul advocated that it was better to marry than to burn.[16] If one could not do without sex, then by all means, one should marry so as to have the appropriate arena for assuaging the urge. (The reader may note how little thoughts of love figure into the equation! Marriage is the license for sexual release.) However, it would be better, he thought, if one could remain free from the entanglements of family life if one could. Of course, not to have to marry would be a boon to those who were not interested in functioning heterosexually. However, one should note that, whether homosexually inclined or not, one would do without sex so as to be free of family responsibilities as well as having to do one's family duty. It was family life that was an unnecessary entanglement. It would take Augustine to make sex the problem, and it would be he who would provide the thought patterns by which homosexuality would come to be framed in the West as the apogee of ungodliness—and perhaps even of unmanliness.

AUGUSTINE OF HIPPO:
SEX, HOMOSEXUALITY, FAITH, AND DEATH

Augustine (354-430 C.E.), a Roman citizen who hailed from North Africa, had at first resisted the Catholic Christianity of his mother because of what seemed to him the rhetorical crudity of its scriptures as well as its more general intellectual poverty in favor of the then much trendier Manichaeanism. However, when he traveled to Rome and beyond in search of fame and fortune, he met the Christian intellectual Ambrose, who impressed him with his intellectual stature. Meanwhile, Augustine began to gain familiarity with the work and thought of Plato—albeit in translation, since Augustine never mastered Greek—an exposure that would eventually undermine his endorsement of what he later called the overly materialistic approach to divinity, good, and evil that characterized Manichaeanism. After the embrace of the Catholic Christianity he had earlier abjured, he soon became one of its bishops and principal intellectual architects, producing a body of work that would set the theological agenda of the Latin West for the next thousand years. When, in the thirteenth century, Saint Thomas Aquinas inquires whether any venereal act can be without sin, he is engaging a problematic bequeathed to him by Augustine.[17] When the Reformation thinker John Calvin insists that the world was a just order in which God showed his mercy by exempting some from the general suffering and damnation deserved by all, he was actually echoing a line of thought first sounded by Augustine.

For medieval thinkers, it was not the homosexual but the sodomite that was the subject of ethical concern. *Sodomy* was a more general and fluid term that could denote a wide range of nonvaginal sex acts, whether they involved members of the same sex or not—as well as any number of sins stemming from incontinent desire. However, when the homosexual was identified and so named in the nineteenth century, the homosexual would attract the opprobrium, hitherto directed at the sodomite, an opprobrium that made sense in the light of the discourse about sex and sexual pleasure that can be traced to Augustine.[18]

At the end of his life, Augustine was embroiled in heated debate with a Pelagian-inspired Italian bishop, Julian of Eclanum. For Julian, some of the suffering to which we humans are vulnerable was simply the price of existence, for, in Julian's mind, whatever was simply natural could not be deemed evil. However, for Augustine, suffering that was not deserved threatened the whole edifice of faith. If anyone suffered for no reason, for not somehow having deserved it, then the affirmation of a just, much less a merciful god, would be illegitimate. Against Julian, he hurls the thought, "You see your whole heresy shipwrecked upon the misery of infants."[19] For Augustine, the suffering of infants only made sense if it could be understood as the punishment for some inherited guilt: "If there were no sin, then, infants, bound by no evil, would suffer nothing harmful in body or soul under the great power of the just God."[20] If Augustine would only come to complete possession of his position late in life, he was nevertheless already capable of recognizing the sinfulness even of infants in his earlier *Confessions,* arguably his first great masterpiece.

Augustine's *Confessions* is not a catalog of sins but actually the world's first autobiography, tracing the lineaments of a life that had been saved for faith. Augustine explores the circumstances of his own conversion, not so much because he thought his own life history was all that compelling but because he was convinced that the particular revealed the general. The movement from sin to faith in any person's life would look much like the same process that he had undergone. Indeed, *Confessions* is a text from which one can glean the contours of what Augustine takes sinful consciousness to be in general, as well as the outlines of faith.

His own infancy escapes his memory. Augustine, then, must turn to observation to recontruct what he must have been like as an infant.[21]

Mothers and babies, he observes, are outfitted by nature with the propensities that serve to guarantee the child's survival. Children are naturally disposed to suckle at the breast, and mothers' breasts are relieved by suckling the child. However, when we look at the child, what do we observe? Do we observe any quiet confidence in the providential arrangement by which the child's existence can be secured? No, the child protests and cries and demands attention, as if he or she was possessed of a fear and anxiety that mother is not there. Look, says Augustine, at the case of twins. As one child observes the other at the breast, he or she is roused to scream and struggle, anxious that what he or she needs will not be there. We are appetitive creatures who need that which is beyond ourselves in order to live. Sin—as distinct from concrete sinful acts—lies in this desperate clutching for experience lest we miss out on life. It seems to come with the territory of being human that we doubt that our destiny is fullness of life, and we clutch at things as if to shore ourselves against such a loss. We are born anxious, rather than trusting, creatures, all too ready to act out of that anxiety rather than out of trust. Therein is a distortion of our divinely given nature.

The plot of *Confessions* is modeled on the story of Genesis. The story of Augustine's personal beginnings in infancy thus gives way to an episode in his childhood that corresponds to the story in which Adam and Eve eat of the forbidden fruit. The distortion of our nature that is already present in our infancy is reinforced and encouraged as we grow up surrounded by those who share our distorted nature. So, in his childhood, Augustine is egged on by his peers to steal some pears from a tree that was near a road they were following. Augustine wills to steal fruit, as it were, for the hell of it, that is to say, for no good reason, since he is not hungry and ends up throwing away the stolen fruit uneaten.[22] From this incident, Augustine draws the picture of the sinful human as engaging in—to echo the felicitous phraseology of Shakespeare—"much ado about nothing." In his or her sin, the human looks out upon the world, seeing not what is actually before him or her, but what today might be called a "projection" onto the world. For Augustine, we do not see the things before our noses such as they really are, but fantastical images in terms of which we find ourselves overly invested in them. Thus, the human is continually reacting to and grasping after trivial things as if they had an importance that they do not in actuality bear. No wonder, Augustine observes, we cry at what happens to characters on the stage as we neglect the need of the neighbor who is at hand. And so it goes. As we grow into adulthood, the objects that we see so distortedly as they are given to our disordered desires and affections may change in content from those that engaged us as children, but the dynamics of sin present in childhood remain and color the life of the adult as well as the child. For such is the way sin operates in the progeny of Adam, who has passed on his disordered affections to them in his semen, or as we latter day people might say, with his genes.

A life that overinvests in the things of the world is, for Augustine, doomed to frustration and disappointment. In one of the most moving passages of *Confessions,* Augustine tells of the pain into which the death of a friend he had come to love early in his career plunged him. "Everything on which I set my gaze was death," he writes. "I hated everything because they did not have him, nor could they now tell me 'look, he is on the way', as used to be the case when he was alive and absent from me."[23] (Is this a love that was merely that of a friend for a friend? It is hard not to hear overtones of homoeroticism.) At the death of his friend, Augustine continues, "I was in misery, and misery is the state of every soul overcome by friendship with mortal things and lacerated when they are lost."[24] We are nourished by our loves, and when we love what is mortal with an intensity that is perhaps due only to the immortal, we are condemned not only to a deadening, perhaps even unconsolable, grief, at the same time, we find ourselves confronted with our own mortality:

> I suppose that the more I loved him, the more hatred and fear I felt for the death which had taken him from me, as if it were my most ferocious enemy. I thought that since death had consumed him, it was suddenly going to engulf all humanty.[25]

To love things of the world with an erotic intensity that only God deserves is to find ourselves shipwrecked on death, and subsumed by loss. For the mature Augustine, it is only when we can love our friends with a love that is ordered by the love for and of God that we can not lose them in the death that the life and power of God can overcome. However, such a love requires a massive reordering of the habit of sinful love and desire.

The process of conversion, by which the dynamics of faith would begin to replace the workings of sin, began for Augustine through familiarization with the thoughts of Plato. Through him, Augustine recognized the existence of the forms and ideals that we invoke as standards of comparison when we set about to judge things in the world as to their desirability. For Augustine, to discover such standards of quality, he had in fact recognized the reality of God, or at least the ideas in the mind of God. He would ever thereafter think of God as the "light that enlighteneth the mind"—that reality which enabled the mind to function above all in judging matters of quality and desirability. However, it was axiomatic in Augustine that precision of sight depends upon the strength of our love. Augustine the sinner could not clearly see what he had, as of yet, so dimly recognized, for he did not yet love it with the intensity that sharpened sight. Plato had, of course, envisioned an ascent to the divine. We begin by loving some one thing in this world, and that love becomes the first step in a process of discovery whereby we rise to love of divine perfection. Love for things in this world and love for the divine are thus arranged in a kind of continuum. Augustine sees the erotic love for God and an eros directed at things in this world simply as opposites, indeed as rivals to one another. Either the weight of his love—as he would call it—was directed upon the ideal, or upon things in the world. One either loved God more than the world, or the world more than God. However, if one loved the world more than God, one could neither see the standards by which to judge the world with any kind of clarity, nor could one see things in the world clearly for what they are. Acuity of sight regarding both the divine and the world depended upon an overriding love of God. Coming to love God more than the world is what he means by conversion. However, Augustine is careful to point out that we are converted to faith, rather than to sight. Conversion signals a basic reordering of our affections. However, conversion sets in motion a process whereby our love is strengthened and our sight improved—conversion is not in and of itself the perfection of sight or of love. Until our love is perfected, our sight will remain cloudly, and we will have to rely on the insights of those whose love and whose sight is more perfect than ours. Hence, the Christian relies on the wisdom of the Christ as it has been deposited in the Church, until one has so grown in love that one can see for oneself through inner "eyes" that have been perfected by the perfection of one's love.

What is salient is that conversion, for Augustine, was preceded by a dream in which he felt himself called to be numbered among virgins, prepubescent children, and widows. Given his psychological disposition, the reordering of the affections that constituted conversion would bring with it the power to say no to sex. Conversion was tantamount to the discovery of the freedom from the seductiveness of sex.

It is not that sexual desire is an evil in and of itself, but it is the case that sinful selves cannot experience sexual desire except sinfully, that is with that distortedness of love he dubs "lust." The object of our desire is always all too desirable, all too seductive, and we love it with a love and desire all too strong. If for Plato, the sexual self was the template for understanding the nature of all desire, for Augustine, the sexual self was evidence of the disorder of our sinful nature. Augustine speaks graphically of his experience as a male. Almost every schoolboy at one time in his life knows that tumescence can occur completely out of context, just when he is called to the board, and the adult male finds that he can grow tumescent at the sight of a forbidden partner, even as he remains flaccid and impotent with his legally married wife. However, it is in the act of sex itself that the shame of our distortion is even more apparent. This, Augustine says, we intuitively recognize. Do we not seek to have sex behind closed doors, and not in the public eye? "The sexual act itself, which is performed with such lust, seeks privacy," Augustine writes. "A natural sense of shame ensures that even brothels make provision for secrecy."[26]

The real embarrassment is the orgasmic self. At the moment of orgasm, the self loses that self-control which is the mark of virtue. The automaticity of the animalistic takes over, and we are carried along by an automatic rhythm that eclipses choice. At the same time, the mind is set adrift in a sea of pleasure, and it loses sight of anything in particular, much less those ideas in virtue of which it is empowered to be the thinking, rational animal that it is. "So intense is the pleasure that when it reaches its climax there is an almost total extinction of mental alertness; the intellectual sentries, as it were, are overwhelmed."[27] For Augustine, we grow like that which we love. He who loves God is immortalized and made happy in that vision. Orgasm eclipses the vision of God and threatens us with the end appropriate to our animal nature. The loss of the sight of God is a herald of death. At the same time, so intense is the pleasure of orgasm that it proves, as with all pleasure for the sinful self, all too pleasurable. Orgasm not only eclipses God from our sight and threatens us with death but seeks to seduce us into a life of God-forgetfulness, the sure and certain pursuit of which carries us away to our eternal death. Thus, Augustine opines that it would be much better if we could take our food as if it were medicine.[28] Even so, he envisions that Adam before his fall into sin would have had an erection only when he wanted children and would have been able to deposit his seed in the vagina without the embarrassing throes of an animal in ecstasy.[29]

So dangerous is sex that anyone in his or her right mind will risk orgasmic ecstasy and the momentary loss of rational self-control only in the most controlled of circumstances. Marriage is indeed just such a controlled circumstance. Marriage is a divine dispensation through which people reproduce and continue to populate the earth. Thus, having sex within marriage is a way of indulging in the dangerous, but doing so only for the sake of the most rational of reasons in the most rational of ways. Sex should be only of a certain sort, namely of the sort that can issue in progeny (that is to say, vaginal intercourse) with the right person (the one to whom one is married) and *only* for the sake of having children. Otherwise, one shows oneself all too given to the pursuit of pleasure.

If sex is to be with one's lawfully married wife only for the sake of children, then homosexual sex cannot be other than the sign of an unhealthy and ungodly interest in pleasure for its own sake. By its very form, homosexual sex can never be procreative and therefore can never be sought for the only legitimate reason for having sex. The person interested in such a "sodomitical" kind of sex cannot be other than a person far too interested in pleasure than it appropriate among the faithful, far too taken with having sex for pleasure, a pursuit that is always all too addictive. The words of Mark Jordan are on point:

> In the history of Christian moral teaching, sexual love was permitted for the sake of procreation and on the condition that it be unerotic, that it strive to suppress so far as possible the intensity of passion. . . . The vehement denunciations of same-sex pleasure are justified explicitly by appeal to the rule that sex must be procreative. But I suspect that the vehemence is also simply a displacement of the negative judgment on all sex that was suspended in the case of procreative marriage. Most Christian moralists have regarded celibacy as the higher calling, the fullness of Christian response to God. Marriage was permitted, though not recommended, for the continuation of the species and as a concession to human weakness in the present day.[30]

It is this fear of sex for the sake of pleasure that is already so prominent in the thought of Augustine.

What seems to be absent, however, is the centrality of the notion of masculinity that has been so much a part of our discussions of other traditions and thinkers. But the absence is only apparent. It is the argument of Mathew Kuefler's *The Manly Eunuch*[29] that, from the start of the third century C.E. to the middle of the fifth century C.E., the transformations that were taking part in the Roman empire currently represented a crisis for Roman masculinity. Christianity responded by clothing its advocacy of chastity with the rhetoric of manliness. The dream that Augustine had before his conversion was a call to join widows and virgins and girls and boys of both sexes. Absent was the "man" of Rome who was almost inconceivable except as sexually active. However, even in Augustine, we find the move to deny that chastity is a feminine virtue, affirming rather that it is in fact the most masculine of dispositions. Indeed, we find Augustine insistent that chaste men are, because of their very chastity, real men. Of those who say that those who have castrated themselves—Augustine is thinking figuratively here—for the sake of the kingdom of Heaven are no longer men, he expostulates "O astonishing madness! . . . let them not deny that holy people are men because they do nothing of a sexual nature."[32] It strikes me that we are not dealing with a new construct of masculinity here. Rather, we are looking at the exploitation of one aspect of the received notion. A real man is one who rules himself and those others who are either not men or are lesser men. (The parallel with the Muslim who rules over the non-Muslim world and the non-Muslim parts of his own soul is striking.) The Roman citizen expressed his masculinity sexually in the penetration of social subordinates— women, boys, and slaves. However, at the same time, masculinity was connoted by control of the emotions and the desires. (Both the Roman and the Greek, we might remember, feared that the youths who were destined for citizenship might be compromised by penetration when young—not by penetration itself, but because of the effeminization that might occur should they come to enjoy pleasure too much. The Greek resolved the issue by assuming the social fiction that the young man would not enjoy, but simply tolerate, being penetrated. The Roman simply denied sexual access to young men destined to be citizens.) The Christian movement exploits and celebrates the idea of masculine self-rule at the expense of the sexual subordination of the other, but it does not break with the complex of ideas in which masculinity is a matter of power and "rule." Fullness of masculinity is exercised in the total avoidance of sex, whereas those who could not give up sex were somehow "lesser" men whose very lack of control made their marriage necessary, for marriage legitimated sex.

Christianity represents a variation on a theme in accordance with which sexually active men, husbands, are "lesser" men. But it was a move that would prove to have ominous consequences for the homosexual. When spirituality is so constructed that fullness of masculinity lay in the pious repudiation of pleasure, those interested in homosexual sex were destined to be thought not merely ungodly in their pursuit of pleasure but the most unmasculine of men as well.

Chapter 7

The Variegated Lotus: Homosexual Sex and Historical Buddhism

THE NIRVANIC TRANSCENDENCE OF DESIRE

To turn to Buddhism from Augustine is to encounter a strikingly similar diagnosis of the human condition unaided by spiritual redirection or cultivation. For both, spiritual maturation lay in a certain kind of transcendence of demanding desire. Yet perhaps because Buddhism was revolutionary in never regarding procreation as a religious obligation incumbent even upon a few, Buddhism was not tempted to see marriage as a safe house for sexual indulgence, and would—at least in its Japanese forms—prove amenable to seeing homosexual forms of sex as contributory to spiritual growth and development.

Indeed, a widely told story about the Buddha is testament to Buddhism's arguable uniqueness among the spiritual traditions of mankind. The Buddha, so the story goes, conceded that questions about whether life might exist after death or whether there was a creator god might be theoretically interesting, but refused to see opinions about such issues as religiously significant. People who indulge in such speculations, he opined, are rather like the man who has been shot with an arrow who then sits down to ask himself where the arrow might have come from and of what it has been made, interesting questions to be sure, but questions that are beside the point, given the circumstances. The issue at hand is the removal of the arrow. Consequently, Buddhism represents itself less as a doctrine to be believed than as a cure for human suffering and pain. Buddhism is above all a path of spiritual therapy.

Dukkha is the Sanskrit term for whatever it is that the Buddhist path is understood to alleviate. The word is normally translated as "suffering," which is not an inappropriate rendering insofar as it comprehends the discomfort that results from the human vulnerability to disease, disappointment, decay, and death. However, the term also covers the frustration of not having what we want, even as it denotes the disappointment at discovering that getting what we wanted does not bring the satisfaction one had anticipated. *Dukkha* also refers to the general sense that we are missing out on life, that life is what is happening to someone else while we are confronted by the difficulties and concerns of our personal situation. It refers to the tedium and ennui to which the routine of life seems to condemn us. In its most encompassing perhaps, *dukkha* can be understood as the discomfort of the ill fit between expectation and reality, the suffering that attends the general unsatisfactoriness of life.[1]

The Buddhist address to *dukkha* lies in what is traditionally known as the Noble Eightfold Path. For our purposes, we can follow tradition and conflate the eight steps into three: Right (or Noble) Thinking, Right (or Noble) Behavior, and (Noble) Insight. In keeping with the general pragmatic nature of Buddhism, right thinking is at first simply the entertainment on faith of the idea that the Buddha was on to something significant and the willingness to follow the path the he charted. Right behavior is tantamount to an ethical practice, where ethics is understood as controlling the self for the sake of something other than the self. Insight is the transformation in the way that one experiences the world that is gained, above all, through meditation. Together right behavior and insight make plausible the Buddhist description of the reality of the world, which in turn reinforces the devotee's practice of right action and meditation. Thus is set up a spiral of reinforcement that has as its end the realization of nirvana.

Meditation is not principally, as one might be tempted to think, a matter of following a chain of reasoning or thinking out a problem. Rather, it covers a range of practices that generally have more to do with the focusing of awareness than any rationative processes. Concentrated, deep breathing is a meditational technique that plays a significant role in the Buddhist repertoire, and is particularly instructive in context. Americans might very well advise one another to take a deep breath before an activity about which we are stressed. Such a deep breath before, say, an exam or a job interview can serve to lessen the anxiety and reduce the stress. So too, the practice of meditation can be seen as a strategy of stress reduction, which when practiced over time putatively becomes habitual. In such a state, a person is more apt to experience the events of his or her life with a certain kind of equanimity in which one can let the good and bad things in life come and go without undo distress, with a certain kind of graceful composure and stability. In such a state one has "blown out" or otherwise "extinguished" the fire that leads one to grasp after experience as if life depended upon it. The extinction of such desperate craving is of the essence in the psychological realization of nirvana.

Buddhist thought, like much Eastern thinking in general, insists that reality is comprised of all those things that are objects of care and concern. However, to the extent that things in one's life cease to be an occasion for anxiety and despair, to that extent they have been stripped of the ponderous reality they otherwise have had. As worry dissipates, so too does the sense of the reality of that about which one is worried. If it is not true to say that it has completely ceased to exist for me, nevertheless its existence has now come to seem but insubstantial and uncompelling. Hence, the attainment of nirvanic psychology is at the same time the recognition of the de facto unreality of all things: the realization of nirvana does not merely signal the extinction of a certain kind of desiring, but the rooting and grounding of the self in the quietness, the stillness, the no-thing-ness, which is the nirvana that underlies and is the real truth at the heart of all things.

Everything that appears to exist is a compound entity. Think of the human who is eating across the table from you. He or she is a cluster of organs, each of which in turn is a community of cells which, further, can be broken down into parts composed in turn of molecules, which in their turn are made up of atoms, which are made up of subatomic particles, and so on. Eventually one reaches a point where the elements that make up compound things are so small that they cease to appear as formed things at all, and the compounds seem to be materializations that are rooted in what we might call no-thing-ness in particular. This means that whatever does give itself to us in our experience is an epiphany that comes from nowhere and nothing. At its base, the world is nothing but the mysterious appearance of nothing substantial. At the same time, whatever does appear is inextricably caught up in the process of change. That person who is seated across the dinner table from us is only apparently stable in time. Given enough scope, we know that this same person was once a baby, and before that a one-celled organism in his or her mother's womb. In time, he or she will wrinkle and grow old and eventually disappear in death. The apparent stability is only a mask for the changes that are going on even as he or she sits across from us. The energy that he or she takes to chew and digest food can be achieved only by the processes of molecular firing. Within a few days, everything that goes into the makeup of our dinner companion will have changed, even though the surface change will have seemingly been minimal. Thus, every formed thing is not merely a mysterious appearance riding upon the surface of no-thing-ness but is itself an evanescent, changing thing. According to Buddhist tradition, the worries and stresses of life derive from mistaking either the self or the things at hand or both as having a substantiality that nothing possesses. And the realization of nirvana is at base the recognition of the true nature of the world, revealing the Buddhist path in turn to be a kind of reality adjustment, a training to see and experience life in the light of what it actually is.

Sexual desire is normally overwhelming in its intensity. Therefore in the Buddhist diagnostic—or at least according to that form of Buddhism which we are exploring presently—sexual desire is one of those drives which tricks us into sensing that we really need what has occasioned our desire. However, to desire so strongly is to believe both in the substantial reality of the self—"I need him or her!" we say, as if there were a real "I" that needed the object of our affectionate longing—and in the substantial nature of the object of our desire, when in fact neither the self or the object of our longing is all that substantial. Sexual desire, then, is something that is to be transcended if nirvana is to be realized.

In Theravadin Buddhism, the "Buddhism of the Elders," which is practiced in Southeast Asia, it is assumed that the realization of nirvana is something that can be achieved only at the end of a whole series of lifetimes, and is so difficult that it requires a full-time occupation. Therefore, laypersons might aspire to lead a life of sufficient ethical integrity so as to merit a reincarnation as a monk in the next life, but it is only the monastic who is truly capable of nearing the realization of nirvana—the goal of enlightenment. Hence, the monk engages himself in a training by which he distances himself from sexual desire. Indeed, sexual penetration of anyone—male or female—on the part of a monk is grounds for dismissal from the monastic community. Other violations of the monastic rules, such as masturbating another to orgasm, are treated less seriously. (Since monastic communities were single-sex ones, it is no wonder that homosexual sex in one form or another would have occasioned some difficulty—as it does in any single-sex living situation.) As Leonard Zwilling observed, however, "When homosexual behavior is not ignored in Indian Buddhist writings it is derogated much to the same degree as comparable heterosexual acts."[2] It is not the sex of the partner, but the fact of sexual desire itself that is the troubling issue. Or at least one would think so.

In Indian Buddhist writings, one also runs across treatments of male persons who are designated *pandakas*. Once again, the term resists easy translation. The Indian thinker Buddhaghosa lists five types, which Peter Harvey translates and characterizes respectively as:

1. the "sprayed" *pandaka* (one who evidently derives sexual satisfaction from fellating another man to ejaculation);
2. the "jealous" *pandaka* (one who is satisfied through watching others have sex, a voyeur);
3. the "by a means" *pandaka* (one whose semen is expelled through some extraordinary means, someone who is into "kinky"—or what would have counted for kink in the cultural setting—sex perhaps);
4. "fortnight" *pandaka* (one who is impotent for half a month at a time); and
5. the "non-male" *pandaka* (one who is somehow lacking [a penis? testicles?] since conception).[3]

Of these, it is only the first, the "sprayed" pandaka, who is of necessity engaged in homosexual sex. Outside of Buddhaghosa, I have never heard of the equivalent of such a thing as a "fortnight" pandaka.

Beyond Buddhaghosa, the *Vinyana Pitaka,* a collection of texts relating to the rules of monastic life, tells the story of how one pandaka who had been ordained a monk approached at first some other monks to "defile him," then some fat monks, then some nonmonks. Although all of the monks resisted his advances, the last group evidently gratified him and then began to spread the word that all monks were really pandakas. Because of this incident, the Buddha forbade pandakas to be ordained and ordered the expulsion of any monk found to be one.[4] Zwilling opines that the Buddha acts as he does "as a practical concession to prevailing conventions to prevent the charge of dissolute conduct from being leveled at the order as a whole."[5] However, the passage is revealing. Pandakas are men who might willingly seek to be "defiled" by other men. We are obviously dealing with some sort of overt homosexual behavior, but it is not clear that we are simply dealing with oral sex, as Buddhaghosa might lead us to expect. In addition, such men are reputedly given over to an overriding pursuit of pleasure that in itself might prove that they are incapable of the transcendence of desire that is required of the Buddhist monastic path. At the same time, if we follow the lead of Buddhaghosa, we have to recognize that such men are viewed as something other than "real" or "full" men, rather as nonmen. In this case, we are looking at a phenomenon not unlike that which we have met before. Those who willingly enact the receptive role in sex have somehow thereby sacrificed the fullness of masculinity, and this sacrifice shows itself in the uncontrollable nature of their desire. Among the Theravadins, women can at best aspire to be reincarnated as males so that they might attain the enlightenment that is otherwise not available to them because of their sex. It also appears that only true or full men are capable of the discipline that leads to enlightenment, in which case pandakas are assimilated to the status of effeminate or womanized men for which the willingness to be sexually "defiled" is a marker.

ENLIGHTENMENT AND HOMOSEXUAL SEX IN JAPAN AND TIBET

The sexual "puritanism"[6] of the Indian Buddhist tradition would find itself on less receptive ground among the Japanese than it had enjoyed in the ascetic atmosphere of the land of its birth. Not all Japanese could be convinced that doing without sex was healthy or spiritually productive. Of course, it was not Theravadin Buddhism that would migrate into Japan by way of China and Korea, but rather the Mahayana. The Mahayana, the "Greater Vehicle," represented a reform movement within the Buddhist tradition which gets its name from the fact that, in the newer tradition, laypersons could aspire to enlightenment as well as monastics. More important, the Mahayana was intellectually innovative as well. Mahayana thinkers found the pursuit of nirvana, the pursuit of spiritual freedom, for oneself all too self-referential and thereby counterproductive. Hence, there emerged the newer ideal of the bodhisattva, the one who seeks enlightenment, not for his or her own sake but for the sake of all. At the same time, the vocabulary of "emptiness" comes to replace the centrality of the notion of nirvana. All things, it is said, are empty, empty of own-being. That is to affirm the same insubstantiality of all things as the doctrine of the truth of nirvana, but does so in a way that gives equal importance to the relative reality that all things have. Although passing things are insubstantial and evanescent, they are nevertheless not completely nothing. All formed, changing things are real in their changingness, even if they have no stable unchanging essence. With the Mahayana, then, salvational enlightenment comes to mean less a matter of freedom from worldliness than the freedom to be a changeling in a changing world. Enlightenment allows people to experience themselves and the world for what it is, an ever-changing, ever-flowing complex, and to allow themselves to be the ever-changing things that they are. Enlightenment is life that is lived without mistakenly taking things as being more substantial than they are. Giving up false expectations about the world and the self brings with it a gracefulness with which the changing self is now free to change and adapt with changing circumstances.

In this context, sexual love can come to represent an education in the "emptiness," which is to say, the changeableness or mutability of all things. (In accordance with the general pragmatic nature of Buddhism in general and of the Mahayana in particular, Mahayana thinkers felt free not only to be intellectually innovative, but also to endorse nontraditional paths to enlightenment.) To the Japanese, fighting against sexual desire can be spiritually counterproductive. One wastes all one's energy fighting the forbidden when, by giving in, one can satisfy one's desire, let it pass, and get on with the wider program of spiritual cultivation. To experience the satiation of desire is to come to experience how it too passes. If one's sexual desire for another leads one into a more enduring relation with him or her, the romance will eventually go out of the relation, and that too is an education in the changing, insubstantial nature of all things. The lover, then, is educated by experience in the mutability of desire and its satisfaction. So, too, does the beloved experience the waxing and waning of the lover's desire, and shares in the education.

If the Mahayana opened the possibility of enlightenment to the layperson, it did not abandon the option of monastic life. Sex with women was generally thought too defiling for a monk. Since monks generally avoided even the association, much less socialization with, women, as in many all male societies, a monk might very well find that it was another male that came to be the object of his desire. A Samurai warrior might have had a page that he was training and with whom he might have a sexual relation. Just so, monkish sexual desire was typically that of an older monk for a younger. Indeed, among the Japanese in general, as among the Greeks, homosexual love was thought of as something that transpired between an older man and a younger.[7] Even if the two were older men, one would have been thought to be the "boy" and the other the man. We noted among the ancient Greeks, who had a similar construction of homosexual relations, the presumption and social fiction that the younger man would not enjoy being sexually penetrated by his adoring lover. In Japanese Buddhist literature, the beloved is either enjoined to satisfy the desires of his smitten admirer out of compassion[8]—or the literature might simply represent him as indulging his lover out of the compassion that he has acquired by virtue of the karmic merit he might have accumulated in past lives.[9] Here the beloved is manifesting the compassion of the Buddha, and we find no hint of erotic desire on his part. Indeed, in some stories, a bodhisattva—figures with which the spiritual world is peopled—manifests himself or herself as a young man who occasions and satisfies the desires of an older monk for the sake of the older monk's spiritual progress.[10]

We are not speaking here of an adventitious development within Japanese Buddhism, but indeed of an established, recognized spiritual path, the way of *shudo* or "boy love," which owes its origins to one of the great cultural figures not only in Japanese Buddhism, but in Japanese culture as well. None other than Kukai, the founder of the Shingon sect of Buddhism, is supposedly to have introduced the way of *shudo* into Japan.[11] We may be speaking here of the stuff of legend, but a legend nonetheless that functioned to sanction and normalize the love of youths in both monastic and samurai culture.

In Tibetan Buddhism, that development from the Mahayana designated the Vajrayana, would go even further, allowing sex as both symbol and vehicle of enlightenment. To understand the logic here, we need to consider another Buddhist idea that we have hitherto avoided, "the interdependent co-arising of all things." To be is not simply to be caught up in the flow of change, but to be conditioned. That is to say, to be is to be situated. Each of us is set within an environment, each of us is embedded within a social network, and each of us finds ourselves, at each point in our lives, confronted by personal problems and issues. To be Buddhist, who I am is determined by my being just this person in just this situation. I and my world "co-arise" together and are not understandable except in relation to one another. I am the one so situated, and my situation cannot be understood except as being my situation. Because I am grounded in mysterious nothingness at the root of all things, I have the freedom to respond and to cope with my situation creatively. Of course, to do so is to change my situation and thereby myself, creating a new self in a new situation demanding and inviting a new creative address.

Insofar as enlightenment means seeing things as they really are, in this context, enlightenment means in part not seeing things in terms of the past. When meeting a new boss, I should allow him to be the novel, unique being that he is, and not view him through the lens of all the other authority figures I have previously dealt with in my life. More important, however, the quality of my responsiveness to my world and my situation depends upon the scope of my sensitivity. Consider, for example, a person engaged in the game of basketball. No doubt, one has to keep one's attention focused upon the ball. However, if I attend exclusively to the ball, I might not be aware of the player next to me who is poised to steal the ball away from me. If I am only aware of the players in my immediate environment, I might miss the fact that one of my teammates is downcourt ready to receive a pass and make the score. Focal attentiveness tends to exclude the peripheral, but if I can soften my focus, then I become more and more aware of the surrounding context, if only peripherally. Maximal responsiveness, and thereby, maximal creativity, depends upon maximal scope of attention.[12]

In Buddhist language, such maximal perceptivity can be called "mindfulness," and presumes a psychological emptiness, or primordial openness and receptivity to what the world presents me with at any given moment. Such "big-sky-mindedness," as a state of ready receptivity, can be thought of as a kind of feminine state. In Buddhism, wisdom, it is said, is the mother of the Buddha. In this context, the wisdom of total receptivity gives rise to intuitive, responsive action that connotes maleness. If compassion is attending to things as they are without distortion, then this male responsiveness is compassionate action. If my awareness, moreover, is totally unselfconscious, then I am totally lost in my attentiveness and responsiveness to my environment. I am nothing but unselfconscious receptivity and responsiveness.

How like the ecstatic loss of self-consciousness I might have in sex this would be! . . . so much so that I can now begin to view enlightenment as the union of wisdom (empty receptivity) in unselfconscious intercourse with compassionate responsiveness. Hence the Buddhist iconography of a female and male joined in sexual congress. At the same time, the ecstasy of orgasm may be the closest experiential equivalent to the total unselfconscious openness to experience that is wisdom. Hence sex can become a training ground for enlightened apprehension. If, for a Western thinker such as Augustine, self-control is the height of rationality, in Tibetan Buddhism, it is the open receptivity that is the essence of reason.[13]

Although it is the image of a man and woman in intercourse that can represent enlightenment, there seems to be no reason why homosexual sex might not be marshaled in service of training for enlightenment. Yet, when we look, the only homosexual sex that is attested in the scholarly literature is that involving the *lDab ldob.* Apparently, these were warriors and athletes who could not, or did not want to, undertake the academic study that a full monastic vocation entailed, who were nevertheless associated with the monasteries as irregular monks who were content to do the grunt work that kept the monasteries functioning. These *lDab ldobs* avoided the defilement of sex with women, as was traditional for monks—and practiced a kind of intercrural sex with younger men, so as to avoid the penetration that was traditionally forbidden to monks.[14] But here too we have an instance of homosexual sex constructed as a matter of a mature man "using" another who is socially inferior by reason of age for sex.

If, at it seems, there is no reason in Buddhism why homosexual sex should be treated any differently than heterosexual sex, it is nevertheless the case that in actual practice Buddhism presumes the cultural bias that assumes that sex is something a man has with a nonman, a woman, or a lesser or younger man. Jeffrey Hopkins has recently adapted Chopel's *Tibetan Arts of Love,* a handbook for using sex as an instrument of enlightenment, to make it usable for homosexual couples.[15] It is noteworthy that his book is a product not of historical Buddhism but of the accommodation of Buddhism to contemporary homophile advocacy. It is the contemporary homophile movement that is forcing Buddhism along new paths, as it may be forcing many other traditional religions. An inquiry into the historical uniqueness of such contemporary movements and their religious import is the topic of the next and final chapter of this book.

Chapter 8

Struggles on the American Front

A GAY AGENDA? AND THE SOCIAL GOOD

It has been quipped, by whom I know not, that "the love that earlier would not speak its name has now become the love that won't shut up." Our quipster may have grown tired of hearing from and about the homosexuals in our midst. But his weariness is a testimony to the on-going struggle on the part of homophilic communities for social tolerance, legal legitimacy, and religious sanction that remains a prominent aspect of the political and cultural scene in America. Those on the so-called Religious Right frequently complain of the "gay agenda." Yet the aims of representatives of the various homophilic communities remain various, and are not infrequently the subject of ongoing debate among homophile activists themselves. Urvashi Vaid can be taken as a representative for a progressive politics that would subsume the search for gay and lesbian rights within a wider movement for social transformation and equality for all minorities, the most immediate neighbors being bisexuals and transgendered peoples (thus giving us the ubiquitously used acronym LGBT), more remotely women and ethnic minorities. Michael Warner, of the queer left among progressives, longs for an even more radical transformation of the shape of society. Warner's queer politics includes defenses of such things as pornography, sex businesses, and what he calls alternatively "sex outside the home" and "public sex"—as well as advocacy for the legal sanctioning of a wide variety of living arrangements, including presumably polyamorous relations.[1] Andrew Sullivan is perhaps the most prominent among the so-called conservatives— sometimes and perhaps more accurately referred to as "classic liberals"—who would center gay and lesbian activism on the struggle for extension of the same set of social rights traditionally reserved for the heterosexual population to gays and lesbians. Such activism is frequently called a gay rights approach to distinguish it from the more progressive aims of gay liberation. However, debate over the following three issues within and without the homophile communities make them flash points in the contemporary "culture wars":

1. antidiscrimination laws;
2. gays in the military; and
3. gay marriage.[2]

Debate over antidiscrimination laws raises issues about the appropriate role of government in protecting the rights of minorities against the majority, certainly one of the functions of government. Moreover, the debate also raises the question of whether certain dimensions of social interaction which if not impervious to are nevertheless not to be the subject of legislative dicta and control. Consideration of such issues would take us well beyond the confines of this study. It seems to me that Richard Mohr is correct in observing that

> [t]he military is nominally intended to *defend* what the country is, but as its racial and gender histories show, it is the chief institution by which the nation *defines* what the country is and what is to count as full personhood and full citizenship.[3]

However, the current "don't ask, don't tell" policy regulating how gays and lesbians are to be incorporated into the military, adopted during the Clinton administration, works to mask the fact that they have been included. By not being asked about their sexual orientation, and importantly not to volunteer such information, soldiers and prospective military personnel are being required to treat their homosexuality as a dirty little secret. Beyond that, a level of chastity which puts them above suspicion is being expected that is not required of their heterosexual counterparts and that fact in itself smacks of unequal treatment. However, because discussions in this area, too, frequently turn on whether knowledge of gay and lesbian soldiers on the part of other soldiers threatens the cohesiveness required to maintain the fighting potential of the units involved, discussion of this issue here takes us well beyond the limitations of this study. However, if anything concentrates the demand that homosexual love be accorded a respect and dignity equal to that of heterosexual love—a demand that is arguably the real heart behind all gay and lesbian politics—it is the struggle for the right of gay men and lesbian women to marry their partners, with all the rights and privileges associated with matrimony.

Not all in the gay and lesbian communities are united in the pursuit of gay marriage. Michael Warner, for example, seems willing to back the political struggle for the right to marry only if it is coupled with the pursuit of other concerns, such as reform in rights extending to intimate association and immigration, and—more characteristically— as a possible prelude to "making available other statuses, such as expanded domestic partnerships, concubinage, or something like PACS [contracts of social union] for property-sharing households, all available both to straight and gay people alike."[4] But there is the rub— "straight and gay people alike." Some straight people might be as equally interested in the legalization of social arrangements other than marriage as might gays and lesbians. It is not clear that, within such a social development, gay love would have been able to cast off its stigma. It is the struggle for the right to marry that is alone capable of accomplishing that. Although the legal privileging of traditional marriage excludes alternative social arrangements among heterosexual and homosexuals alike, marrriage is the institution from which gays and lesbians are distinctly excluded. The blockage of gays and lesbians from the estate of marriage constitutes a legal disenfranchisement that points to the social dishonor in which gay and lesbian love is held. By establishing the right to marry, gays and lesbians can gain public recognition of the moral equivalence of gay and heterosexual love.

Theorist Kathleen Sands helpfully distinguishes sexual ethics from sexual regulation, arguing that whatever one's personal ethical positions, however widely shared,

> only a small part of these ethics could be used to justify sexual regulation—only when it is established that public interests are at stake, when it is agreed what those public interests are, and when the interests are sufficiently vital to justify coercive measures.[5]

Developing her insight, we might say that continuance of the refusal to extend to gays and lesbians the right to marry cannot legitimately be justified on the basis of the ethical perspectives even of the majority but only on the basis of real, demonstrable public interest. We are right to ask ourselves about the public consequences of extending the right to marry to gays and lesbians, whether they be good or ill. Should there appear no evident deleterious social consequences that would follow from the extension of right to marry to gays and lesbians, the withholding of such a right would be proven manifestly illegitimate.

It is hard to see the drawbacks to such an extension. It may be popularly touted that gay and lesbian marriage would undermine heterosexual marriage. I must confess, however, that I find it hard to see how that might be the case unless, given the option, many men or women would be tempted to enter into homosexual unions rather than heterosexual ones. But that is clearly preposterous. It is true that some men can be attracted to other men when they are denied access to women, as is notoriously the case in prison for example, presumably, however, such men would not be the ones seeking gay marriage outside the confines of a single-sex environment. At the same time, the vast majority of men would not even find the prospect of gay marriage palatable or tempting in any event. Rather than undermining traditional heterosexual marriage, it seems more evidently the case that, by extending gays the right to marry, society might even help to shore up the failing institution of marriage. By doing so, it would create an atmosphere in which such legally sanctioned, committed-pair bonding would be held up as a desirable ideal for all lovers—if indeed we think that it is so.

Jonathan Rauch has advocated what is, I think, one of the most compelling arguments for the social desirability of gay marriage.[6] It is true, as he argues, that religions have shaped what we understand marriage to be, a committed partnership in which each party can expect sexual fidelity from the other. Otherwise, adultery could not be grounds for the dissolution of the marriage. It is not written in stone or in nature that this is how things must be. One could imagine a society in which people bond but whose relationship would not necessarily be sexual. Sexual satisfaction might be thought of as something quite apart from the ends of marriage. However, it is in and through the received traditions stemming chiefly from the Bible that marriage in America has been thought of, and hence institutionalized, as an exclusive sexual relationship. However, Rauch argues that, whether marriage proves to be a social arrangement that receives religious blessing and sanction, a society—a religiously pluralistic society, in particular—needs to frame its understanding of, and establish grounds for, marriage quite independently of any religious construction that the various traditions might make of it.

Rauch therefore asks himself, why marriage? What social good does marriage fulfill? He declines to yoke love and marriage together as "horse and carriage," finding that society has no real stakes in an ideology which would hold that marriage is the appropriate venue for love to express itself. Nor does he find that marriage exists for the sake of children. Indeed, society allows the marriage of sterile couples. (To amend his argument, it is well to note that although the marriage of nonsterile couples may produce children, marriage is not, in and of itself, sufficient grounds to adopt. Society demands that married couples provide a good home before adoption is allowed. So, too, it would seem, that pragmatic considerations might control whether gay married couples might adopt. Society might want to see that all children are placed in married homes, but marriage, as a social institution, is not primarily for the sake of raising, much less producing, children.) Rather, Rauch argues that marriage is society's chief bulwark against the male potential for roguishness and the first—maybe even second and third—line of defense in providing caregivers when and where fortune brings not the better but the worse. For the first point he animadverts to the observation of John Wilson that the male is innately predisposed to hunt, defend, and attack, with Rauch arguing finally "for taming males, marriage is unmatched."[7] He is *not* claiming that men are naturally brutish and need to be controlled. The taming or domestication involved here is not a matter of undoing of the natural, but of giving it channel and focus. In having a family, the male has something to care for and defend—and is less likely to express his native exuberance in socially destructive ways. It is the unattached male, Rauch points out, who typically goes "wilding" in Central Park, who joins in the hooliganism of British soccer games, or who takes part in grope lines in military gatherings, and, significantly, in the wanton gay sex of the 1970s. Although admitting that it is probably true that it is women and children who help domesticate the male, Rauch asserts

> that hardly means that the effect of marriage on homosexual men is negligible. To the contrary, being tied into a committed relationship plainly helps stabilize gay men. Even without mar-

riage, coupled gay men have steady sex partners and relationships that they value, so they tend to be less wanton.[8]

He adds that, when those relationships are recognized legally and sanctioned as "marriages," other stabilizing influences come to bear, not the least of which is the way societal expectations channel and support that relationship:

> Around the partners is [woven] a web of expectations that they will spend nights together, go to parties together, take out mortgages together, buy furniture at Ikea together, and so on—all of which helps tie them together and keep them off the streets and at home.[9]
> ("It's 1:00 a.m.; do you know where your husband is?" Chances are you do.)[10]

At the same time—and certainly not less important—marriage provides, when illness or some other misfortune strikes, someone whose job it is to care for the stricken:

> Absent a spouse, the burdens of contingency crushingly falls upon people who have more immediate problems of their own (relatives, friends, neighbors), and then upon charities and welfare programs that are expensive and often not very good. From the broader society's point of view, the unattached person is an accident waiting to happen.[11]

Marriage is even psychologically salutary, since the married partner can assume that a social "net" is waiting to catch him or her should illness strike or some other misfortune befall. Perhaps this knowledge, in and of itself, provides the psychological security which accounts for the widely held view that married people tend to live longer.

Of course, society could hardly extend the right to marry as long as gay sexual relations were themselves forbidden under law by virtue of so-called antisodomy legislation. In 2003, the U.S. Supreme Court struck down all residual antisodomy laws. By the time this book was going to press, Vermont had already approved civil unions to be offered to gay and lesbian persons as an alternative to traditional marriage, and Massachusetts was poised to begin issuing marriage licenses to same-sex couples. Of course, the federal Defense of Marriage Act (identified with the acronym DOMA), signed into law in 1996, in effect provides that no state need recognize a marriage contracted under the laws of another state that is not the union of one man with one woman. At the same time that the Massachusetts high court was moving to find the exclusion of gay and lesbian couples from marriage unconstitutional according to the provisions of its state constitution, the legislature of Ohio was moving to prohibit such marriages through legislation. In addition, federal legislators are pondering the wisdom of an amendment to the U.S. Constitution which would ban gay marriage (and possibly even the newly accorded right to form civil unions like that provided by Vermont) nationally. Therefore, although the debate over gay marriage is very much to the fore in the present, arguments for and against antisodomy legislation seem a thing of the past. However, a consideration of what seemed to be at stake in the repeal of such legislation is instructive, not the least because of the perspective it lends to the dynamics underlying the ongoing debate over the extension of the right to marry.

In a wide-ranging chapter with the intriguing title " 'Knights, Young Men, Boys': Masculine Worlds and Democratic Values," in his book *Gay Ideas: Outing and Other Controversies,* Richard Mohr[12] advanced an idea—reminiscent of those of Pausanias in Plato's *Symposium*—that the gay subculture, together with its one-night stands and bathhouses, is both a school for, and symbol of, democracy. He disregards the ranking of persons that results from different degrees of "sexiness," and concentrates rather on the fact that, in experiencing other men as fellow searchers of sexual partners and sexual happiness, the normal distinctions between persons that hold in society outside the subculture—distinctions of wealth, status, ethnicity—fall by the wayside. Men who experience one another as fellow seekers of sexual happiness experience one another as equals. Among other features of gay society, Mohr observes "a lack of violence in gay male sexual institutions and acts, despite fantasies to the contrary, and despite the trappings of S&M styles, [which] both betokens and generates respect and equality between gay men."[13] Going further, he argues,

> In their recognition and promotion of personality and material completeness, self-sufficiency and attentive independence, in rankless friendship and intimate knowledge, and in their non-

possessive valuing wrought of robust mutual pleasure, gay male relations serve as a general model of equal respect.[14]

To be sure, Mohr is celebrating those very aspects of current sexual practice in the gay subcultures of the major cities of the United States which many critics find dehumanizing and fear is lurking behind the advancement of the social and legal tolerance of gay and lesbian love and its expression. Such critics, for their own part, are overlooking the degree to which furtive sex can itself be a product of social intolerance and the lack of legal sanction for gay relationships. More important, however, the culture is all too immured in the habit of thinking of sex that is not authorized by a prevenient relational commitment as a form of "abuse" in which one person is simply using another for his or her pleasure. Lurking in the background is the highly questionable presumption that when I "use" another for my pleasure, I am necessarily treating them as an "object" and not as a person. At the very least, such a view can be maintained only by disregarding that two people who agree to mutual "use" of each other are contracting for pleasure, and thus not necessarily treating each other as other than fully personal beings at all.

More to the point, however, it may be that the gay subculture is simply embodying a cultural shift in the way contemporary people are beginning to experience sex. Heretofore, sex was something that marriage legitimated. However, wherever sex involves a mutual choice of partners, it is highly unlikely to be an unalloyed instance of impersonal disregard. Perhaps what is aborning is a view of sex as "meeting" and greeting. Having sex might be a way of hailing another ("I like what you offer to my view, body, and other personal matters inclusive") and a way of getting to know him or her. One sexual encounter may lead to the desire to have more sex and to "meet" the other more fully—or maybe not. The delightfully miraculous occurs when the other remains a turn-on even as he or she continues to reveal more and more about himself or herself. In this light, sex within a relationship is not different in kind from a one-night stand, but simply in degree. What I meet and greet in a spouse is fuller and more complex than what is revealed to me by a person whom I have only just met, but I am still meeting and appreciating what the other has revealed for me to "see" and appreciate. What I am saying is that sex is becoming, not only in gay culture but in the culture at large, one of the vehicles of mate selection. In Mohr's graphic way of putting it, "Love—the real thing—at first fuck is not unusual."[15]

However, our critic continues, does not the availability of sex, and indeed the social acceptance of sex outside marriage, undermine the importance of committed relationships? It is as if our critic fears that, if people did not need to get married to have sex, they would not get married. Nor would they be encouraged to stay together once committed. This strikes me as preposterous. If sex is understood as a vehicle of mate selection, mate selection still remains the aim of the game. And a culture of sex does not necessarily support a culture of divorce. The problem here is not the availability of sex, but the fact that our culture seems unwilling—or unable—to celebrate sticking it out together with the same intensity with which it celebrates the wonderous delight of falling in love.

The fear of gay sexual institutions and practices on the part of many of those resisters to gay sex, I am arguing, is really a fear of the way sex is coming to be understood and experienced not merely by gay men only, but the wider culture at large. Resistance to gay rights, then, mistakes the symbol for the reality. It confuses gay sexual practice with what is in reality a cultural sexual practice. To find an argument as to how the tolerance of man-sex explicitly threatens the social order, we have to look back to the complex of ideas we found lurking behind Native American practices and Levitical homophobia: men who penetrate other men are weakening either the fighting unit or threatening the integrity of the wider society by "creating" penetrable soldiers and men respectively. Those who allow themselves to be penetrated are willingly complicitous in that same weakening of the fighting force and/or society at large. Of course, this is magical thinking that has no real grounds in contemporary science. Indeed, contemporary conditions of warfare are such that this form of magical association between sexually penetrable persons and the integrity of a group can finally be debunked and its psychic appeal weakened. The mere presence of women in the armed services is sufficient to disavow us of the idea that one who can be sexually penetrated thereby weakens the group. Moreover, war is no longer a matter of penetrating enemy bodies by spear, lance, arrow, or bayonet, and thus the analogy of warfare and fighting has ceased to be fully persuasive. Even the gun has ceased to be the principal weapon in modern warfare. Today, we seek to blow up targets quite as much as shooting our "loads" into enemy bodies. To the extent that warfare becomes a matter of aerial bombardment, the association of sex and warfare is to that extent weakened. Even if the fear of gay sex remains a psychologically compelling one on the part of many people, the rationale fails to be sufficiently demonstrable to warrant social control.

That this "magical" kind of association between sex and war is to be debunked, it seems to me, should go without question. Mohr has, I believe, overstated his case about the social contribution that gay democratic sexual practice can contribute to society at large. However, that a sea change is happening in the way in which our culture is coming to think about sex—whether welcome or not—is, I think, undeniable. However, it still remains the case that antisodomy legislation is open to the charge of being manifestly unfair and distinctly undemocratic. We are a culture that celebrates intimate relations. Indeed, most of our lives are given over to the creation of such relationships, and then "working at" them to make them continue to "work" for us. We are encouraged to do so by so much that emanates from the popular media, not to mention the pulpit. Indeed, relational intimacy is one of those great goods of life that is celebrated and honored in popular culture and in religious culture as well.[16] Sexual desire controls those with whom we can find and establish relational intimacy. Although most people will find themselves interested in members of the opposite sex, there is nevertheless a minority who can establish such intimacy only with a member of the same sex. By making the sexual expression of their desire illegal and/or refusing them the right to marry, society denies to a significant minority the right to relational intimacy that it otherwise holds up as one of the great goods in life. This, I submit, is an inherently antidemocratic stance, inhibiting important drives, if not to life and liberty, certainly to the pursuit of happiness. However patently unfair such legal prejudice is in the contemporary context, few legislatures were quick to repeal those antisodomy laws on the books, nor did the highest court of the land agree to find the moral and legal grounds to rule such legislation unconstitutional until quite recently.

GAY RIGHTS AS A FREEDOM OF RELIGION ISSUE

Up until 2003, the most recent U.S. Supreme Court decision regarding the constitutionality of antisodomy legislation had been rendered in the case of *Bowers v. Hardwick*. Hardwick was charged with violating Georgia's statute prohibiting "unnatural acts" when a policeman, who had come to the defendant's home about an unpaid ticket for public drunkenness, was allowed into the house by a roommate and found the unfortunate Mr. Hardwick in his bed with another man in a sexually compromising position. The case made it to the U.S. Supreme Court, where it was held that homosexual sodomy is not protected by any constitutional right of privacy. A great deal has been written on why the justices missed the mark in *Bowers*.[17] What is important in this context, however, is the explicitly religious dimension of the reasoning behind the original decision.

Although the Court has held on other occasions that "mere public intolerance or animosity cannot constitutionally justify the deprivation of a person's physical liberty,"[18] it decided to the contrary in *Bowers*. It has held that only those activities which can be understood as "fundamental" can be protected by a right to privacy, and that such rights are only those that are "'deeply rooted in this Nation's history and tradition.'"[19] Apparently, the desire of homosexuals to find happiness in the arms of one another was not sufficiently fundamental, nor sufficiently consistent with the nation's moral traditions to be protected by the U.S. Constitution. Both presumptions proved to be and remain questionable. Since homosexual desire limits those persons with whom one can establish intimacy, it would seem to be a very fundamental element in the personal life of those living in a culture that values relationships as one of the primary goods of life. That homosexuality is in fact inconsistent with the moral—and ultimately mainstream religious traditions—of America is a question to be addressed. What is apparent in context, however, is the way the opinion of the justices virtually "established" a particular, even if widely held, religious persuasion as grounds for denying homosexuals the right to private congress. In defending their decision in the Bowers case, the justices claimed that the condemnation of homosexuality "is firmly rooted in Judeo-Christian moral and ethical standards."[20] However, the appeal to the Judeo-Christian tradition as the standard for justifying the law of the land seems to be a violation of the constitutional mandate prohibiting the establishment of any given religion—especially if it could be shown that being gay involves its own kind of alternative "religious" persuasion.

During its 2002-2003 term, the U.S. Supreme Court returned to the issue of state antisodomy legislation. By then, of the twenty-five states that had antisodomy legislation on the books when *Bowers v. Hardwick* was decided, only thirteen remained—four criminalizing homosexual "sodomy" only, and nine criminalizing "sodomy" in general. The case before the court, *Lawrence v. Texas,* involved a Texas law banning homosexual sodomy. In a decision rendered in June 2003, Justice Sandra Day O'Connor—who had agreed in *Bowers v. Hardwick* that homosexual activity was not covered by any right to privacy—concurred with the majority decision to strike down the Texas law, in holding that the law, by criminalizing sexual activity when done by one group of people without holding the same activity criminal when done by others, was a violation of the constitutional guarantee of equal protection under the law. By her reasoning, the Court's decision would have applied only to those states that had banned homosexual sodomy alone. However, the Court cast its net wider. Justice Anthony Kennedy, writing on behalf of five other justices (who together made a majority even without the concurrence of Justice O'Connor), penned what amounts to a scathing repudiation of the Court's ruling in *Bowers v. Hardwick* in its denial that homosexual activity, among others, was protected under a claim to any right of privacy which the Court held to be implied by the due process clause of the U.S. Constitution. Justice Kennedy avers that, in their reasoning in *Bowers v. Hardwick,* the majority had oversimplified the historical record. Justice Burger, in his appeal to "Judeo-Christian moral and ethical standards" had failed to take into account "other authorities pointing in an opposite direction,"[21] to wit, a report to the Parliament advising the 1957 repeal of the British laws outlawing homosexual conduct. (Of course, the Court had decided—and Justice Kennedy was himself writing—prior to the Episcopal Church's elevation of V. Gene Robinson, a noncelibate homosexual man living in a relationship with another man, to the episcopacy in November, 2003, a glaring example of counterevidence to Judeo-Christian unanimity on the issue.) However, even in the face of historical precedent, Kennedy quotes the earlier dissent of Justice Stevens approvingly:

> The fact that the governing majority in a state has traditionally viewed a particular practice as immoral is not a sufficient reason for upholding a law prohibiting the practice; neither history nor

tradition could save a law prohibiting miscegenation from constitutional attack.[22]

The real thrust of Justice Kennedy's opinion, however, lay in the charge that, in *Bowers v. Hardwick,* the justices had overlooked the substance of the claim. The case did not simply involve the banning of a particular act, but had symbolic ramifications. In effect, antisodomy legislation is a way by which the state, to use Justice Kennedy's word, "demeans" a class of citizens.

One cannot read Justice Kennedy's views without thinking of the arguments of Richard Mohr's *Gays/Justice.* For Mohr, whether or not antisodomy legislation is actually enforced, the mere existence of such laws constitutes a harrowing threat of arrest, which amounts to governmental disrespect in that it inappropriately undermines and interferes with a person's ability to make responsible choices, forcing him or her to become unduly circumspect.[23] More important, however,

> the largest class of insults and assaults to dignity arise when a person is held in low esteem for widely irrelevant features and without regard to anything he himself has done. These violate a person's essential desert for equal respect as a moral agent. Equal respect is violated because a person's desires, plans, aspirations, and sense of the sacred are not considered worthy of social care and concern on a par with those of others. . . . Unenforced sodomy laws are invective by government.[24]

That is to say, insult was the real point and intended effect of antisodomy legislation. In Mohr's telling turn of phrase, "unenforced sodomy laws are the chief systematic way that society as a whole tells gays they are scum."[25] Justice Kennedy says that, after *Bowers,* in the case of *Planned Parenthood of Southeastern Pa. v. Casey,* the Court has held that

> at the heart of liberty is the right to define one's own concept of existence, of meaning, of the universe, and of the mystery of human life. Beliefs about these matters could not define the attributes of personhood were they formed under compulsion of the State.[26]

In retrospect, the *Bowers* decision is seen as according the state just such compulsion and interference in personal self-definition, which meant it had failed to uphold the import of the due protection clause of the Constitution. Consequently, the Court has repudiated its decision in *Bowers,* now striking down all antisodomy legislation as unconstitutional.

What is salient in the context of this study is the way in which the discussion turns to and invokes the language of person-defining beliefs and convictions, or of a person's sense of the sacred, the language of religion. In the interval between *Bowers v. Hardwick* and *Lawrence v. Texas,* and perhaps with fear that the Court might not choose to reverse its denial of protection to homosexual sex under the due process clause in the background, recent years have seen the birth of an alternative line of reasoning in such thinkers as Andrew Koppelman, Michael W. McConnell, Phillip E. Hammond, and David A. J. Richards, the construction of gay rights as a freedom of religion issue.[27] Such a defense was neither argued before the Court, nor did it seem to figure into the Court's reasoning in any substantive way in its ruling in *Lawrence.* However, although the present author makes no claim to be a master of the intricacies of constitutional law, at least in general terms, it seems a case could be made that denying homosexuals the right to sex and perhaps even marry by an appeal to Judeo-Christian tradition as commonly understood is a violation of the proscription against the establishment of a religion. At the same time, the argument gains further strength if it can be shown that the denial of such gay rights amounts to the inhibition of the free practice of religion which the Constitution also mandates. According to the so-called Sherbert test,[28] only a pressing social interest or need can justify the suppression of the free practice of religion; and our earlier discussion has perhaps been sufficient to suggest ways in which such a protest against gay rights may be undercut. It may seem strange to think of being gay as a kind of religion, or at least what could count as "religion" for the purposes of legal sanction. Yet, Phillip E. Hammond has argued that the court has been moving in the direction whereby it would be hard not to recognize being gay as having a claim to being recognized as religious. Speaking of the founding fathers, he writes:

> While probably nobody at the time would have articulated the matter this way, those favoring liberty of conscience over mere

toleration were creating a perspective in which *conviction,* rather than the *substance* of the conviction, was to be honored. It was not to be *what* a person felt compelled to do, or *why* a person felt compelled, but the *fact of compulsion* that deserved special treatment.[29]

Hammond goes on to argue that the course of judicial review has led the Supreme Court along a trajectory that finds its terminus ad quem in the recognition of conscience as itself the substance of religion. Having been freed from its moorings in the institutions and conceptuality that have traditionally been the locus of religion, in the modern world conscience has become religion's functional equivalent. The decisive move came with the decision in *United States v. Seeger,* in which a self-avowed nonreligious person was accorded the status of conscientious objector to war, even though that status had previously been recognized only for those who identified with a traditional religious body that preached pacifism.[30] In short, Hammond argues that the court is progressively moving toward the recognition of religion as the language of conscience. It is not a matter of the language in which conscience speaks that makes conscientiousness religious, but the fact of the compulsion of conscience itself. Hammond appeals to a number of passages from Andrew Sullivan to suggest that homosexual rights "reflect the rights of conscience":

> The vast majority of people engaging in homosexual acts regard those acts as an extension of their deepest emotional and sexual desires, desires which they do not believe they have chosen and which they cannot believe are always and everywhere wrong (1995: 30). . . . When the subject of homosexuality emerges, it is always subject to emotive passion, and affects matters of religious conscience (1995:158). . . . The act of openly conceding one's homosexuality is in some ways an act of faith, of faith in the sturdiness of one's own identity and the sincerity of one's own heart (1995: 166). . . . Marriage is not simply a private contract; it is a social and public recognition of a private commitment. As such, it is the highest public recognition of personal integrity (1995: 179).[31]

Hammond admits that Sullivan draws back from explicitly claiming being homosexual is an explicit "religious calling." For that, he might very well have consulted an even stronger argument of this author:

> [T]he mere acknowledgment of the presence of . . . an erotic responsiveness to masculine beauty as part of oneself does not a gay man make. Nor does it ground the courage to come out. The gay man is one who finds that these realities are to a great extent his anchors to life and to the world at large—and one who treats them as foundational realities for a good life by giving them prominence in how he goes about leading his personal life.[32]

Long continues with explicit appeal to the language of religion:

> [T]o echo the clarion shout of an earlier generation, . . . "Gay is Proud!" The gay man refuses the abject status that society seeks to assign him. He refuses to be ashamed of what is so deeply important to him. But these are refusals that are part of his discovery of gay dignity, gay pride. His love for male beauty and his love for males, these are not things to be ashamed of, but venerable realities to be celebrated and revered. Indeed, these things are realities, the neglect of which is felt to result in the impoverishment of life, the very essence of "sacrality." A gay man is one who recognizes and lives by the "sacrality" of masculine beauty and homo-sex. And "coming out" is a gay man's refusal to live a life that belies the sacrality of what he holds sacred.[33]

If Hammond, Sullivan, and Long are right, then contemporary homophile movements are not simply social or political in thrust, but religious as well.

THE SPIRITUAL CHALLENGE OF CONTEMPORARY HOMOPHILE MOVEMENTS

To invoke freedom of religion as the grounds for the legal sanctioning of homosexual sex and nuptial relations is, of course, to cast them as evidencing an "alternative" religious tradition at variance with the ethicoreligious values of many mainstream traditions. Indeed, most mainstream religious traditions in the culture seem convinced that, if not homosexual persons, at least homosexual practice is not only wrong, but ungodly and inconsistent with the faith they arguably profess.

However if, as I have argued, it is the depth of personal self-involvement in a basic way of valuing such that infidelity is experienced as a compromise of selfhood that constitutes the essentially religious, that it is—as Augustine said—one's loves that define who one is, it is still nevertheless true that any such religious valuation will have recourse to a rhetoric by which those values can be seen to be fitting and appropriate. In Hammond's more concise language, religion is the language of conscience. It is not any particular language— whether God-talk, the language of emptiness, appeals to the way of the world, or any number of other rhetorical strategies—that makes for the religiosity of religion. It is conscience that is the definitively religious. But conscience will speak to defend and justify itself. More often than not, conscience will avail itself of the cultural forms, the languages immediately available to it, to articulate itself. However, this need not be the case. Conscience may seek alternative rhetorics to that immediately at hand.

Since it is the concrete religions that provide the cultural supports for conscience, it should come as no surprise that gay men, convinced that their loving impulses toward one another are sacred and not to be renounced without self-betrayal, should have recourse to the language and forms of traditional institutional religion to articulate their sense of their own legitimacy. Some might identify themselves with alternative traditions they think are less homophobic than the religions that they are apt to have experienced in growing up, finding themselves, like gay novelist Fenton Johnson, much too gentlemanly to crash a party from which they have been so explicitly disinvited.[34] A significant number, however, will claim to be of and for God, and in the name of God challenge those very institutions and ways of thinking that would condemn and exclude them.

It is the "unapologetic" gay theologian Gary David Comstock who has perhaps given the gay community the theological charter for such a challenge. (The word "unapologetic" used with reference to gay theology refers to the presumption that homosexual impulses are morally equivalent to heterosexual ones, and thus represents a style of theological thinking that is uncompromising in its refusal to prove the religious legitimacy of gay love.) In his *Gay Theology Without Apology*,[35] Comstock, a Protestant chaplain at Wesleyan University, has adapted the perspective of lesbian-feminist Carter Heyward to his own ends. Heyward, herself a priest of the Episcopal Church, has, over the years, advanced a trinitarian way of thinking about divinity or the sacred.[36] We are born interrelated with other beings and realities. This is the divine matrix within which we live and move and have our being, the first dimension of the sacred. But we are discomforted when our relationships are less than just and can be inspired, in fidelity to a holy spirit, to try to establish right relation in their place. At the same time, as we succeed in establishing ever more just relations among us, we are empowered and filled with life. In Comstock's hands, this view is rendered as a conceit: we are born among relations, and our job is to turn our relations into friends. Since friends do not merely support one another, but challenge one another to be all that they can be, so too gay men and lesbians can think of themselves as "friends of religion," challenging their traditions of birth or choice to live up to their God-given potential and true calling. Such friends would be more than a loyal opposition, for they would claim to speak for and try to nurture forth the better natures of their respective traditions.

Thus it is that representatives of the homosexual communities, as friends of religion, may look at Saint Paul and accuse him of a failure of nerve, indeed an infidelity to his Christ, in stopping short of rendering sexual impurity a matter of taste rather than sin as he had done with dietary impurity. It is as friends of religion that gay men and lesbians can commend biblical commentator Robert Gagnon for the impressiveness of his argument that, all arguments to the contrary, the biblical texts are uniformly dismissive of homosexual relations, but then chide him for his overly narrow view of biblical authority. It has been a staple of post-Reformation biblical interpretation to recognize that not all passages of the Bible are of equal authority, and concrete passages are to be evaluated in the light of the drift of the whole.[37] Gagnon insists, however, that one can only overrule one explicit biblical passage by another.[38] Since the Bible is uniformly homophobic, then homosexuality must be against the will of God. However, gay friends of Christianity can chide Gagnon for his insistence on the letter over and against the spirit. By his argument, one wouldn't know that killing modern Amalekites was wrong if Jesus had not commanded his followers to love their enemies. Nor would we know that stoning adulteresses to death was wrong had Jesus not commanded that only those without sin should cast the first stone. Indeed, such a narrow view of biblical authority seems to unduly restrict the way in which the spirit might indeed speak through holy writ.

Gay and lesbian friends of the Roman Catholic tradition might accuse their tradition of a number of self-betrayals as well. In Catholic thought, homosexual acts are "unnatural." However, we have seen earlier that such an appeal to what is natural is no real argument at all, simply the college-educated way of name calling, condemning homosexual acts as being essentially deformed, impure, and, shall we say, distasteful? When in the "Letter to the Bishops of the Catholic Church on the Pastoral Care of Homosexual Persons"[39] (sometimes referred to as the Halloween Letter because of the date of its issuance) the Roman Church finally recognizes that there is such a thing as a homosexual condition and homosexual persons, but then proceeds to characterize such people as "objectively disordered," given to do unnatural things, it is clear that their language is simply another way of calling homosexuals "sick"—something the American Psychiatric Association ceased to do when it stopped classifying homosexuality as a psychological illness. Let us allow, for the moment, that the claim that the unnaturalness of homosexual acts is an argument. A number of things follow. Such a line of thinking really compromises one of the essential claims of the faith, that humans are not simply creatures of nature, but are made in the "image of God." If humans are condemned to learn from and simply imitate the ways of nature, surely the human is being subjugated by a slavery to the standards of an amoral natural system. Human realms of meaning may build upon nature, but to insist that humans form their intentions in accordance with nature is to compromise the human calling to judge nature by their powers of conscience. To put the matter bluntly, are we simply to imitate the animals? Or can humans marshal their natural impulses in the name of their calling to be the crown, indeed the judge, of nature, to use them for the emergence of a truly humane world in the midst of, at best, a morally neutral natural environment?

Within nature, sex may exist for the sake of reproduction, but human beings more often than not have sex for reasons other than conception. Sex may be, for example, a way of saying "I love you" or a way of comforting another. Moreover, to insist that sex be "natural" is to insist that sex take the form of penis in vagina. Such a demand overlooks the many different ways in which humans actually have

sex and, more significantly, runs the risk of making homosexual loving sex (which by its very form is "unnatural") a sin far more serious
than heterosexual rape (which, after all, has the form sex is "intended" to have in the natural scheme of things). Not only is such a
position counterintuitive in its force, it fails to meet the bar of acceptability by any humane standard. That is why thinkers such as Angli-
can theologian John Macquarrie argue that natural law is not a matter
of how nature works, but how things ought to work in accordance
with the nature of humane judgment: "natural law" is not to be identified with the law(s) of nature![40]

At the same time, the Roman tradition has insisted that lifelong
chastity is a special calling expected only of those who are called to a
special vocation within the Church. Although it holds out the ideal of
sexual abstinence for unmarried people, heterosexual and homosexual alike, heterosexual people are accorded the right to marry and
thus are relieved of the necessity of a lifelong chastity. By denying
homosexuals the right to marry, the Church is imposing a life of self-
denial, one it otherwise admits is a heroic way not to be expected of
any but the religious, on a whole group of people who are not called
to a special vocation within the Church. Contemporary Roman Catholic ethics recognizes two ends of marriage: unitivity and procreativity. Consequently, sex within marriage is seen as an aid in the
bonding of spouses, but it is to be of a form that is open to procreation. Interestingly, the Church does not deny marriage to impotent
heterosexual couples, nor couples who are past the age at which they
can sire and bear children. Procreativity should then be understood
metaphorically, as André Guindon argued it should,[41] or dropped as a
condition for the religious blessing of marriage. Of course, to do so
would require the recognition of gay marriages, since they would be
on a par with impotent heterosexual ones. Yet the Roman Church resists such a move. In its eyes, at least impotent heterosexual sex involves a penis in a vagina, whereas homosexual sex fails to conform
to that paradigm. Once again, homosexuals are being singled out for a
life of heroic virtue because of the "unnaturalness" of homosexual
sex. Calling homosexual sex unnatural is thus revealed to be what it
is, simply a way of denying homosexuals the right to marry.

The Protestant tradition has not proven as insistent as the Catholic
tradition in holding that potential procreativity—however miraculous
such procreativity might be—is one of the essential ends and there-

fore one of the conditions for marriage. The idea that marriage was the appropriate context of sex had long been part of the Christian tradition. But the idea that love—rather than the desire for sex or reasons of family or state—would be a reason to marry was one that had only really begun to percolate in Western culture at the time of the Renaissance. Historians can trace the lineage of the "companionate marriage"—the idea that marriage partners are chiefly helpmates—in the theological tradition back to the writings of John Calvin, one of the great thinkers of the Reformation and fountainheads of the Protestant tradition. If companionship, and ultimately love, is why the institution of marriage exists, there is no reason, of course, why homosexuals could not marry. Faced with the incipient homophile movements that had begun to appear by the turn of the last century, and fearing this very prospect, Protestants began to insist that marriage partners be gender complements to one another. As Karl Barth would classically put it,

> the male is a male in the Lord only, but precisely, to the extent he is with the female, and the female likewise. . . . [T]heir humanity can consist concretely only in the fact that they live in fellow humanity, male with female and female with male. . . . [H]umanity as fellow-man is to be understood in its root as the togetherness of man and woman . . .[42]

Although one might concede that we are humanizied only through encountering one another in our "otherness," our difference from one another, it is another thing to hold that it is the difference between male and female that counts in defining our fellow humanity and yet another to insist that it is the defining difference that counts when it comes to who can marry whom. Surely, this line of thinking disregards completely the otherness that we all confront in the mysterious depths of one another, despite our sex. It would simply remain stillborn as a contentiously modern reading of passages in Genesis could it not be refracted through the contemporary evangelical understanding of family. Indeed, it is only when refracted through the lens of what Kathy Rudy has dubbed the "cult of domesticity" that this biblical interpretation attains whatever plausibility it might seem to enjoy.

As Rudy so compellingly points out in her book *Sex and the Church: Gender, Homosexuality, and the Transformation of Christian Ethics,*[43] industrialization occasioned a sea change in how people came to experience family in America, and how men and women experienced themselves and their respective significance. As more and more men began to seek work in the cities and ultimately move their families there, the change from being a self-sufficient farming community transformed the family into a social unit of townies. Under the new conditions of town life, children who were once additional unpaid (!) hands who could help to work the fields now became one more mouth to feed. Women who might once have played a vital role in keeping a large farm organization going now saw themselves exercising influence over a much smaller domain, becoming "housewives"—even as the men came to make their living in the factories and, more important, in business and commerce.

The new social conditions associated with town life transformed how men and women were to experience and think about their gender. Men came to be seen as natively "aggressive, cold-hearted, and self-interested,"[44] ideally suited to the competitive atmosphere of business and the marketplace. Although having a wife might provide our businessman a regular sex partner, sexual relief might have hardly seemed a sufficient reason to marry. Indeed, having a family might be experienced as unduly burdensome unless the family had a more significant role to play in a man's life. Ultimately, a family would come to be valued as a "haven in a heartless world," a place of respite for world-weary men. It would be the soft touch of a woman who could turn the house into a home. However, as with the man who would come to be seen as naturally disposed to the world of business, providing such a soft haven for her man would not merely be women's work, but a work that was ideally suited to a woman's nature. Women were coming to be seen as characterized more naturally by love, compassion, and humility—in a word, more naturally Christian. As women came to be seen as more natively Christian, they would also be responsible for "Christianizing" not only whatever children might come of the marriage, but their husbands as well. The result would be that religion would undergo what some scholars have called a "feminization of religion."[45] Religion became more of an affair of women than of men, and religious virtue was often seen as "feminine" virtue.

Although this "cult of domesticity" would be threatened by social developments of the 1920s and beyond, such as a new sexual permissiveness and the rise of the so-called New Woman, it would reassert itself in the popular culture immediately following World War II. It is no surprise that today's leading evangelicals grew up under the tutelage of such television shows as *Father Knows Best, Leave It to Beaver, Little House on the Prairie*—shows that embody, to one degree or another, this very nineteenth-century view of the relations of the sexes—and that such tutelage would be reflected in their teaching about marriage. Under such a regime of thinking, a man needs a family—he needs to be married, especially to a wife who can "domesticate" and Christianize him. A woman belongs in the home, attending to the Christianization of her man and his children—for otherwise how can the culture be Christianized? Indeed, a woman is a man's pathway to God, and without a wife, a man stands in danger of loss of salvation.

It goes unnoticed all too easily how untraditional this is. First, it puts an importance upon being married that is at variance with the status marriage has traditionally had in classical Christianity. As argued earlier, Christianity was a revolutionary religious movement that effectively dethroned the moral hegemony of the ancient family, whether Greek, Roman, or Hebrew. One did not need to be married to be a member of the Church, and, derivatively, one did not need to be married to be a fully adult person. Not only was Jesus himself unmarried, but as early as the New Testament Christianity insisted that marriage was optional, not incumbent on the Christian. One might be a eunuch for the kingdom of God. Indeed, earliest Christianity saw marriage as second best. As Saint Paul put it, "Better to marry than to burn."[46] Better to remain unmarried. For much of Christian history, the unmarried estate was regarded more highly than the married one. If, at the Reformation, the condition of being unmarried and its incumbent sexual chastity lost some of its religious preeminence, it was still not thought that marriage was an essential condition of salvation. But here, in the renovated cult of domesticity, it is.

More problematic is the way this "cult" recasts the Reformation doctrine of the total depravity of man as a matter of gender. In Catholic tradition, original sin entailed a loss of an explicit relation with God. This means that a person, apart from God, would be living without the "theological" virtues of faith, hope, and charity. However, even without the theological virtues, a person could live a relatively virtuous life—characterized by the virtues of wisdom (prudence), temperance, courage, and justice. The absence of the theological virtues might distort and compromise one's potential for full virtue, but it does not completely undermine it. The graced life, infused with the theological virtues, recontextualizes the so-called cardinal virtues and gives them a perfection they might otherwise not attain, but in the telling catchphrase of the Catholic tradition, grace perfects nature, it does not remake it totally. In the Reformation view, without faith, a person is seen to be so thoroughly compromised as to be constitutionally unable to be virtuous. Without faith, the "natural" person is, in the language of the tradition, "totally depraved." It seems to me that what we have been calling the cult of domesticity refracts this Reformation doctrine of the "total depravity of man" through the lens of gender. When seen through the prism of the evangelical construction of family, the total depravity of man elides into the total depravity of the male. It is the male who is naturally without faith, whereas the female is naturally more religious. However, because Christian virtue is thus feminine, it actually means that a man who is "christianized" is effectively unmanned and feminized. Since becoming Christian means a total makeover of the natural person, the idea of being a Christian and masculine is at best an oxymoron, if not an outright contradiction in terms. The identification of manhood and unregenerate humanity is, to my knowledge, nowhere explicitly made. It nevertheless represents an inescapable symbolic confusion. This symbolic difficulty underlies, I believe, the struggle of the Promise Keepers to try to find a way of being Christian men. It also makes evangelicals strange bedfellows with the otherwise hated radical feminists.

Modern feminism represents a threat to the evangelical idea of gender, for it threatens to allow women to move out of the house and into the workforce, thus depriving children and men of one of the essential conditions for their christianization. At the same time, radical feminists have seen masculinity as so implicated in and complicitous with the patriarchal order against which they war that, under their influence, males such as John Stoltenberg are "refusing to be" men,[43] aspiring to be but penis-bearing persons in a gender-blind society instead. What is interesting, in my view, is the way that both radical feminists and modern evangelicals have reinscribed what should be apparent to the reader at this point as being a very ancient understanding of men as essentially aggressive, predatory penetrators. Indeed, for feminists such as Andrea Dworkin, all heterosexual intercourse is an exercise in domination and is thus actually a form of rape, while for the evangelicals, men are unregenerate aggressors naturally suited for the cutthroat world of business. Both seek to redeem men from their masculinity. However, the evangelicals, as a religious group, are the exception to the story that I have been telling, for they represent a religion which does not seek to support the masculinity of men but rather to unmake and regenerate it.

I would argue it is among modern gay men that a new and potentially more salutary construction of masculinity has been born which portends to finally shatter the equation of sex and war, the analogy that underlies the notion of masculinity which makes men warriors on the battlefield and in the bedroom.

TOWARD A NEW POETIC OF MASCULINITY

Not all commentators on the gay scene are convinced of the liberatory potential of what we might call the gay movement. Steven Zeeland, for example, has published a series of books in which he recounts his interviews with men in the military about their sexual experiences,[48] and on that basis, argues that fear of being classed as "homosexual" has served to limit the erotic freedom and exploration among men. However, there are, after all, men who are gay, whose sexual desire is predominately or exclusively directed to members of his own sex. It may be but an exercise in vain nostalgia to lament the tendency of modern society to recognize their existence by virtue of a classificatory nomenclature. Being gay is a very important dimension of a gay man's life, because it names the range of persons with whom he can effectively establish intimacy. One sometimes hears lesbians who speak of their sexuality as a matter of choice. They choose the company of women. A man's sense of his own sexuality is much more profoundly bound to physiological responsiveness. While being gay is much more than a matter of simply conceding to the self and others the kind of person with whom one can enjoy sexual intimacy, involving as it does the refusal of shame, for a man—and I suspect a large number of gay women—being gay is a matter of honesty about who one is and who can turn one on. The problem is not the classification, but the social stigma that accompanies the classification. If no stigma was attached, one could dare to be thought gay since it would not be such a bad thing to be. Although it is unlikely that the social stigma can be eradicated totally, it seems to me that the legalization of gay marriage, and perhaps after that the defeat of the "don't ask, don't tell" policy that limits the gay presence in the military, would go a long way in creating a climate in which the stigmatization of being gay would find itself increasingly alien.

Those who call themselves "queer" rather than "gay" have adopted a moniker that underscores the failure to be "normatively masculine" and, at the same time, is meant to establish an identification with all others who fail the regnant standards of normality in other ways. "Queer theorists" delight in seeking conceptual ways of undermining contemporary norms of thinking and practice. Pointing out historical variation is but one way of doing so. Mark Simpson is particularly adept at the alternative strategy of revealing the homoeroticism that underlies traditional masculinity and the heterosexual constructions operative in homosexual desire and practice, leaving one with the dizzying sense of not knowing whether anything can be said that does not carry the prospects of its own undoing.[49] Ultimately, queers and queer theories together conspire to destabilize and ultimately "deconstruct" not merely a particular way of thinking about how men and women ought to be, a particular understanding of normative gender, but the sense that gender norms should exist at all.

I am not sure, of course, that we can live without gender norms, even if it was desirable. In the typical course of growing up, children of both sexes often bond with their mothers. Eventually, the task of disidentifying with Mother and of becoming something other than Mother will fall to the boy.[50] It seems impossible that boys would not frame some idea, some paradigm, some aspirational ideal, to define the direction into which they are to move and grow, some idea of what it means to be other than Mother, what it is to be in fact a man. This idea is what we mean by normative gender.

It seems to me that the contemporary gay movement is historically unique in the world. What has been traditional is the idea that fully adult men are penetrators of their social underlings. If George Chauncey is right, Americans prior to the 1920s tended not to think that their masculinity was compromised were they to have sex with a man, as long as they were sexual tops. It was their receptive partners who would carry the stigma of being other than real men, other than fully masculine. The introduction of the "homosexual" label resulted in classifying a group of men whose masculinity had not hitherto been put into question by having sex with a man with the perverts/inverts. What this realignment of classification potentiated was the possibility for homosexual men as a class, whether they were sexual tops or sexual bottoms, to lay claim to the full masculinity that had hitherto been accorded only to the top. I can hardly understate the importance of this idea. By identifying tops with their bottoms, a realignment had taken place by which the bottom could now be identified with their formerly unstigmatized tops. It seems to me that this is precisely what modern homophile movements represent, sexual bottoms for the first time in history laying claim to the nonstigmatized masculinity of the top. It is as if gay pride was announcing that bottoms are real men too.

It is hard to overestimate the importance of World War II in facilitating this shift.[51] Before mobilization, boys from the countryside who had thought themselves unique in bottoming for, or merely wanting to bottom, for the local rural boys might very well have been all too conscious of their difference from the norm. However, World War II involved such massive mobilization that the kid from down on the farm who had thought himself as uniquely queer now found himself among many another similarly disposed young men, with the result that their queerness no longer seemed quite so unique and outside the norm. For the first time, it became possible to see the penetrated war buddy as "butch." However important World War II was in nurturing this sea change, I do not think it was fully accomplished until the mid-1970s. Tom Bianchi has written of this change of sensibility, which he saw happen as the 1960s gave way to the 1970s. The sixties, he says, were

> a time when boys or men with muscles were rare and desired, but were probably at best "trade." Queers, hungry as they were for the embrace of strong arms, did not realize their own physical potential. Some time in the 1970's, some of them got tired of the emotionally unavailable. They began to find they could create sexual attractiveness in themselves, and present each other with increasingly accurate realizations of their fantasies.[52]

To put the matter in other words, it was one thing when potential bottoms had to seek our their sexual partners among those who were "trade." It was quite another to realize gay men could play the role of trade for one another. This potentiated the possibility of recognizing the bottom equal to his top in masculinity and masculine dignity. In such a light, gays who think of themselves as "girls" in anything other than a humorous light are really throwbacks to an earlier time in which sexually receptive men were thought of as effeminate inverts. Queers who seek to overthrow the idea of normative gender are really undoing the revolutionary potential that is inherent in the homosexual/heterosexual classification. For homosexuals are bearers into the world of the revolutionary potential not of deconstructing, but actually reconstructing, the idea of normative masculinity. To be sure, one could say that gay bottoms are masculine despite their sexual proclivities. That is to say, masculinity is a concept that is sufficiently vague and/or a reality sufficiently malleable that some minor failures to fully embody the ideal are insufficient to undermine the general applicability of the ascription. On the other hand, one might think that the masculinity that sexual bottoms claim for themselves is not claimed in spite of their sexual behavior, but inclusive of sexual bottoming. In other words, "real men can get fucked!" To entertain the possibility of the fully masculine bottom is to begin to think about gender and masculinity in a new way. In turn, masculine gay bottoms can be thought of as the avant-garde for a new way of being a "real" man in the world, a way that is liberative for all men, whether straight or gay—not to mention for women as well. But how can this be so?

The religious traditions that we have explored in the course of this book resemble nothing so much as a set of variations upon a common theme. When we looked to Sambia, fully adult men were semen providers. In their scheme of thinking, only the adult male who might want to be sexually receptive is somehow perverted. Chinese Taoists drew on a similar line of thinking when they allowed that young men or women were equally threatening as "sexual vampires," even as they could be the occasion for strengthening the life force through sex—as long as the penetrator did not ejaculate. However, the Taoist adept is regularly thought of as the insertive partner in such life-enhancing sex. In Greece, a male lover was "constructed," regularly thought of, as a mature men whose beloveds, by social convention, should not be at all interested in their lovers sexually lest their desires compromise their masculine futures. Plato and the Islamic Sufis who followed his lead, although officially frowning on sex between males, nevertheless held that homoerotic attraction could be marshaled in the service of religious insight. At work in all these cases is the fact that masculinity is defined in terms of sexual role. A sexually receptive male is somehow other than a real man. In modern Western culture in general, the sexually receptive male would be assimilated to that which is paradigmatically "other" than masculine, i.e., the female. Thus, such men would be thought of as effeminate, failed men, as "sissies." In other cultures, the receptive partner in sex could be thought of as a "boy"—or perhaps, where slaves existed, humiliated or servile men, again something other than being fully masculine. It was the analysis of Native American berdaches and the proscription against homosexual anal intercourse among the Hebrews that revealed the dynamic at work in all this. The berdache was filled with holy power because he was sexually penetrated. His penetration was a violation, an act of war, against his person. Thus, he could accompany a war party into battle, allowing them to engage the enemy already victorious. And it was ultimately the fear of rape at the hand of enemy soldiers that fueled the Levitical proscription of anal intercourse, which could further presume that a sexually penetrated or penetrable soldier correspondingly threatened the social body. Paul's protest against homosexual sex, we argued, simply left unquestioned the presumption that sexual penetration connoted subordination. If Augustine seems, at times, to have freed himself from this complex of ideas, we need only remember that he construed masculinity as a matter, above all, of control and domination—even if such control was directed at the self rather than another.

Over and again in our study, we have had the occasion to make repeated recourse to an idea that echoes the stance of much contemporary feminism, that the personal is the political. Here, we might say that the sexual is the political. Full adult masculinity has been thought regularly to be sexually enacted in the penetration of social inferiors, and penetration thus signified, if it does not cause, subordination. By extension, homosexual sex cannot be constructed as other than the subordination of one man to another, whether sanctioned by virtue of his actual social position or not. Some religious traditions have simply presumed such an understanding of masculinity, as seems to have been the case with Buddhism. Others have exploited it in the interest of specifically religious ends, either in the pattern of the Sambians or of the Platonists. Religious thinkers such as Paul may, in the argument that they mount against homosexual sex, however unknowingly, implicitly invoke the paradigm in the process. It seems inescapable that religious traditions have in the past proved to be social mediators of a common construction of masculinity, and the consequent understanding of homosexual penetration as a matter of domination. Ultimately, such a construction of homosexual sex is grounded, I would argue, in a double analogy that would make war a kind of sex and sex a kind of war: war involves the assault upon others in which one penetrates the enemy with one's weapons as one might penetrate another with one's penis, even as sex is a kind of war in which one plays the aggressor against one who is at best a passive, at worst a defeated, other. In the final analysis, it is this double analogy that war is sex and sex is war that grounds the sense that of all the things a man might do with his body, it is his sexual penetration alone that defines what it means to be a real man. A real man is a warrior on the battlefield and in the bedroom, and sexual love is inextricably bound up with the assertion of rank over one's receptive partner. Real men are aggressive tops who penetrate passive bottoms. Therefore, bottoms cannot be understood as fully adult, "real men." They might be failed men, lesser men, boyish men, womanly men, but not men!

It is the sense that sexual receptivity constitutes at best an active abandonment of masculine will in sexual submission to the will of another that is at stake here. (And it is a very short step indeed to the modern popular view that sex outside of a committed relationship is somehow simply a matter of the "abuse" of another, a top's use of another for his sexual pleasure.) Tibetan Buddhism does challenge the sense that the loss of will in orgasmic pleasure is dehumanizing, but it is the gay bottom's claim to masculinity that effectively threatens to bring the edifice down, undermining the presumption that sexual penetration and penetration in war should be analogized.

We have already had occasion to note several times how the conditions of modern warfare undermine the sense that war is sexual. To the degree war ceases to be a matter of hand-to-hand combat, or even a matter of shooting another body, but is instead more and more a matter of aerial bombardment, the analogy is undercut. But it is actually the presence of women in the military in other than supportive roles that undermines not only the fear that a soldier who can be sexually penetrated threatens the whole, but also the presumptive idea that being penetrated sexually is tantamount to a kind of defeat of one's person. If the presence of women in the military thus threatens the analogy that war is a kind of sex, what we need is a new way of thinking about sex so as to shatter to presumption that sex is a kind of war, the analogy which grounds the denial of masculinity to the gay bottom.

Bernadette Brooten has pointed the way forward here. What we need, she argues, are new metaphors for sex. With regard to heterosexual sex, we might "conceptualize the woman swallowing the male penis—enfolding, encircling, embracing, or otherwise taking in the penis."[53] Perhaps there is a way of reconceiving the act of penetration as something other than a matter of aggressive assault upon the body of another, and thrusting as something other than a pushing of one's point into another, thus dissolving the applicability of the metaphorics of war entirely.[54] Here I think we can have recourse to the metaphors that are used by ethologists to describe animal behavior. It is common knowledge that simian males will try to frighten away potential interlopers by a "display" of their penis. The kinesthetics of penile display in the human correspond exactly to the kinesthetics of penile thrusting. The hips are rotated such that the erect penis moves outward, upward, and forward. Of course, such penile display is implicitly an aggressive act. However, ethologists also speak of display behavior on the part of males animals in other animal species as their way of attracting mates. Perhaps, then, we are not bound to equate penile display in the human male with its aggressive counterpart among his simian cousins. We could think of penile display as a matter of attracting the attentions, indeed the sexual attentions, of another. The homosexually inclined male observer may respond with an appreciative fascination, an admiration that shows itself in the desire to touch, manipulate, or insert wherever possible what the admirer is so captivated by—much as a baby might play with something he or she has been intrigued by. Thus, we might free ourselves from thinking of homosexual sex as a matter of one man pushing himself into the body of a subordinate, and therefore subdued, man. Homosexual sex could instead be seen to embody an interplay of gestures of display and admiration. If we then continue to define masculinity on the basis of male roles in sex, and men who have sex with men are both to be considered masculine, whether their role be top or bottom, then masculinity must lie in a dialectic, a rhythmic alternation, of display and mutual admiration.

I am not sure that we need think of heterosexual relations in the same way. Ethologists speak not of female display, but of female presentation. So too, it might not be inappropriate to think that male display elicits a different kind of sexual response in the female than in the male. Perhaps penile display elicits embracive behavior in the female. Perhaps the female is given less to fascination and to playful manipulation than to playing the host to the other with her body. In this line of thinking, the act of sex between heterosexual couples is likewise freed from any implication of dominance and submission. In addition, along these lines, we can also conceive how men having sex with men would not necessarily be behaving like females having sex with men.

At the very least, the compulsion to see intercourse as a matter of fucking someone, doing something to someone else who has been rendered passive, to see sex as a kind of war, would be broken, and our sexual swords will have been beaten into plowshares.

Seen in the context of the sweep of historical religions, modern male homophile movements thus prove to be not only social movements of sexual liberation, nor are they simply political movements for the extension of democratic rights, but first and foremost—as the British gay cleric turned social critic Edward Carpenter first hailed them many years ago[55]—spiritual movements for a liberation that promises to transform the common life for the good. It is only as such that they can constructively engage and challenge the churches and synagogues and mosques as well as society at large. A male homophile movement that insists upon the masculinity even of gay sexual bottoms is the beachhead of a movement for the spiritual liberation of all men. It is the bearer of a revolutionary idea of what it means to be a man, the advance guard for a masculinity that is enacted not as power over social underlings, but a masculinity enacted in an interplay of display and fascination. If there are times in which men must perform as soldiers, gay men represent the freedom from having to be soldiers in the bedroom. Freed to discover and explore the erotic potential of their own bodies without fear of losing their masculinity, men will discover that they can be lovers as well as soldiers. By giving into the temptation to try to make war in the bedroom rather than love, gay men may all too often betray the cause that they truly represent. Those gay men—be they sexual tops or bottoms or both—who embrace and insist upon their uncompromised masculinity are effectively champions of the revolutionary insight that war is not sex, nor sex war. Although Chesterton is no doubt right when he writes that coming to love something is at the same time the discovery of something one is willing to fight and to die for,[56] that love and defense may imply each other in human experience, it is nevertheless a mistake to conflate one with the other. Since truth lies at least in part in seeing difference where difference lies, the truth of the difference between love and war cannot but help to set us all—both men and women, whether straight, bi-, or gay—free to be fully human. Free at last! Free at last! Free to make love as well as war!

Notes

Chapter 1

1. Frank E. Turner, *The Greek Heritage in Victorian Britain* (New Haven: Yale University Press, 1981), p. 427.

2. As quoted in Bernard Faure, *The Red Thread: Buddhist Approaches to Sexuality* (Princeton: Princeton University Press, 1998), p. 208.

3. Henry Fielding, *The History of Tom Jones, a Foundling* (New York: Vintage, 1950), p. 84.

4. Apparently, my father's friend was echoing the lyrics of a bluegrass gospel song made famous by The Carter Family, the refrain to which ran:

> Oh, come to the church by the wildwood
> Oh, come to the church in the dale

I believe the song is a traditional one that was adopted and performed by The Carter Family. The lyrics are accessible through Internet sites such as <bluegrasslyrics. com>.

5. The phrasing here derives from Phillip E. Hammond, *Freedom for All: Freedom of Religion in the United States* (Lousville, KY: Westminster John Knox, 1998), pp. 50-54. It is a handy summary expression which, as I see it, unites two lines of thinking—on the one hand the idea that religion is an individual or group's basic way of valuing and, at the same time, the final "court of appeals." My definition of religion as a person's basic way of valuing depends principally upon the still-relevant definitional strategy advanced by Frederick Ferre, *Basic Modern Philosophy of Religion* (New York: Charles Scribner's Sons, 1967), see especially pp. 2-3. However, the idea to include the "realities" that constitute a final court of appeals reflects the methodological considerations developed by Russell T. McCutcheon, "A Default of Critical Intelligence? The Scholar of Religion As Public Intellectual," in his *Critics Not Caretakers: Redescribing the Public Study of Religion* (Albany: State University of New York Press, 2001), pp. 21-39. Also relevant is the important essay in definition by Michael LaFargue, "Radically Pluralist, Thoroughly Critical: A New Theory of Religions," *Journal of the American Academy of Religion* 60(4), pp. 693-713.

6. Plato, *Symposium,* translated with an introduction by Robin Waterfield (New York: Oxford World Classics, 1994). For the translation of the relevant Greek passages of the speech of Pausanias, 182a-185b, see pp. 15-19. See Chapter 3 in this book for a fuller account of Athenian sexual mores.

7. Kristen Bjorn, interview (June 6, 1999).

8. As quoted and discussed in David M. Friedman, *A Mind of Its Own: A Cultural History of the Penis* (New York: Free Press, 2001), p. 17.

9. This is a widely reprinted article and can be found among such other sources as George Chauncey Jr., "Christian Brotherhood or Sexual Perversion? Homosexual Identities and the Construction of Sexual Boundaries in the World War I Era," in Gary David Comstock and Susan E. Henking, eds., *Que(e)rying Religion: A Critical Anthology* (New York: Continuum, 1997), pp. 156-178. It is included in the earlier Martin Duberman, Martha Vicinus, and George Chauncey Jr, eds., *Hidden from History: Reclaiming the Gay and Lesbian Past* (New York: Meridian, 1990), pp. 294-317.

Chapter 2

1. The myth is recounted and discussed by Gilbert H. Herdt, *Guardians of the Flutes: Idioms of Masculinity* (New York: Columbia University Press, 1981), pp. 255-294.

2. Use of other inmates for sex is notorious among prison populations. For more "respectable" parallels, see the instances of the taking of "boy wives" provided by Stephen O. Murray, *Homosexualities* (Chicago: University of Chicago Press, 2000), pp. 161-168, as yet another variation on a theme.

3. For a fuller account of such male initiation among the Sambians, see David D. Gilmore, *Manhood in the Making: Cultural Concepts of Masculinity* (New Haven: Yale University Press, 1990), pp. 146-168.

4. L. L. Langness, "Semen and Bone," in his *Men and "Women" in New Guinea* (Novato, CA: Chandler and Sharp Publishers, 1999), pp. 109-134 and passim.

5. When the anthropologist Gilbert Herdt asked whether older brothers were sent to their younger ones for oral intercourse for the sake of the younger boys' development or for the relief of the older boys' sexual tension, he was greeted with a laugh from his tribal informants, suggesting the latter is a strong motivation for, if not the "real" rationale behind, the practice.

6. Bret Hinsch, *Passions of the Cut Sleeve: The Male Homosexual Tradition in China* (Berkeley: University of California Press, 1990), p. 53.

7. See the discussion of religious Taoism, among others, by Laurence G. Thompson, *Chinese Religion: An Introduction,* Fifth Edition. (Belmont, CA: Wadsworth Publishing, 1996), pp. 80-94.

8. For cross-cultural parallels with Taoist thinking, see Elizabeth Abbot, *A History of Celibacy: From Athena to Elizabeth I, Leonardo da Vinci, Florence Nightingale, Gandhi, and Cher.* New York: Scribners, 2000), pp. 197-230.

9. So concludes Giovanni Vitiello, "Taoist Themes in Chinese Homoerotic Tales," in Michael L. Stemmeler and Jose Ignazio Cabezón, eds., *Religion, Homosexuality, and Literature* (Las Colinas, TX: Monument Press, 1992), p. 102.

10. Murray cites the Nkundó of Africa as unique among traditional societies in allowing boys to be tops of their older lovers and, by his formulation, suggests that it is the semen of the young man that has medicinal value. Cf., Murray, *Homosexualities*, p. 197.

11. This is the view of Jolan Chang, *The Tao of Sex and Love: The Ancient Chinese Way to Ecstasy* (New York: Arkana, 1991), p. 48.

Chapter 3

1. For the passage from Strabo, see Will Roscoe, *Queer Spirits: A Gay Men's Myth Book* (Boston: Beacon, 1995), pp. 229-231.

2. William Armstrong Percy III, *Pederasty and Pedagogy in Archaic Greece* (Urbana and Chicago: University of Illinois, 1996), pp. 62-64.

3. Robert Koehl, "The Chieftain Cup and a Minoan Rite of Passage," *Journal of Hellenic Studies* 106 (1986), pp. 99-110.

4. The language of patronage is drawn from the admirable introduction of Robin Waterfield to his very readable translation of the *Symposium.* The introductory essay, which covers the social background, interpretive issues, as well as basic content of the dialogue, is perhaps the best of the short, accessible introductions into the contemporary reading of the *Symposium,* at least in my experience.

5. Ibid., 191d, p. 28.

6. Ibid.

7. Ibid., 192b., p. 28.

8. Ibid., 192c, p. 28.

9. This is the famous argument of K. J. Dover, *Greek Homosexuality* (New York: Vintage, 1978). See especially p. 99.

10. See, for example, Martti Nissinen, *Homoeroticism in the Biblical World: A Historical Perspective,* translated by Kirsi Stjerna (Minneapolis: Fortress Press, 1998), p. 65.

11. Plato, *Symposium,* 192b-d, tr. Waterfield, pp. 28-29.

12. For one scholar's attempt to unravel the irony here, see David M. Halperin, "Why Is Diotima a Woman?" in his *One Hundred Years of Homosexuality, and Other Essays on Greek Love* (New York: Routledge, 1990), pp. 113-151.

13. Martha Nussbaum, "The Speech of Alcibiades: A Reading of Plato's *Symposium,*" in Nussbaum's *The Fragility of Goodness* (Cambridge: Cambridge University Press, 1986), pp. 165-199.

14. Plato, *Symposium,* "Introduction" by Waterfield, p. xl.

15. Quran 26:165-166, 173 in *The Meaning of the Glorious Koran,* explanatory trans. by Mohammed Marmaduke Pickthall (New York: Mentor, n.d.), pp. 269-270. Other Quranic passages referring to the people of Lot include 7:80-84; 11:77-83; 21:74; 22:43; 27:56-59; and 29:27-33.

16. Quran 4:16, Pickthall, p. 81.

17. As cited in Jim Wafer, "Muhammad and Male Homosexuality," in Stephen O. Murray and Will Roscoe, *Islamic Homosexualities: Culture, History, and Literature* (New York: New York University Press, 1997), p. 89.

18. Khalid Duran, "Homosexuality and Islam," in Arlene Swidler, ed., *Homosexuality and World Religions* (Valley Forge, PA: Trinity Press International, 1993), p. 184.

19. Stephen O. Murray, "The Will Not to Know: Islamic Accommodations of Male Homosexuality," in Murray and Roscoe, *Islamic Homosexualities,* pp. 14-54.

20. Wafer, "Muhammad," p. 90.

21. Duran, "Homosexuality," p. 182.

22. Wafer, "Muhammad," p. 90.

23. William C. Chittick, *Faith and Practice of Islam: Three Thirteenth Century Sufi Texts* (Albany: State University of New York, 1992), p. 39.

24. Here I am briefly following an argument developed at great length and to powerful effect in Robert Nozick, *The Examined Life: Philosophical Mediations* (New York: Simon and Schuster, 1989). See, for example, his discussion of the reality of literary characters, p. 130.

25. Seyyed Hossein Nasr, "Spiritual Chivalry," in S. H. Nasr., ed., *Islamic Spirituality: Manifestations* (New York: Crossroads, 1997), p. 304.

26. "The Tale of Kamar and the Darwish" in Henry M. Christman, *Gay Tales and Verses from the Arabian Nights* (Austin, TX: Banned Books, 1972), pp. 47-53.

Chapter 4

1. Richard C. Friedman, *Male Homosexuality: A Contemporary Psychoanalytic Perspective* (New Haven: Yale University Press, 1988), p. 239. The parallels with this work and the thrust of my own research are striking. Friedman argues that although homosexuality may result from a sense of a lack of masculinity at a decisive point in life, psychological health is achieveable through a later reclamation of one's own masculinity. The present work avers that contemporary gay pride is dependent upon a strong sense of homosexual manliness.

2. Kristen Bjorn, Interview (June 16, 1999). Murray, *Homosexualities,* p. 409, cites Jared Braiterman on the same phenomenon, who argues that penetration by a "queen" is no threat to a man's reputation since no one would believe a queen who claimed he topped a "man." I rather think that men do not generally choose their sexual partners on such narrow pragmatic grounds: the queen must be safe on deeper grounds.

3. For the general picture of the berdache in these paragraphs, I have relied on the summary discussion of Robert M. Baum, "Homosexuality and the Traditional Religions of the Americas and Africa," in Arlene Swidler, ed., *Homosexuality and World Religions* (Valley Forge, PA: Trinity Press International, 1993), pp. 8-17 especially.

4. Ibid., p. 14.

5. Ibid., p. 15.

6. It is not clear what to make of this fact. Among the Zunis, for example, the berdache was assigned the role of what Baum calls "androgynous gods" in the ritual reenactment of a tribal myth (ibid., p. 16). By implication, this would have been an honor. Ramón Gutiérrez, however, argues that the role was that of a defeated prisoner god. Hence, the role may have fallen to the berdache not as an honor, but by default; perhaps in the ruggedly masculinist society of the Zunis, no warrior would want to play the role of a cosmic loser. See Ramón Gutiérrez, "Must We Deracinate Indians to Find Gay Roots?" *Out/look* 1(4) (Winter 1989), p. 65. The difference in interpretation reflects the different approaches to the berdache, which is the subject of my entire chapter devoted to the same.

7. E.g., Will Roscoe; see his "We'wha and Klah: The American Indian Berdache As Artist and Priest," in Comstock and Henking, *Que(e)rying Religion,* pp. 89-106.

8. Ibid., see pp. 105-106 especially.

9. This is the rationale advanced by David F. Greenberg, *The Construction of Homosexuality* (Chicago: University of Chicago Press, 1988), pp. 52-53.

10. Micah 6:8.

11. Peter Byrne, *Natural Religion and the Nature of Religion* (London: Macmillan, 1989).

12. Walter L. Williams, *The Spirit and the Flesh: Sexual Diversity in American Indian Culture* (Boston: Beacon Press, 1986), p. 243.

13. I owe this forumlation to Victoria McLaughlin.

14. Gutiérrez, "Deracinate," pp. 61-67. See also Richard C. Trexler, *Sex and Conquest: Gendered Violence, Political Order, and the European Conquest of the Americas* (Ithaca, NY: Cornell University Press, 1995).

15. Trexler, ibid., p. 71.

Chapter 5

1. George Weinberg, *Society and the Healthy Homosexual* (New York: St. Martin's Press, 1972).

2. Leviticus 18:22. The translation is that of Saul M. Olyan, " 'And With a Male You Shall Not Lie the Lying Down of a Woman': On the Meaning and Significance of Leviticus 18:22 and 20:13," in Comstock and Henking, *Que(e)rying Religion,* p. 398.

3. Lev. 20:13. Again, the translation is by Olyan, Ibid.

4. Israel Finkelstein and Neil Asher Silberman, *The Bible Unearthed: Archaeology's New Vision of Ancient Israel and the Origin of Its Sacred Texts* (New York: The Free Press, 2001), p. 150.

5. Jacob Milgrom, *Leviticus* (The Anchor Bible), 3 volumes, New York: Doubleday, 1991-2000.

6. See, for example, Calum M. Carmichael, *Law, Legend, and Incest in the Bible: Leviticus 18-20* (Ithaca, NY: Cornell University Press, 1997), p. 6.

7. Ibid.

8. Derrick Sherwin Bailey, *Homosexuality and the Western Christian Tradition* (Hamden, CT: Archon Books, 1955), pp. 9-28.

9. Here, I am following Milgrom, *Leviticus,* Volume 1, pp. 42-44, while leaving the claim that it is the impurity of death that compromises the God who is Life for later consideration.

10. This is the argument of Olyan, "And with a Male," pp. 412-414.

11. The story is recounted in Tsuneo Watanabe and Jun'ichi Iwata, *The Love of the Samurai: A Thousand Years of Japanese Homosexuality* (Boston: Alyson Publications, 1987), pp. 32-33.

12. G. Bownas, "Shinto," in R. C. Zaehner, *The Concise Encyclopedia of Living Faiths* (Boston: Beacon, 1967), p. 357.

13. Barbara C. Sproul, *Primal Myths: Creating the World* (San Francisco: Harper and Row, 1979), p. 142.

14. Milgrom, *Leviticus,* Volume 2, p. 1567.

15. It was the anthropologist Mary Douglas who pioneered the structuralist understanding of impurity as dirt, "matter out of place," in her classic study *Purity and Danger: An Analysis of the Concepts of Polution and Taboo* (London: Routledge Kegan Paul, 1966). It has been suggestively applied by L. William Countryman, *Dirt, Greed, and Sex: Sexual Ethics in the New Testament and Their Implications for Today* (Philadelphia: Fortress Press, 1988), pp. 11-44.

16. Gen. 1:1a, 2a: "In the beginning . . . The earth was without form and void."

17. I have not been able to ascertain the exact source of the saying, but the quote is widely attributed to Bishop Joseph Butler. See, among others, the "Introduction" by Ernest C. Mossner for Joseph Butler, *The Analogy of Religion* (New York: Frederick Ungar Publishing, 1961), p. x.

18. John Boswell, *Christianity, Social Tolerance, and Homosexuality* (Chicago: University of Chicago Press, 1980).

19. Mark D. Jordan, *The Invention of Sodomy in Christian Tradition* (Chicago: University of Chicago Press, 1997), pp. 10-28.

20. The figure one in ten that is so ubiquitously bandied about is derived from the study of Alfred Kinsey et al., *Sexual Behavior in the Human Male* (Philadelphia: W. B. Saunders Company, 1948). As recounted in Richard A. Isay, *Being Homosexual: Gay Men and Their Identity* (New York: Farrar, Straus, Giroux, 1989), pp. 12-13, of the approximately five thousand men surveyed by Kinsey, approximately four percent could be numbered among those whose sexual activity and interest were exclusively homosexual for the whole of their lives after adolescence, whereas approximately ten percent were exclusively homosexual for a period of at least three years after adolescence.

21. Such Egyptian paintings were discussed by John Barclay Burns in his "Devotee or Deviate: The 'Dog' (keleb) in Ancient Israel as Symbol of Male Passivity and Perversion," a paper presented before the Gay Men's Issues Group at the Annual Meeting of the American Academy of Religion, Boston, Massachusetts, 1991.

22. Wafer's entire discussion is well worth reading. See Jim Wafer, "Muhammad," pp. 87-96.

23. Countryman, *Dirt,* pp. 5-6.

24. Ibid., p. 150.

25. K. J. Dover, *Greek Homosexuality* (New York: Vintage, 1980), p. 19.

26. Countryman, *Dirt,* p. 147.

27. Richard D. Mohr, *A More Perfect Union: Why Straight America Must Stand Up for Gay Rights* (Boston: Beacon, 1994), p. 116.

28. Cf., Trexler, *Sex and Conquest,* p. 71.

Chapter 6

1. Steve Bolerjack, "Casting the First Stone," *New York Blade News* 3(44) (October 29, 1999), p. 18.

2. Mark 8:34; cf., Matt. 10:38; Luke 9:23, 14:27.

3. Matt. 5:17.

4. Mark 2:27. The phrase "plucking heads of grain" comes from the preceding lines, Mark 2:23.

5. For a discussion of Paul's actual arguments, consult Countryman, *Dirt,* pp. 101-104.

6. Friedman, *A Mind of Its Own,* p. 25.

7. Craig A. Williams, *Roman Homosexuality: Ideologies of Masculinity in Classical Antiquity* (New York: Oxford University Press, 1999), p. 18.

8. Ibid., pp. 83-86.

9. Curio the Elder, *Julius* 49.51-21, as translated in John Boswell, *Christianity, Social Tolerance, and Homosexuality: Gay People in Western Europe from the Beginning of the Christian Era to the Fourteenth Century* (Chicago: University of Chicago Press, 1980), p. 75.

10. Romans 1:24-27.

11. *Timaeus* 91. See the translation by Henry Bettenson, *Plato's Cosmology: The "Timaeus" of Plato* (Indianapolis: Boss-Merrill, n.d.), pp. 356-357. I credit Roy Bowen Ward with pointing out that Plato offers one of the earliest rationales for the long-standing presumption that homosexual sex is "contrary to nature." See Ward's "Why Unnatural? The Tradition Behind Romans 1:26-27," *Harvard Theological Review* 90:3 (1997), pp. 264-269.

12. Countryman, *Dirt*, pp. 109-123.

13. Bernadette J. Brooten, "Paul's Views on the Nature of Women and Female Homoeroticism," in Clarrissa W. Atkinson, Constance H. Buchanan, and Margaret R. Miles, eds., *Immaculate and Powerful: The Female in Sacred Image and Social Reality* (Boston: Beacon Press, 1985), pp. 61-87.

14. Dale B. Martin, "*Arsenokoites* and *Malakos:* Meanings and Consequences," in Robert L. Brawley, ed., *Biblical Ethics and Homosexuality: Listening to Scripture* (Louisville, KY: Westminster John Knox Press, 1996), p. 123.

15. Robert Jewett, "The Social Context and Implications of Homoerotic References in Romans 1:24-27," in Davd L. Balch, ed., *Homosexuality, Science, and the "Plain Sense of Scripture"* (Grand Rapids, MI: William B. Eerdman's Publishing, 2000), pp. 239-240.

16. 1 Cor. 7:9 (King James Version).

17. For the discussion of the question and the number of times Thomas quotes Augustine, see Thomas Aquinas, *Summa Theologica,* Quaest. 153.2: Art 1-2, as excerpted in Edward Batchelor Jr., ed., *Homosexuality and Ethics* (New York: Pilgrim Press, 1980), pp. 39-42.

18. This is the general argument of Mark Jordan, *Sodomy.*

19. Augustine, *Opus Imperfectum Contra Julianum* 3.109, as quoted in Elaine Pagels, *Adam, Eve, and the Serpent* (New York: Random House, 1988), p. 135.

20. Augustine, *Opus Imperfectum,* in ibid.

21. Augustine, *Confessions* 1.7.11, translated by Henry Chadwick (New York: Oxford World Classics, 1992), pp. 8-9.

22. Ibid. 2.4.9, pp. 28-29.

23. Ibid., 4.4.9, p. 57.

24. Ibid., 4.6.11, p. 58.

25. Ibid., 4.6.11, p. 59.

26. Augustine, *City of God* 14.18, translated by Henry Bettenson (New York: Penquin Classics, 1984), p. 579.

27. Ibid. 14.16, p. 577.

28. Augustine, *Confessions* 10.31.44, pp. 204-205.

29. Augustine, *City of God* 14.23, pp. 585-587.

30. Jordan, *Sodomy,* p. 175.

31. Mathew Kuefler, *The Manly Eunuch: Masculinity, Gender Ambiguity, and Christian Ideology* (Chicago: University of Chicago Press, 2001).

32. Augustine, *De Opere Monarchorum,* in ibid., p. 274.

Chapter 7

1. In this characterizaion of *dukkha*, I am following the lead of Michael Carrithers, "The Buddha," in Michael Carrithers, Raymond Dawson, Humphrey Carpenter, and Michael Cook, *Founders of Faith* (New York: Oxford University Press, 1986), pp. 52-53.

2. Leonard Zwilling, "Homosexuality As Seen in Indian Buddhist Texts" in José Ignazio Cabezón, ed., *Buddhism, Sexuality, and Gender* (Albany: State University of New York Press, 1992), p. 209.

3. Peter Harvey, *An Introduction to Buddhist Ethics* (New York: Cambridge University Press, 2000), pp. 414-415.

4. Zwilling, "Homosexuality," pp. 207-208. See also his "Avoidance and Exclusion: Same-Sex Tradition in Indian Buddhism," in Winston Leyland, ed., *Queer Dharma: Voices of Gay Buddhists* (San Francisco: Gay Sunshine Press, 1998), pp. 45-54. The latter is an excellent collection of essays on historical and contemporary Buddhism.

5. Ibid., p. 209.

6. The term is from John Stevens, *Lust for Enlightenment: Buddhism and Sex* (Boston: Shambhala, 1900), pp. 22ff.

7. Paul Gordon Schalow, "Male Love in Early Modern Japan: A Literary Depiction of the 'Youth,'" in Martin Duberman, Martha Vicinus, and George Chauncey Jr., eds., *Hidden from History: Reclaiming the Gay and Lesbian Past* (New York: Meridian, 1900), pp. 118-128.

8. Paul Gordon Schalow, "Spiritual Dimensions of Male Beauty in Japanese Buddhism," in Stemmeler and Cabezón, ed., *Religion*, p. 77. This essay also appears in Leyland, ed., *Queer Dharma*, pp. 107-124.

9. Ibid., p. 76.

10. For examples of this as well as all the above, see Ihara Saikaku, *The Great Mirror of Male Love*, translated with an introduction by Paul Gordon Schalow (Stanford: Stanford University Press, 1990), passim.

11. Paul Gordon Schalow, "Kukai and the Tradition of Male Love in Japanese Buddhism," in Cabezón, ed., *Buddhism, Sexuality*, pp. 215-230. Reprinted in Leyland, ed., *Queer Dharma*, pp. 91-106.

12. My description here follows the lead of Newman Robert Glass, who argues that Buddhist meditation encourages the shift from figure-dependent apprehension to field-dependent perception. See his *Working Emptiness: Toward a Third Reading of Emptiness in Buddhism and Postmodern Thought* (Atlanta, GA: Scholars Press, 1995), pp. 90-91.

13. This is the theme of the famous article by Jeffrey Hopkins, "The Compatibility of Reason and Orgasm in Tibetan Buddhism: Reflections on Sexual Violence and Homophobia," in Comstock and Henking, eds. *Que(e)rying Religion*, pp. 372-383. Also included in Leyland, *Queer Dharma*, pp. 335-347. In the essay, Hopkins argues that homophobia may result from a psychological projection of the fear of being out of control.

14. José Ignazio Cabezón, "Homosexuality and Buddhism," in Swidler, *Homosexuality*, pp. 81-101. Also in Leyland, *Queer Dharma*, pp. 29-44.

15. Jeffry Hopkins, *Sex, Orgasm, and the Mind of Clear Light: The Sixty-Four Arts of Gay Male Love* (Berkeley, CA: North Atlantic Books, 1998).

Chapter 8

1. See Michael Warner, *The Trouble with Normal: Sex, Politics, and the Ethics of Queer Life* (New York: The Free Press, 1999), passim.

2. Until 2003, the repeal of antisodomy legislation had to have been a central element of any gay or queer politics. However, the overthrow of all such laws by the U.S. Supreme Court has rendered the continued pursuit of this aim anachronistic.

3. Richard Mohr, *Perfect Union,* p. 115.

4. Warner, *Trouble,* p. 146.

5. Kathleen Sands, "Public, Pubic, and Private: Religion in Political Discourse," in Kathleen M. Sands, ed., *God Forbid: Religion and Sex in American Public Life* (New York: Oxford University Press, 2000), p. 68.

6. Jonathan Rauch, "Who Needs Marriage?" in Bruce Bawer, ed., *Beyond Queer: Challenging Gay Left Orthodoxy* (New York: Free Press, 1996), pp. 296-313. The essay can also be found in John Corvino, ed., *Same-Sex: Debating the Ethics, Science, and Culture of Homosexuality* (Lanham, MD: Rowan and Littlefield Publishers, 1999), pp. 304-316. "Who Needs Marriage?" is a version of an article that originally appeared in *The New Republic* (May, 1996) under the title, "For Better or Worse: The Case for Gay (and Straight) Marriage." This version has been reprinted as "For Better or Worse?" in Andrew Sullivan, *Same-Sex Marriage: Pro and Con, A Reader* (New York: Vintage Books, 1997), pp. 169-181.

7. Rauch, "Marriage?" in Bawer, ed., *Beyond Queer,* p. 307.

8. Ibid., pp. 308-309.

9. Rauch, "For Better or Worse?" in Sullivan, ed., *Marriage,* p. 178.

10. Rauch, "Marriage?" in Bawer, ed., *Beyond Queer,* p. 309.

11. Ibid., p. 308.

12. Richard D. Mohr, *Gay Ideas: Outing and Other Controversies* (Boston: Beacon Press, 1992), pp. 129-218.

13. Ibid., p. 200.

14. Ibid., p. 201.

15. Ibid., p. 200.

16. For some general perspectives and relevant parallels here, one might consult Anthony Giddens, *The Transformation of Intimacy: Sexuality, Love, and Eroticism in Modern Societies* (Cambridge, UK: Polity, 1992). See also John D'Emilio and Estelle B. Freedman, *Intimate Matters: A History of Sexuality in America* (New York: Harper and Row, 1988).

17. Richard Mohr is an informed, learned, and morally sensitive guide in the relevant issues here. See especially Richard D. Mohr, *Gays/Justice: A Study of Ethics, Society, and Law* (New York: Columbia University Press, 1988), cc. 2-4 especially.

18. *O'Connor v. Donaldson,* 422 US 563, 575 (1974), as cited in Mohr, ibid., p. 205.

19. *Bowers v. Hardwick,* 478 U.S. 190, 190-92, 192 (1986), as cited in Mohr, *Ideas,* p. 64.

20. *Bowers v. Hardwick,* 478 U.S. 186, 196 (1986) (Burger, C. J., concurring), as cited in Andrew Koppleman, "Sexual and Religious Pluralism," in Saul M. Olyan and Martha C. Nussbaum, eds., *Sexual Orientation and Human Rights in American Religious Discourse* (New York: Oxford University Press, 1998), pp. 218, 230 note 27.

21. "Excerpts from Supreme Court's Decision Striking Down Sodomy Law," *New York Times,* Friday, June 27, 2003, p. A18.

22. Ibid.

23. Mohr, *Gays/Justice,* p. 59.

24. Ibid.

25. Ibid, p. 60.

26. "Excerpts from Supreme Court," p. A18.

27. Koppelman, ibid., pp. 215-233; as well as Michael W. McConnell, "What Would It Mean to Have a 'First Amendment' for Sexual Orientation" in the same volume, pp. 234-260; Phillip E. Hammond, *Liberty;* David A. J. Richards, *Identity and the Case for Gay Rights: Race, Gender, Religion As Analogies* (Chicago: University of Chicago Press, 1999).

28. Hammond, *Liberty,* pp. 43-44.

29. Ibid., p. 40.

30. Ibid., p. 50.

31. The quotations are all from Andrew Sullivan, *Virtually Normal: An Argument About Homosexuality* (New York: Vintage, 1995), as quoted in Hammond, p. 78.

32. Ronald E. Long, "The Sacrality of Male Beauty and Homosex: A Neglected Factor in the Understanding of Contemporary Gay Reality," in Comstock and Henking, *Que(e)rying Religion,* p. 273.

33. Ibid.

34. The words have stayed with me over the years, though I have forgotten where I first encountered them.

35. Gary David Comstock, *Gay Theology Without Apology* (Cleveland, OH: Pilgrim Press, 1993).

36. Cf., especially Carter Heyward, *Touching Our Strength: The Erotic As Power and the Love of God* (New York: Harper and Row, 1989).

37. Cf., Robert McAffee Brown, *The Spirit of Protestantism* (New York: Oxford University Press, 1956), p. 77:

> The Reformers made a great deal of the principle *Scriptura scripturae interpres* (Scripture is the interpreter of Scripture). By this they meant that there is a consistent witness shining though Scripture *as a whole.* When the character of that central thrust and concern has been discerned, it is then possible to interpret the rest of Scripture in the light of it. . . . On these terms we know very well that we are not to slay the modern Amalekites, that dashing children's heads against the rocks is no part of the divine plan.

38. "In cases where the church deviates in its moral practices from portions of the Bible, one can usually find a trajectory within the Bible itself that justifies a critique or moderation of such texts," Robert Gagnon, *The Bible and Homosexual Practice: Texts and Hermeneutics* (Nashville, TN: Abingdon Press, 2001), p. 442. It seems clear to me that, in context, Gagnon understands by "trajectory" something which is explicit rather than implicit.

39. The full text, together with considered responses, can be found, among other places, in Jeannine Gramick and Pat Furey, eds., *The Vatican and Homosexuality:*

Responses to the "Letter to the Bishops of the Catholic Church on the Pastoral Care of Homosexual Persons" (New York: Crossroads, 1988).

40. John Macquarrie, "Rethinking Natural Law," in Macquarrie's *Three Issues in Ethics* (New York: Harper and Row, 1970), pp. 82-110. See p. 107f especially.

41. André Guindon, *The Sexual Creators: An Ethical Proposal for Concerned Christians* (Lanham, MD: University Press of America, 1986).

42. Karl Barth, *Church Dogmatics,* Part III, Vol. IV (Edinburg: T and T Clark, 1961), pp. 164-166, as excerpted in Edward Batchelor, ed., *Homosexuality and Ethics* (New York: Pilgrim Press, 1980), pp. 48, 50.

43. Kathy Rudy, *Sex and the Church: Gender, Homosexuality, and the Transformation of Christian Ethics* (Boston: Beacon, 1997), p. 17ff.

44. Ibid., p. 21.

45. Cf., Ann Douglas, *The Feminization of American Culture* (New York: Doubleday, 1988).

46. 1 Cor. 7:9 (King James Version).

47. John Stoltenberg, *Refusing to Be a Man: Essays on Sex and Justice* (New York: Meridian, 1990). For a not dissimilar view from a thinker who fancies himself a "male lesbian," see J. Michael Clark with Bob McNeir, *Masculine Socialization and Gay Liberation: A Conversation on the Work of James Nelson and Other Wise Friends* (Las Colinas, TX: Monument Press, 1992).

48. See especially Steven Zeeland's, *Sailors and Sexual Identity: Crossing the Line Between "Straight" and "Gay" in the U.S. Navy* (Binghamton, NY: Harrington Park Press, 1995) and *The Masculine Marine: Homoeroticism in the U. S. Marine Corps* (Binghamton, NY: Harrington Park Press, 1996).

49. Mark Simpson, *Male Impersonators: Men Performing Masculinity* (New York: Routledge, 1994). A "queer" approach to Christianity delights in pointing to the homoeroticism that is seemingly an inescapable part of Christian devotion. See, for example, Richard Rambuss, *Closet Devotions* (Durham, NC: Duke University Press, 1998) and Stephen D. Moore, *God's Beauty Parlor, and Other Queer Spaces in and Around the Bible* (Stanford: Stanford University Press, 2001). Chapter 2, "Christian Homodevotion to Jesus," of Robert E. Goss, *Queering Christ: Beyond Jesus Acted Up* (Cleveland, OH: Pilgrim Press, 2002), is a good summary of many of the other scholarly observations in this regard.

50. Cf., Elisabeth Badinter, *XY: On Masculine Identity,* translated by Lydia Davis (New York: Columbia University Press, 1995), pp. 43-66 especially.

51. The classic study is Alan Berube, *Coming Out Under Fire: The History of Gay Men and Women in World War Two* (New York: Plume, 1990). For a more compact discussion, see John D'Emilio, "Forging a Group Identity: World War II and the Emergence of an Urban Gay Subculture," in his *Sexual Politics, Sexual Communities: The Making of a Homosexual Minority in the United States, 1940-1970* (Chicago: University of Chicago Press, 1983), pp. 23-39.

52. Tom Bianchi, "Better Read Than Dead: A Reply," *The Harvard Gay and Lesbian Review* 4(3) (summer 1997), pp. 13-14.

53. Bernadette Brooten, with Eugene Fontenot, "Of Love Spells and Lesbians in Ancient Rome," *The Harvard Gay and Lesbian Review* 1(2) (spring 1994), p. 11.

54. For an early statement of the argument I develop here, see Ron Long, "The Fitness of the Gym," *The Harvard Gay and Lesbian Review* 4(3) (summer 1997), p. 14. For my further speculations on the subject of gay masculinity, see Ron Long,

"Becoming the Men We're Ceasing to Be: A Gay Agenda for Aging in a Youth Culture," *Theology and Sexuality* 15 (September 2001), pp. 94-113.

55. For an overview of the truly sweeping and prophetic work of Carpenter, see Frank Leib, *Friendly Competitors, Fierce Companions: Men's Ways of Relating* (Cleveland, OH: Pilgrim Press, 1997). Although I am unsure of many of the specific parallels Leib draws between Carpenter and contemporary positions, the copiousness of the quotations make this a good introduction to the ideas of Carpenter himself. Cf., also the use to which Carpenter is put in the important work by David Nimmons, *The Soul Beneath the Skin: The Unseen Hearts and Habits of Gay Men* (New York: St. Martin's Press, 2002), pp. 138-139.

56. G. K. Chesterton, *Collected Works. Vol. XV. Chesterton on Dickens* (San Francisco: Ignatius Press, 1989), p. 255.

Bibliography

Abbott, Elizabeth. *A History of Celibacy: From Athena to Elizabeth I, Leonardo da Vinci, Florence Nightingale, Gandhi, and Cher.* New York: Scribner's, 2000.

Abraham, Ken. *Who Are the Promise Keepers? Understanding the Christian Men's Movement.* New York: Doubleday, 1997.

Augustine, Saint *City of God.* Translated by Henry Bettenson. New York: Penquin Classics, 1984.

————. *Confessions.* Translated and Introduction by Owen Chadwick. New York: Oxford World Classics, 1992.

Badinter, Elisabeth. *XY: On Masculine Identity.* Translated by Lydia Davis. New York: Columbia University Press, 1995.

Bailey, Derrick Sherwin. *Homosexuality and the Western Christian Tradition.* Hamden, CT: Archon Books, 1955.

Balch, David L., ed. *Homosexuality, Science, and the "Plain Sense of Scripture."* Grand Rapids, MI: William B. Eerdmans Publishing, 2000.

Batchelor, Edward Jr., ed. *Homosexuality and Ethics.* New York: Pilgrim Press, 1980.

Baum, Robert M. "Homosexuality and the Traditional Religions of the Americas and Africa," in Arlene Swidler, ed., *Homosexuality and World Religions* (pp. 1-46). Valley Forge, PA: Trinity Press International, 1993.

Bawer, Bruce, ed. *Beyond Queer: Challenging Gay Left Orthodoxy.* New York: Free Press, 1996.

Berube, Allan. *Coming Out Under Fire: The History of Gay Men and Women in World War Two.* New York: Plume, 1991.

Bianchi, Tom. "Better Read Than Dead: A Reply. *The Harvard Gay and Lesbian Review* 4(3) (summer 1997), pp. 13-15.

Bolerjack, Steve. "Casting the First Stone." *New York Blade News* (October 29, 1999), p. 18.

Boswell, John. *Christianity, Social Tolerance, and Homosexuality: Gay People in Western Europe from the Beginning of the Christian Era to the Fourteenth Century.* Chicago: University of Chicago Press, 1980.

————. *Same-Sex Unions in Premodern Europe.* New York: Villard Books, 1994.

Bouhdiba, Abdelwahab. *Sexuality in Islam.* Translated by Alan Sheridan. London: Routledge and Kegan Paul, 1985.

Bouldrey, Brian, ed. *Wrestling with the Angel: Faith and Religion in the Lives of Gay Men.* New York: Riverhead Books, 1995.

Bownas, G. "Shinto," in R. C. Zaehner, ed., *The Concise Encyclopedia of Living Faiths* (pp. 348-364). Boston: Beacon, 1967.

Brawley, Robert L., ed. *Biblical Ethics and Homosexuality: Listening to Scripture.* Louisville, KY: Westminster John Knox, 1996.

Brooten, Bernadette J. *Love Between Women: Early Christian Responses to Female Homoeroticism.* Chicago: University of Chicago Press, 1996.

————. "Paul's Views on the Nature of Women and Female Homoeroticism," in Clarissa W. Atkinson, Constance H. Buchanan, and Margaret R. Miles, eds., *Immaculate and Powerful: The Female in Sacred Image and Social Reality* (pp. 61-87). Boston: Beacon Press, 1985.

Brooten, Bernadette J. with Edouard Fontenot. "Of Love Spells and Lesbians in Ancient Rome." *The Harvard Gay and Lesbian Review* 1(2) (summer 1994), pp. 11-14.

Brown, Peter. *Augustine of Hippo: A Biography.* Berkeley: University of California Press, 1969.

Brown, Robert McAfee. *The Spirit of Protestantism.* New York: Oxford University Press, 1965.

Bull, Chris and John Gallagher. *Perfect Enemies: The Religious Right, the Gay Movement, and the Politics of the 1990s.* New York: Crown, 1996.

Burns, John Barclay. "Devotee or Deviate: The 'Dog' (keleb) in Ancient Israel As Symbol of Male Passivity and Perversion." Paper delivered before the Gay Men's Issues Group. Annual Meeting. American Academy of Religion, Boston, November 21, 1999.

Butler, Joseph. *The Analogy of Religion,* with an introduction by Ernest C. Mossner. New York: Frederick Ungar Publishing, 1961.

Byrne, Peter. *Natural Religion and the Nature of Religion.* London: Macmillan, 1989.

Cabezón, José Ignazio, ed. *Buddhism, Sexuality, and Gender.* Albany: State University of New York, 1992.

————. "Homosexuality and Buddhism," in Arlene Swidler, ed. *Homosexuality and World Religions* (pp. 81-101). Valley Forge, PA: Trinity Press International, 1993.

Carmichael, Calum M. *Law, Legend, and Incest in the Bible: Leviticus 18-20.* Ithaca, NY: Cornell University Press, 1997.

Carrithers, Michael, Raymond Dawson, Humphrey Carpenter, and Michael Cook. *Founders of Faith.* New York: Oxford University Press, 1986.

Chang, Jolan. *The Tao of Love and Sex: The Ancient Chinese Way to Ecstasy.* New York: Arkana, 1991.

Chauncey, George. "Christian Brotherhood or Sexual Perversion? Homosexual Identities and the Construction of Sexual Boundaries in the World War I Era," in Gary David Comstock and Susan E. Henking, eds. *Que(e)rying Religion: A Critical Anthology* (pp. 156-178). New York: Continuum, 1997.

Chesterton, G. K. *Collected Works: Chesterton on Dickens,* Volume XV. San Francisco: Ignatius Press, 1989.

Chittick, William C. *Faith and Practice of Islam: Three Thirteenth Century Sufi Texts.* Albany: State University of New York Press, 1992.

Christman, Henry M., ed. *Gay Tales and Verses from the Arabian Nights.* Translated by Powys Mathers. Austin, TX: Banned Books, 1989.

Clark, J. Michael with Bob McNeir. *Masculine Socialization and Gay Liberation: A Conversation on the Work of James Nelson and Other Wise Friends.* Las Colinas, TX: Monument Press, 1992.

Comstock, Gary David. *Gay Theology Without Apology.* Cleveland, OH: Pilgrim Press, 1993.

————. *Unrepentant, Self-Affirming, Practicing: Lesbian/Bisexual/Gay People Within Organized Religion.* New York: Continuum, 1996.

Comstock, Gary David and Susan E. Henking, eds. *Que(e)rying Religion: A Critical Anthology.* New York: Contiuum, 1997.

Corvino, John. *Same Sex: Debating the Ethics, Science, and Culture of Homosexuality.* Lanham, MD: Rowman and Littlefield, 1999.

Countryman, L. William. *Dirt, Greed, and Sex: Sexual Ethics in the New Testament and Their Implications for Today.* Philadelphia: Fortress, 1988.

Davidson, James. *Courtesans and Fishcakes: The Consuming Passions of Classical Athens.* New York: St. Martin's Press, 1997.

D'Emilio, John. *Sexual Politics, Sexual Communities: The Making of a Homosexual Minority in the United States, 1940-1970.* Chicago: University of Chicago Press, 1983.

D'Emilio, John and Estelle B. Freedman. *Intimate Matters: A History of Sexuality in America.* New York: Harper & Row, 1988.

Douglas, Ann. *The Feminization of American Culture.* New York: Doubleday, 1988.

Douglas, Mary. *Purity and Danger: An Analysis of the Concepts of Pollution and Taboo.* London: Routledge and Kegan Paul, 1966.

Dover, K. J. *Greek Homosexuality.* New York: Vintage, 1980.

Duberman, Martha Vicinus and George Chauncey Jr., eds. *Hidden from History: Reclaiming the Gay and Lesbian Past.* New York: Meridian, 1990.

Duran, Khalid. "Homosexuality and Islam," in Arlene Swidler, ed., *Homosexuality and World Religions* (pp. 181-198). Valley Forge, PA: Trinity Press International, 1993.

Dynes, Wayne R., ed. *Encyclopedia of Homosexuality,* two volumes. New York: Garland Publishing, 1990.

Eilberg-Schwartz, Howard. *Gods' Phallus, and Other Problems for Men and Monotheism.* Boston: Beacon Press, 1994.

Engberg-Pedersen, Troels. *Paul and the Stoics.* Louisville, KY: Westminster John Knox, 2000.

Excerpts from Supreme Court's Decision Striking Down Sodomy Law. *New York Times,* Friday, June 27, 2003, p. A18.

Faure, Bernard. *The Red Thread: Buddhist Approaches to Sexuality.* Princeton, NJ: Princeton Unversity Press, 1998.

Ferre, Frederick. *Basic Modern Philosophy of Religion.* New York: Charles Scribner's Sons, 1967.

Fielding, Henry. *The History of Tom Jones, a Foundling.* New York: Vintage, 1950.

Finkelstein, Israel and Niel Asher Silberman. *The Bible Unearthed: Archaeology's New Vision of Ancient Israel and the Origin of Its Sacred Texts.* New York: Free Press, 2001.

Friedman, David M. *A Mind of Its Own: A Cultural History of the Penis.* New York: Free Press, 2001.

Friedman, Richard C. *Male Homosexuality: A Contemporary Psychoanalytic Perspective.* New Haven, CT: Yale University Press, 1988.

Gagnon, Robert A. J. *The Bible and Homosexual Practice: Texts and Hermeneutics.* Nashville, TN: Abingdon Press, 2001.

Gilmore, David D. *Manhood in the Making: Cultural Concepts of Masculinity.* New Haven, CT: Yale University Press, 1990.

Glass, Newman Robert. *Working Emptiness: Toward a Third Reading of Emptiness in Buddhism and Postmodern Thought.* Atlanta, GA: Scholars Press, 1995.

Goldstein, Joshua A. *War and Gender: How the War System Shapes Gender and Vice Versa.* New York: Cambridge University Press, 2001.

Goss, Robert E. *Jesus Acted Up: A Gay and Lesbian Manifesto.* San Francisco: HarperSanFrancisco, 1993.

———. *Queering Christ: Beyond Jesus Acted Up.* Cleveland, OH: Pilgrim Press, 2002.

Goss, Robert E. and Amy Adams Squire Strongheart, eds. *Our Families, Our Values: Snapshots of Queer Kinship.* Binghamton, NY: Harrington Park Press, 1997.

Gould, Thomas. *Platonic Love.* New York: Free Press, 1963.

Gramick, Jeannine, and Pat Furey, eds. *The Vatican and Homosexuality: Reactions to the "Letter to the Bishops of the Catholic Church on the Pastoral Care of Homosexual Persons."* New York: Crossroads, 1988.

Greenberg, Davd R. *The Construction of Homosexuality.* Chicago: University of Chicago Press, 1988.

Gross, Rita M. *Buddhism After Patriarchy: A Feminist History, Analysis, and Reconstruction of Buddhism.* Albany: State University of New York Press, 1993.

Guindon, André. *The Sexual Creators: An Ethical Proposal for Concerned Christians.* Lanham, MD: University Press of America, 1986.

Gutiérrez, Ramón A. "Must We Deracinate Indians to Find Gay Roots?" *Out/Look* 1(4) (winter 1999), pp. 61-67.

Halperin, David M. *One Hundred Years of Homosexuality, and Other Essays on Greek Love.* New York: Routledge, 1990.

Hammond, Phillip E. *With Liberty for All: Freedom of Religion in the United States.* Louisville, KY: Westminster John Knox, 1998.

Harvey, Peter. *An Introduction to Buddhist Ethics.* New York: Cambridge University Press, 2000.

Helfing, Charles, ed. *Our Selves, Our Souls, and Bodies: Sexuality and the Household of God.* Boston: Cowley Publications, 1996.

Helminiak, Daniel A. *What the Bible Really Says About Homosexuality.* San Francisco: Alamo Press, 1994.

Herdt, Gilbert H. *Guardians of the Flutes: Idioms of Masculinity.* New York: Columbia University Press, 1981.

Herdt, Gilbert H., ed. *Ritualized Homosexuality in Melanesia.* Berkeley: University of California Press, 1984.

Herman, Didi. *The Antigay Agenda: Orthodox Vision and the Christian Right.* Chicago: University of Chicago Press, 1997.

Heyward, Carter. *Touching Our Strength: The Erotic As Power and Love of God.* San Francisco: Harper and Row, 1989.

Hinsch, Bret. *Passions of the Cut Sleeve: The Male Homosexual Tradition in China.* Berkeley: University of California Press, 1990.

Hopkins, Jeffrey. "The Compatibility of Reason and Orgasm in Tibetan Buddhism: Reflections on Sexual Violence and Homophobia," in Gary David Comstock and Susan E. Henking, eds. *Que(e)rying Religion: A Critical Anthology* (pp. 372-383). New York: Continuum, 1997.

———. *Sex, Orgasm, and the Mind of Clear Light: The Sixty-Four Arts of Gay Male Love.* Berkeley, CA: North Atlantic Books, 1998.

Horner, Tom. *Jonathan Loved David: Homosexuality in Biblical Times.* Philadelphia: Westminster, 1978.

Isay, Richard D. *Being Homosexual: Gay Men and Their Development.* New York: Farrar, Straus, Giroux, 1989.

Jewett, Robert. "The Social Context and Implications of Homoerotic References in Romans 1:24-27," in David L. Balch, ed., *Homosexuality, Science, and the "Plain Sense of Scripture"* (pp. 223-241). Grand Rapids, MI: William B. Eerdmans Publishing, 2000.

Jordan, Mark D. *The Ethics of Sex.* Malden, MA: Blackwell Publishers, 2002.

———. *The Invention of Sodomy in Christian Theology.* Chicago: University of Chicago Press, 1997.

Koppelman, Andrew. "Sexual and Religious Pluralism," in Saul M. Oylan and Martha Nussbaum, eds., *Sexual Orientation and Human Rights in American Religious Discourse* (pp. 215-233). New York: Oxford University Press, 1998.

Kuefler, Mathew. *The Manly Eunuch: Masculinity, Gender Ambiguity, and Christian Ideology in Late Antiquity.* Chicago: University of Chicago Press, 2001.

LaFargue, Michael. "Radically Pluralist, Thoroughly Critical: A New Theory of Religions." *Journal of the American Academy of Religion* 60(4), pp. 693-713.

Langness, L. L. *Men and "Women" in New Guinea.* Novato, CA: Chandler and Sharp Publishers, 1999.

Leib, Frank B. *Friendly Competitors, Fierce Companions: Men's Ways of Relating.* Cleveland, OH: Pilgrim Press, 1997.

Leonard, Arthur S. "Poised for History." *Gay City News* (December 6-12, 2002), pp. 1, 11.

Leupp, Gary P. *Male Colors: The Construction of Homosexuality in Tokugawa Japan.* Berkeley: University of California Press, 1995.

Leyland, Winston, ed. *Queer Dharma: Voices of Gay Buddhists.* San Francisco: Gay Sunshine Press, 1998.

Long, Ron[ald E.] "Becoming the Men We're Ceasing to Be: A Gay Agenda for Aging in a Youth Culture." *Theology and Sexuality* 15 (September 2001), pp. 94-113.

————. "The Fitness of the Gym," in *The Harvard Gay and Lesbian Review* 4(3) (summer 1997), pp. 20-22.

Long, Ronald E. "The Sacrality of Male Beauty and Homosex: A Neglected Factor in the Understanding of Contemporary Gay Life," in Gary David Comstock and Susan E. Henking, eds., *Que(e)rying Religion: A Critical Anthology* (pp. 266-281). New York: Continuum, 1997.

Maccoby, Hyam. *Ritual and Morality: The Ritual Purity System and Its Place in Judaism.* New York: Cambridge University Press, 1999.

Macquarrie, John. *Three Issues in Ethics.* New York: Harper and Row, 1970.

Martin, Dale B. "*Arsenokoites* and *Malakos:* Meanings and Consequences," in Robert L. Brawley, ed., *Biblical Ethics and Homosexuality: Listening to Scripture* (pp. 117-136). Louisville, KY: Westminster John Knox, 1996.

McConnell, Michael W. "What Would It Mean to Have a 'First Amendment' for Sexual Orientation?" in Saul M. Oylan and Martha C. Nussbaum, eds., *Sexual Orientation and Human Rights in American Religious Discourse* (pp. 234-260). New York: Oxford University Press, 1998.

McCutcheon, Russell T. *Critics Not Caretakers: Redescribing the Public Study of Religion.* Albany: State University of New York Press, 2001.

McNeill, John J. *The Church and the Homosexual,* Third Edition. Boston: Beacon, 1988.

Milgrom, Jacob. *Leviticus: A New Translation and Commentary.* Three volumes. Anchor Bible. New York: Doubleday, 1991-2000.

Mohr, Richard D. *Gay Ideas: Outing and Other Controversies.* Boston: Beacon, 1992.

————. *Gays/Justice: A Study of Ethics, Society, and Law.* New York: Columbia University Press, 1988.

————. *A More Perfect Union: Why Straight American Must Stand Up for Gay Rights.* Boston: Beacon Press, 1994.

Moore, Stephen D. *God's Beauty Parlor, and Other Queer Spaces in and Around the Bible.* Stanford: Stanford University Press, 2001.

Murata, Sachiko and William C. Chittick. *The Vision of Islam.* New York: Paragon House, 1995.

Murray, Stephen O. *Homosexualities.* Chicago: University of Chicago Press, 2000.

———. "The Will Not to Know: Islamic Accommodation of Male Homosexuality," in Stephen O. Murray and Will Roscoe, eds., *Islamic Homosexualities: Culture, History, and Literature* (pp. 14-54). New York: New York University Press, 1997.

Murray, Stephen O. and Will Roscoe, eds. *Islamic Homosexualities: Culture, History, and Literature.* New York: New York University Press, 1997.

Nasr, Seyed Hossein. *Islamic Spirituality: Manifestations.* New York: Crossroads, 1997.

Nimmons, David. *The Soul Beneath the Skin: The Unseen Hearts and Habits of Gay Men.* New York: St. Martin's Press, 2002.

Nissinen, Marti. *Homoeroticism in the Biblical World: A Historical Perspective.* Translated by Kirsi Stjerna. Minneapolis, MN: Fortress, 1998.

Nozick, Robert. *The Examined Life: Philosophical Meditations.* New York: Simon and Schuster, 1989.

Nugent, Robert, ed. *A Challenge to Love: Gay and Lesbian Catholics in the Church.* New York: Crossroad, 1984.

Nussbaum, Martha C. *The Fragility of Goodness.* Cambridge: Cambridge University Press, 1986.

Olyan, Saul M. " 'And with a Male You Shall Not Lie the Lying Down of a Woman': On the Meaning and Significance of Leviticus 18:22 and 20:13," in Gary David Comstock and Susan E. Henking, eds., *Que(e)rying Religion: A Critical Anthology* (pp. 398-414). New York: Continuum, 1997.

Olyan, Saul M. and Martha C. Nussbaum. *Sexual Orientation and Human Rights in American Religious Discourse.* New York: Oxford University Press, 1998.

Pagels, Elaine. *Adam, Eve, and the Serpent.* New York: Random House, 1988.

Percy, William Armstrong III. *Pederasty and Pedagogy in Archaic Greece.* Urbana: University of Illinois Press, 1996.

Pickthall, Mohammed Marmaduke. *The Meaning of the Glorious Koran.* New York: Mentor, n.d.

Plato. *Plato's Cosmology: The "Timaeus" of Plato.* Translated and Commentary by Francis MacDonald Cornford. Indianapolis: Boss-Merrill, n.d.

———. *Symposium.* Translated and Introduction by Robin Waterfield. New York: Oxford World's Classics, 1994.

Price, A. W. *Love and Friendship in Plato and Aristotle.* New York: Clarendon/Oxford University Press, 1990.

Rambuss, Richard D. *Closet Devotions.* Durham, NC: Duke University Press, 1998.

Rauch, Jonathan. "Who Needs Marriage?" in Bruce Bawer, ed., *Beyond Queer: Challenging Gay Left Orthodoxy* (pp. 296-313). New York: Free Press, 1996.

Richards, David A. J. *Identity and the Case for Gay Rights: Race, Gender, Religion As Analogies.* New York: Chicago: University of Chicago Press, 1999.

Roscoe, Will. *Queer Spirits: A Gay Man's Myth Book.* Boston: Beacon, 1995.

————. "We'Wha and Klah: The American Indian Berdache as Artist and Priest," in Gary David Comstock and Susan E. Henking, eds., *Que(e)rying Religion: A Critical Anthology* (pp. 89-106). New York: Continuum, 1997.

Rudy, Kathy. *Sex and the Church: Gender, Homosexuality, and the Transformation of Christian Ethics*. Boston: Beacon Press, 1997.

Saikaku, Ihara. *The Great Mirror of Male Love*. Translated with an Introduction by Paul Gordon Schalow. Stanford: Stanford University Press, 1990.

Sands, Kathleen M., ed. *God Forbid: Religion and Sex in American Public Life*. New York: Oxford University Press, 2000.

Schalow, Paul Gordon. "Kukai and the Tradition of Male Love in Japanese Buddhism," in José Ignazio Cabezón, ed., *Buddhism, Sexuality, and Gender* (pp. 215-230). Albany: State University of New York Press, 1992.

————. "Male Love in Early Modern Japan: A Literary Depiction of the 'Youth'" in Martin Duberman, Martha Vicinus, and George Chauncey Jr., eds., *Hidden from History: Reclaiming the Gay and Lesbian Past* (pp. 118-128). New York: Meridian, 1990.

————. "Spiritual Dimensions of Male Beauty in Japanese Buddhism" in Michael L. Stemmeler and Jose Ignacio Cabezón, eds., *Religion, Homosexuality and Literature* (pp. 75-93). Las Colinas, TX: Monument Press, 1992.

Schimmel, Annemarie. *Mystical Dimensions of Islam*. Chapel Hill: University of North Carolina Press, 1975.

Scroggs, Robin. *The New Testament and Homosexuality: Contextual Background for Contemporary Debate*. Philadelphia: Fortress, 1983.

Shilts, Randy. *Conduct Unbecoming: Gay & Lesbians in the U.S. Military*. New York: St. Martin's Press, 1993.

Simpson, Mark. *Male Impersonators: Men Performing Masculinity*. New York: Routledge, 1994.

Sproul, Barbara C. *Primal Myths: Creating the World*. San Francisco: Harper and Row, 1979.

Stemmeler, Michael L. and Jose Ignazio Cabezón, eds. *Religion, Homosexuality and Literature*. Las Colinas, TX: Monument Press, 1992.

Stevens, John. *Lust for Enlightenment: Buddhism and Sex*. Boston: Shambhala, 1990.

Stoltenberg, John. *Refusing to Be a Man: Essays on Sex and Justice*. New York: Meridian, 1990.

Stuart, Elizabeth. *Just Good Friends: Toward a Lesbian and Gay Theology of Relationships*. New York: Mowbray, 1995.

Sullivan, Andrew, ed. *Same-Sex Marriage: Pro and Con, a Reader*. New York: Vintage, 1997.

————. "Unnatural Law: We're All Sodomists Now." *The New Republic* 228:4601 (March 24, 2003), pp. 18-23.

————. *Virtually Normal: An Argument About Homosexuality*. New York: Knopf, 1995.

Swidler, Arlene, ed. *Homosexuality and World Religions.* Valley Forge, PA: Trinity Press International, 1993.

Tafel, Richard. *Party Crasher: A Gay Republican Challenges Politics As Usual.* New York: Simon and Schuster, 1999.

Thompson, Laurence G. *Chinese Religion: An Introduction,* Fifth Edition. Belmont, CA: Wadsworth, 1996.

Thorton, Bruce S. *Eros: The Myth of Ancient Greek Sexuality.* Boulder, CO: Westview Press, 1997.

Tombs, David. "Honor, Shame and Conquest: Male Identity, Sexual Violence, and the Body Politic," *Journal of Hispanic/Latino Theology* 9(4) (May 2002), pp. 21-40.

Trexler, Richard C. *Sex and Conquest: Gendered Violence, Political Order, and the European Conquest of the Americas.* Ithaca, NY: Cornell University Press, 1995.

Turner, Frank E. *The Greek Heritage in Victorian Britain.* New Haven: Yale University Press, 1981.

Vaid, Urvashi. *Virtual Equality: The Mainstreaming of Gay and Lesbian Liberation.* New York: Anchor Books/Doubleday, 1995.

Vanita, Ruth, and Saleen Kidwai, eds. *Same-Sex Love in India.* New York: Palgrave, 2000.

Vasey, Michael. *Strangers and Friends: A New Exploration of Homosexuality and the Bible.* London: Hodder and Stoughton, 1995.

Vitiello, Giovanni. "Taoists Tales in Chinese Homoerotic Tales," in Michael L. Stemmeler and José Ignazio Cabezón, eds., *Religion, Homosexuality and Literature* (pp. 95-103). Las Colinas, TX: Monument Press, 1992.

Wafer, Jim. "Mohammed and Male Homosexuality" and "Vision and Passion: The Symbolism of Male Love in Islamic Mystical Literature," in Stephen O. Murray and Will Roscoe, eds., *Islamic Homosexualities: Culture, History, and Literature* (pp. 87-89; 107-131). New York: New York University Press, 1997.

Ward, Roy Bowen. "Why Unnatural? The Tradition Behind Romans 1:26-27." *Harvard Theological Review* 90(3) (1997), pp. 263-284.

Warner, Michael. *The Trouble with Normal: Sex, Politics, and the Ethics of Queer Life.* New York: Free Press, 1999.

Watanabe Tsuneo and Iwata Jun'ichi. *The Love of the Samurai: A Thousand Years of Japnaese Homosexuality.* Translated by D. R. Roberts. Boston: Alyson Publications, 1989.

Weinberg, George. *Society and the Healthy Homosexual.* New York: St. Martin's Press, 1972.

Williams, Craig. *Roman Homosexuality: Ideologies of Masculinity in Classical Antiquity.* New York: Oxford University Press, 1999.

Williams, Walter L. *The Spirit and the Flesh: Sexual Diversity in American Indian Culture.* Boston: Beacon Press, 1986.

Wilson, Nancy. *Our Tribe: Queer Folks, God, Jesus, and the Bible.* San Francisco: HarperSanFrancisco, 1995.

Zeeland, Steven. *The Masculine Marine: Homoeroticism in the U.S. Marine Corps.* Binghamton, NY: Harrington Park Press, 1996.

———. *Military Trade.* Binghamton, NY: Harrington Park Press, 1999.

———. *Sailors and Sexual Identity: Crossing the Line Between "Straight" and "Gay" in the U.S. Navy.* Binghamton, NY: Harrington Park Press, 1995.

Zwilling, Leonard. "Homosexuality As Seen in Indian Buddhist Texts," in Jose Ignazio Cabezón, ed., *Buddhism, Sexuality, and Gender* (pp. 203-214). Albany: State University of New York, 1992.

Index

Order a copy of this book with this form or online at:
http://www.haworthpress.com/store/product.asp?sku=5096

MEN, HOMOSEXUALITY, AND THE GODS
An Exploration into the Religious Significance of Male Homosexuality in World Perspective

_____in hardbound at $34.95 (ISBN: 1-56023-151-3)

_____in softbound at $16.95 (ISBN: 1-56023-152-1)

Or order online and use special offer code HEC25 in the shopping cart.

COST OF BOOKS_____

POSTAGE & HANDLING_____
*(US: $4.00 for first book & $1.50
for each additional book)*
*(Outside US: $5.00 for first book
& $2.00 for each additional book)*

SUBTOTAL_____

IN CANADA: ADD 7% GST_____

STATE TAX_____
*(NY, OH, MN, CA, IL, IN, & SD residents,
add appropriate local sales tax)*

FINAL TOTAL_____
*(If paying in Canadian funds,
convert using the current
exchange rate, UNESCO
coupons welcome)*

☐ **BILL ME LATER:** (Bill-me option is good on
US/Canada/Mexico orders only; not good to
jobbers, wholesalers, or subscription agencies.)
☐ Check here if billing address is different from
shipping address and attach purchase order and
billing address information.

Signature_____

☐ **PAYMENT ENCLOSED: $_____**

☐ **PLEASE CHARGE TO MY CREDIT CARD.**

☐ Visa ☐ MasterCard ☐ AmEx ☐ Discover
☐ Diner's Club ☐ Eurocard ☐ JCB

Account #_____

Exp. Date_____

Signature_____

Prices in US dollars and subject to change without notice.

NAME_____

INSTITUTION_____

ADDRESS_____

CITY_____

STATE/ZIP_____

COUNTRY_____ COUNTY (NY residents only)_____

TEL_____ FAX_____

E-MAIL_____

May we use your e-mail address for confirmations and other types of information? ☐ Yes ☐ No
We appreciate receiving your e-mail address and fax number. Haworth would like to e-mail or fax special
discount offers to you, as a preferred customer. **We will never share, rent, or exchange your e-mail address
or fax number.** We regard such actions as an invasion of your privacy.

Order From Your Local Bookstore or Directly From
The Haworth Press, Inc.
10 Alice Street, Binghamton, New York 13904-1580 • USA
TELEPHONE: 1-800-HAWORTH (1-800-429-6784) / Outside US/Canada: (607) 722-5857
FAX: 1-800-895-0582 / Outside US/Canada: (607) 771-0012
E-mailto: orders@haworthpress.com

For orders outside US and Canada, you may wish to order through your local
sales representative, distributor, or bookseller.
For information, see http://haworthpress.com/distributors

(Discounts are available for individual orders in US and Canada only, not booksellers/distributors.)

PLEASE PHOTOCOPY THIS FORM FOR YOUR PERSONAL USE.
http://www.HaworthPress.com   BOF04